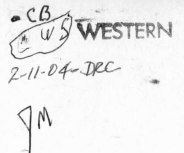

76 A

Large Print Bra

Brand, Max, 1892-1944.

Max Brand's best Western
  stories

MAX BRAND'S
BEST WESTERN STORIES

Also available in Large Print
by Max Brand:

MAX BRAND'S
Best Western Stories

Edited with a Biographical
Introduction by

William F. Nolan

G.K. HALL & CO.
Boston, Massachusetts
1988

The stories in this volume were originally published in
the following magazines: *This Week Magazine* ("Wine on
the Desert"), *The Elks Magazine* ("Virginia Creeper"),
Western Story Magazine ("Macdonald's Dream," under
the title "Sunset Wins"), *American Magazine* ("Partners"
and "Dust Across the Range") and *Argosy* ("The Bells of
San Carlos").

Published in Large Print by arrangement with
Dodd, Mead & Company.

British Commonwealth rights courtesy of
A. M. Heath & Co. Ltd.

G.K. Hall Large Print Book Series.

Set in 18 pt. Plantin.

Library of Congress Cataloging-in-Publication Data

Brand, Max, 1892–1944.
  [Best Western stories]
  Max Brand's best Western stories / edited with a biographical introduction by
William F. Nolan.
     p.   cm.—(G.K. Hall large print book series)
  1. Western stories. 2. Large type books. I. Nolan, William F., 1928–
II. Best Western stories.
III. Title.
[PS3511.A87A6   1988]
ISBN 0-8161-4435-4
813'.52—dc19   88-11028

To Robert Easton and Jane Faust Easton with respect and affection

CONTENTS

Acknowledgments

The dedication page of this book reflects my gratitude to Robert Easton and to his wife, Jane Faust Easton (Frederick Faust's eldest daughter). Mr. Easton's definitive, superbly written biography, *Max Brand: The Big Westerner* (University of Oklahoma Press, 1970), is still in print, and is highly recommended. I have quoted from it in my introduction.

And, although it is not available for general sale, Jane Faust Easton's privately printed *Memories of the '20s and '30s* (Santa Barbara, 1979) has also been of great value, providing many special insights into her early life with Frederick Faust. It is charming, straightforward and informative, written with a grace and style Faust himself would surely have appreciated.

My personal debt to Mr. Easton is considerable. He arranged for this book's publication, supplied copies of missing stories, cleared rights, helped select material, and functioned as an editorial consultant on the final manuscript. His generosity is deeply appreciated.

The six stories in this collection originally appeared in *American Magazine, Argosy, Elk's Magazine, This Week* and *Western Story Magazine*, and are reprinted through the courtesy of Brandt & Brandt and the Estate of Frederick Faust.

My thanks also to the Bancroft Library, University of California at Berkeley, for access to the Faust Papers — and finally to Dodd, Mead and Company.

W.F.N.

MAX BRAND'S
BEST WESTERN STORIES

INTRODUCTION

Western Giant

A book is on the desk in front of me as I write. The pages are sun-faded, yellowed with age. It has no dust jacket, and its cheap red binding is spotted, frayed at the corners.

The book is Max Brand's *The Rancher's Revenge,* in a 1938 Triangle reprint edition, equivalent to today's mass-market paperback. I was fourteen in March of 1942 when I received this book as a birthday present from my boyhood pal Jack Morgan, who had absolutely no idea of the atomic chain reaction he was initiating. I opened its pages, dived into the book and, in one sense, never came out. My young mind responded to this sweeping saga of a decent, hard-working rancher, John Saxon, forced to take up arms to pursue and destroy the powerful villian known as the Solitaire.

Now, all these long years later, I open

the book to its final page — and find myself emotionally stirred at the closing scene, in which Saxon and his beloved Mary Wilson are finally united:

He pointed to the blue nakedness of the upper mountains. "It's a cold winter up here," he told her.

"It'll be a happy winter, though," she said, "if only — if only you don't grow restless, John."

"I'll never be restless again," said Saxon.

He took off his hat. His face showed pale and drawn, years older, and the bandage around his head was a thin strip of white. These months had left many scars, more in the spirit than in the flesh.

He pointed to a small spot of newly-turned ground. "The restlessness is buried there," he said.

"What is it, John?" she asked.

"John Saxon's gun," he said.

I later discovered that Max Brand was a pen name. The man himself was Frederick Schiller Faust, who used more than a dozen pseudonyms. I began to read and collect the books of Max Brand. His highly charged, romantic novels of the Old West fired my young imagination. A particular favorite, in this early collecting stage, was his *Singing Guns*, with its haunting friendship between sheriff and outlaw. Soon I was devouring book after book, lost in Faust's magic aura of romance and adventure.

When he died on the Italian front, in May of 1944, I was a sixteen-year-old high school student. His death stunned me; on the afternoon when I learned that he'd been killed in action as a war correspondent, I remember the tears as I stood by my locker in the hallway of Lillis High — tears from a schoolboy for a man he'd never met.

These tears were deeply rooted. The books of Frederick Faust formed a large emotional part of my young life. His tales of high adventure had given me a sense of idealism, of strength and endurance, of knightly honor — a sense of what Faust called "the god in man."

He believed implicitly in these things. "There is immense power in every soul," he declared, "if it can be set properly in action." To his daughter Jane he wrote: "It is the nature of flame to rise, just as it is the nature of the human spirit to rise. Never forget this. It is the only essential truth behind all that men have thought and dreamed. . . . Truth, beauty and kindness are the important weights to carry until they carry you. Decency, friendship, faith and courage are the only actualities. The people who don't believe in the beauty of life are really the defeated ones."

At his death, I made myself a promise — and in my high school yearbook that promise is quoted beneath my graduation photo: "To carry on for Max Brand."

I kept the promise. Early in 1954, at twenty-five, I sold my first story and embarked, in the Max Brand tradition, on the job of writing to entertain. I became, as twenty-five-year-old Fred Faust had become in 1917, a professional storyteller.

My style owes much to Max Brand, in its speed of narrative and technique of creating character-within-action. My first novel, *Logan's Run*, published in 1967, is dedicated in part:

To Frederick Schiller Faust, who was Max Brand who was Evan Evans who was George Challis who was . . .

Now, in this particular moment of time, writing the introduction to this collection of his best western stories, I have returned to Max Brand, not as an idol-struck teen-aged boy but as a seasoned fellow professional, to celebrate the special skills and rare genius of this American giant of western fiction.

A definitive study of Frederick Faust's western output is long overdue, and I have no doubt that such a study, relating his work to the popular culture of this century, will be written. Certainly, Faust's influence on the commercial western story has been enormous, and while he wrote successfully in many other genres of popular fiction, he is best known as a writer of the West.

Even the bare statistics are impressive. In all, he wrote a western wordage equal to 215 full-length novels. Into 1981, including this present collection, his published books in the western genre total 164 — meaning that a sizable portion of his output still remains in original magazine format. Each year, more of it sees book publication, and "new" Max Brand westerns will likely still be appearing when we've colonized the moon and landed on Mars!

This is because Max Brand's West was timeless. He wrote legendary tales, using the land as a stage backdrop for his incredible sagas of magic deeds and godlike feats of heroism. His rangeland was the sea of Odysseus. And although he had grown up in the real West and later, as a professional writer, maintained an extensive card file of western facts, he preferred to re-create it in his imagination, to invest it with a sense of heroic myth, based on his lifelong passion for the Arthurian knights of Malory and the mythological gods of ancient Greece.

The year of Frederick Faust's birth was 1892; the place, Seattle, Washington. Faust remembered his mother as "pure Irish, possessing a deep, soft voice and wonderfully gentle hands. . . . She had a haunting fear that I would prove to be weak-minded, since I found my early school lessons impossibly difficult. But, at 7, I discovered Malory's *Morte d'Arthur*, and my life was changed."

A year later, when he was eight, Faust's mother died.

"I grew up tall, gangling, and as the 'new kid' in each of the nineteen schools I attended there were always the bruising fistfights. I went for years with a swollen, scarred face . . . losing the few friends I found when my father changed jobs and I moved to a new school. In defense, I withdrew utterly into a world of books and daydreams. I veritably *lived* the printed lives of others."

The Uriels, his mother's family, were Welsh-Irish, and Faust believed that this linked him with Celtic lore. King Arthur, in fact, had been a Celtic hero. The boy was proud of his bardic roots; they provided the bridge to a romantic past.

He was not an only child, but he *was* alone most of the time, since his younger brother, Tom (who died of pneumonia in 1923), and older sister, Pauline, lived with relatives. Therefore, young Faust withdrew deeper into himself, learning to exist independently.

He also began to value strength in its own right as a wall against pain: If you were strong, truly strong, no one could harm you.

The boy's stern German father had once been a successful lawyer, but had lost everything in the California land boom. Bad luck continued to hound him. He died in 1905, five years after his Irish wife, leaving young Frederick parentless at thirteen.

"Aeschylus' plays based on myths were among his favorites," says Max Brand's biographer, Robert Easton. "He identified strongly with the fatherless Orestes, obliged to make his way alone in the world."

As an orphan, young Faust was bound out to a dirt farmer in the central valley of California, the San Joaquin. Big and husky for his age, the boy earned his meals by pitching hay, feeding hogs, working the tired, stubborn black dobe soil by day, reading by lamplight each night in a loft, acquiring his father's love for classical literature.

In his midteens, Frederick began to attend high school in Modesto, scraping together enough to buy a few books by working a hay press, earning a dollar and a half for a cruel sixteen-hour day under a blazing California sun. He learned to handle haywagons, tie bales, tame unruly horses, and swear like a trooper. And, slowly, he was putting words on paper — thoughts, fragments, bits of verse.

"During these years," says Easton, "he talked to cowboys who had ridden in from the big ranches of the Coast Range to the west, and to prospectors down for supplies from the Mother Lode country . . . and he liked to visit the hobo jungles along the Tuolumne River."

The West, for young Fred Faust, was indeed real.

As a young man in his midtwenties, fresh from academic writing honors at the University of California in Berkeley (and on the heels of some overseas adventures as a newspaper reporter in Honolulu), Faust began his professional fiction career with the Munsey Company in New York in 1917.

The editor who first purchased his work was the fabled Robert Hobart Davis, whose acute understanding of popular fiction contributed a great deal to the success of the Munsey chain of pulp magazines. The pen name "Max Brand" was created that year in the Munsey offices — since Faust hoped to sell verse under his real name — and was used as the by-line on his first book-length serial, "Fate's Honeymoon," blurbed on the cover of *All-Story Weekly* as a tale of "the West at its bravest and best."

Actually, this was a mining story, not really a western in the traditional sense of the term, but it convinced Bob Davis that his new protégé could function in this genre.

"Davis handed me copies of Zane Grey's *Lone Star Ranger* and *Riders of the Purple Sage*," Faust later recalled. "Told me to read 'em and see what I could do along those lines."

Faust did just that and, by December of 1918, *All-Story Weekly* was serializing *The Untamed*, Max Brand's saga of "Whistlin' Dan" Barry, a hero figure derived from the god Pan, who combined Faust's passion for myth with his attempt to produce a commercial action western. In this epic, which became his first published book (from Putnam's in 1919), he moved immediately beyond the more realistic fiction of Zane Grey with a sharply personalized, romantic view of the Old West as a land of fable and legend, containing heroes and villains of Homeric proportion.

The Untamed was a hit, and western screen idol Tom Mix starred in a silent film version in 1920. Dan Barry appeared in two sequels, *The Night Horseman* and *The Seventh Man*, firmly establishing Max Brand as a major western talent.

In jubilation, with his first book and film earnings, he married his college sweetheart, Dorothy Schillig, and embarked on a career of full-time writing. He did not find it difficult to turn out large amounts of wordage for the pulps, and was soon forced to use other pen names beyond Brand.

This popular success, however, created a lasting split in Faust's life and career. He desired, desperately, to become a published poet, and had dreams of winning extensive critical and public acclaim as a master of classical verse. "Prose is writing about life," he declared. "Poetry *is* life."

A natural storyteller, Faust was able to sell his fiction as fast as he produced it, but his delicate verse, written on classic themes, was being rejected with crushing regularity. (One notebook entry of the period: "38 poems out to market . . . 38 poems back, unsold.") The pattern was quite clear: Editors did not want epic verse from Frederick Faust, they wanted action tales from Max Brand.

As a married man and a father (his first daughter, Jane, had been born in 1918, and a second daughter and son would follow), Faust accepted the fact that he must turn out a large amount of popular fiction in order to pay the bills.

In late 1920 he began a truly amazing business arrangement with Frank E. Blackwell, a former feature writer with the New York *Sun,* who was then at the helm of Street & Smith's new weekly pulp, *Western Story Magazine.* Faust agreed to supply

Blackwell with over a million words a year for an indefinite period; in return, he was to receive premium rates. At five cents a word, he was paid more than any other pulp writer of the era. Over the next fourteen years, under eleven pen names, Faust's work appeared in 622 issues. In all, he wrote thirteen million words of western fiction for Frank Blackwell! During the dark Depression era, when $5,000 was considered a substantial annual income, Faust earned $100,000 a year from his work, blasting out nearly two million words of fiction annually for *Western Story* and several other pulps.

Blackwell was eventually paying him $5,000 for a serial Faust could turn out in under a week. For years, he averaged a full-length novel every ten days. They called him the King of the Pulps — and no other American ever produced more saleable wordage in a shorter period. He was, literally, a one-man fiction factory. And he did it all without help of any kind, pounding out each story, two-finger style, on a battered typewriter he called "my oldest friend."

He kept a careful page count of his fiction each day, and would often extend his heavy afternoon work schedule into darkness in order to finish a particular assignment. This is reflected in a typical diary entry: "9:05 p.m. Only 19 pages to go — and it is running like a song! End of the story's in sight, and it's a peach. I'm going to finish it before midnight. . . . 11:15. Finished."

The split in Frederick Faust's creative life saw him devoting each morning to verse, each afternoon to fiction. Overwhelmed with the beauty of Italy, he leased a seven-acre villa in the hills above Florence, writing both poems and wild western tales in this classical romantic atmosphere.

Easton describes the morning poet: "Faust sat in a straight-backed wooden chair in his book-lined Florentine study, working at a massive antique table of dark oak, a genuine Renaissance piece from a Benedictine monastery. For his verse, he used a quill pen on extra-long, extra-heavy sheets of white paper, custom-cut to his measure. If, in four hours, he produced three lines that satisfied him it was a good morning's work."

In the afternoon, hunched over his typewriter, sleeves rolled up, he became Max Brand, and (in the same four-hour period) slammed out some thirty pages of adventure fiction, first draft, and style be damned! Thus, the careful maker of verse gave way to the pulp high-wordage wonder.

In the evening, after dinner, Faust often read aloud to his family and friends, declaiming Shakespeare (he had memorized more than 25,000 lines!) or reading from expensively bound volumes of Milton and Chaucer. He would follow with a rendition of his latest verse, modeled after these masters.

Carl Brandt, who became Faust's agent in 1925 and remained a lifelong friend, was present at some of these readings, recalling that "Faust had a beautiful speaking voice and read poetry musically, with passion and conviction. I would sit and listen to him read. Drugged by the spell of his voice, at three in the morning, I'd be convinced that his verse was great. But in the next day's cold white light, reading the same lines, it became clear how personal a thing his poetry was, and how little of it was really publishable."

Aside from a few scattered magazine verses, only two slim volumes of Faust's poetry saw print in his lifetime, and one of these *Dionysus in Hades*, his most mature work, was paid for by Faust himself and privately published in England.

When asked how he could possibly produce so many pages of fiction each day, Faust declared that "the average man is only 40 to 50% efficient, but when he's backed into a corner . . . he can be as high as 90% efficient. Financially, I'm in that corner."

This was true. Despite his high earnings, Faust's lavish style of living kept him in constant debt. He never believed in moderation; Fred Faust was, heart, soul and body, a man of excess. He launched himself full-tilt into many arenas of life: he rode fence-jumping thoroughbreds in Ireland, prowled the great art museums of Paris, raised a stable of fighting bulldogs in the States, kept a staff of ten servants busy in his Italian villa, swam in a lake-sized pool of his own design, entertained in royal splendor, played vigorous golf and tennis, gloried in Bach, took fencing lessons, raced his custom Isotta-Fraschini along Italian roads at Grand Prix speeds, gardened with a passion, bottled wine from his own vineyards, collected rare prints, mastered chess, taught himself Greek and Italian in order to read Homer and Dante in the original, was an amateur astronomer, boxed, arranged private tutoring for his three children ("I swell with pride because John is reading Homer at 14!") — and often drank and partied late into the night.

All this, while maintaining his prodigious daily work rate.

The strain affected his health. Even giants can break, and beginning in 1921 Faust suffered a series of damaging heart attacks. His doctors warned him that he must slow down or die. Faust's unique solution: *more* play, *more* work! "The heart is a muscle," he claimed. "It responds best to exercise."

He confounded the experts with his killing routine, but, for him, it seemed to make sense and they shrugged, writing up his case in specialized journals. Faust was a medical marvel!

Dorothy Faust, his patient, long-suffering wife, proofread all of Max Brand's manuscripts before they went off to the Brandt agency for marketing. If he sent six men into a canyon and only five came out, Dorothy caught the error and corrected it, since Faust never bothered to revise his pulp westerns.

At night, when he would awake from nightmares of suffocation caused by pressure from his damaged heart, Dorothy was there to read him back to sleep. She worried about his murderous work schedule, his drinking, his late-night parties. "It's a strain," she confessed to her daughter Jane, "living with such a tempestuous giant of a man."

Bitter quarrels often resulted from this strain, yet their marriage endured; Faust claimed he could never love another woman as he loved Dorothy.

Faust's most famous western hero was created during these Blackwell–*Western Story* years. In February of 1930 a Max Brand serial, "Twelve Peers," was featured in *Western Story Magazine*. It was a story of vengeance. After an innocent man is released from prison he rides to hunt down the "twelve peers" on the jury who sent him there. The fellow's name was Destry — and Dodd, Mead published the fast-action serial in book format that same year as *Destry Rides Again*.

When Faust completed the 80,000-word manuscript late in 1929, he'd been writing for *Western Story* for nine years, and this was just one more gaudy adventure whipped out for Blackwell's top rate. He dismissed it from his thoughts the moment it left his typewriter.

He had no idea that the story would become an all-time western classic, sell millions of copies in book form, be chosen as the first talking western to star Tom Mix, attain legendary status in the filmed remake, starring James Stewart, be filmed a third time with Audie Murphy, become a full-scale Broadway musical with Andy Griffith and finally emerge on television in 1964, starring John Gavin in the title role.

Unlike Dan Barry, the Montana Kid, and other of his creations, Destry was never a Faust series character. The only story written about Harrison Destry was this single novel, but it firmly placed Max Brand in the ranks of all-time best sellers alongside Zane Grey and other major genre names.

During 1932, a peak year for Faust in *Western Story*, his work was printed in every weekly issue, and Blackwell was now depending on him as the magazine's major source of fiction.

Under the heading "Banner Issue Next Week!" Blackwell bragged about four of his top authors:

First installment of a great serial by George Owen Baxter . . . "Lucky Larribee" . . . Then there's a complete novel by Max Brand . . . "Speedy's Crystal Game" . . . and it's as fast as its name! Next comes the second installment of "The Golden Spurs" by David Manning . . . Then, folks, we're beginning a serial by a new man, Evin Evan, called "Montana Rides" . . . and the folks on this here editorial ranch have declared this yarn to be something special. . . . She sure does move, that's for certain!

Of course, Baxter, Brand, Manning and the "new" man, Evan, were *all* Frederick Faust. (In book format, Evin Evan became Evan Evans — the real name of Faust's heart specialist in New York, pressed into service as a Faust pseudonym!)

By the mid-1930s Faust had moved away from Blackwell and *Western Story* to concentrate on the higher-paying slick paper markets. Under the direction of Carl Brandt, he began selling to *The Saturday Evening Post, American Magazine*, and *Collier's*. He also continued to turn out a sizable amount of fiction for *Argosy* and other pulps during this same breakthrough period.

Earlier, in April of 1932, he had complained to Brandt: "When I come to the writing of western stories I have so thoroughly exhausted most of my possibilities that I don't find new scenes to describe, or new emotions, or a new lingo for new ideas."

Faust was convinced that he had come to the end of his western output — but, in truth, much of his best work in the genre lay ahead.

In September of 1932 he completed *Montana Rides!*, the first of his superb trilogy of border westerns featuring the Montana Kid. And, in November of the same year, he wrote *Silvertip*, the first of thirteen novels detailing the adventures of Jim Silver, a roving gunman whose nickname derived from two tufts of silver set into his dark hair like the horns of a devil. For this series, his most extensive, Faust created the fabled stallion, Parade, who became as important as the title character himself. Parade was possessed of near-human powers, could read Jim Silver's moods, and often stood guard at night as Silver slept, eyes and ears alert for his master's enemies.

This great stallion was the end product of Faust's deep love of thoroughbred horses, and his novels are filled with these dazzling, wind-swift creatures, as godlike as the heroes who rode them.

"A horse is a glorious animal," Faust declared. "It can understand more of one's speech than most men."

He produced another outstanding border western in mid-1935, in book form as *Smugglers' Trail,* and capped the year with his *Argosy* magazine serial "The Streak," written that September. It was the last of his full-length traditional action-westerns. After this, his work in the genre became far more polished as he concentrated on shorter tales of superior quality and craftsmanship. Of his final eight western tales, including his long 1937 novella, *Dust Across the Range,* five are collected in this book — and I have provided a special preface to each, relating it to the body of his western fiction career.

What *was* Frederick Faust's ultimate contribution to the American western story in our century?

In his study of the Street & Smith empire, *The Fiction Factory,* journalist Quentin Reynolds stated: "Max Brand's best work may well become a permanent part of western folklore."

Biographer Robert Easton credits Faust with "introducing old world myth into the new world West. In his work, king-sized heroes ride in pursuit of queen-sized heroines on a landscape of mythological dimensions . . . elevated by a distinctive epic tone."

Critic Jack Nachbar adds: "In Faust, the western landscape becomes an elemental place in which to recast the ancient and medieval myths."

Another critic, in praising the Montana Kid novels, called him "the Homer of the western story."

Indeed, Fred Faust's adventure tales could, in many cases, be traced directly to classical themes. In *Hired Guns*, he utilized the plot and characters of *The Iliad;* his *Garden of Eden* contains obvious elements of the Odysseus legend; *Trailin'* recounts the Oedipal search for a father; and in *Pillar Mountain* he retold the Greek myth of Theseus.

As Easton has pointed out: "Faust introduced most of the Olympian hierarchy, as well as Norse gods, Celtic master-spirits, and Arthurian knight-heroes . . . yet he had few conscious thoughts about writing myth. These elements flowed naturally from his interests."

Max Brand's pulp readers were, of course,

totally unaware of these buried classical roots since Faust made certain to deliver nonstop action, keeping his outlaw gunmen, as he once phrased it, "jumping through fiery hoops." Asked for the key to successful pulp fiction, he replied, "Action, action, action!" Few writers have ever been able to move a narrative along at a faster pace.

"In the early 1920s," wrote critic Samuel Peeples, "the western story was rapidly gaining mass appeal, and it is impossible to say how many writers came under Faust's influence. Certainly, the breathless pace set by other pulp writers was a direct result of his wide popularity. Yet Faust's amazing ability to blend characterization *within* action made his work unique."

And John Schoolcraft, who edited a book of Faust's letters and verse, stated: "He made himself a major figure in our most American kind of writing, a definite current in the great stream of world literature. The dime novels which began in the 1860s, James Fenimore Cooper's Leatherstocking tales, Mark Twain's work, Owen Wister's *The Virginian*, the novels of Zane Grey — all are peaks in the same high chain. And in that chain Frederick Faust created a kind of Everest of his own, bringing to the field his poetic style, his quality of imagination and his fascinating preoccupation with strength." Faust said of his own work: "My men are fifty feet high, and my women bear twenty-five pound babies."

He made no secret of his vast preference for verse over fiction and would complain bitterly in letters to friends of having to "drudge out" story after story. Yet he was, to the bones and blood, a born storyteller, and admitted that he often found himself "caught up in the suspense and sheer narrative drive of a yarn." On his best days, fiction writing was far more satisfying than he liked to admit.

There is no doubt that, on a conscious level, he greatly favored the careful creation of verse to the machine-gun production of commercial fiction (he once spent six years on a single epic poem), but one has only to sample his best work to see the sheer joy, the vigor and vast enthusiasm exhibited in his top action tales. No writer can fake such basic elements.

In truth, Frederick Faust and the western genre were ideally matched. This field provided the epic scope his romantic imagination demanded. In the legendary Old West, where grand deeds were the order of the day, Faust had free rein in the creation of his demigod heroes, magicians with gun and knife, fabled horsemen who championed lost causes, toppled epic villains, laughed and swaggered and fought — loving danger for its own "bright face" (as Faust once described it) and finding a kind of primitive glory in the proven strength of body and mind.

As Peeples has said of Faust's western fiction: "In it, we find a sense of exhilaration, of freedom from normal bounds and physical limits. The intense vibrancy of the man is evident in these stories, reflecting the apparently limitless source of energy he drew upon."

Defying his erratic heart, Faust was a giant who wrote of giants. Weighing 220 pounds, with solemn features chiseled into a massive head, he stood six-feet-three, and carried his tall body lightly, with a pride in his step. His hands were tough and blunt-fingered from early years of hard labor, and his eyes were direct and penetrating. Gifted with a natural bent for the dramatic, he could easily have portrayed any one of his many stalwart heroes, but in public was actually a shy man who always avoided photos and personal interviews.

"I dream of money," he told his agent. "Endless amounts of money." And he made these dreams into reality. Had he invested his vast earnings, aimed for profit, he would have been a very rich man. But to Faust, money was for spending — to be shared lavishly with others. All of Faust's friends speak of his boundless generosity. He was a "soft touch" for starving fellow professionals or beginning writers seeking his aid.

"Anyone who'd been kind to him in the early days could always count on him for help," declared Carl Brandt. "He had me send several thousand dollars to an old pulp editor who'd become an invalid — and in all the years I knew him there was never a time when he was not supporting several lame-duck writers. He'd say to me, 'Carl, you've got to send a check from me every month to Johnny Doe. There's a man who really *can* write. He'll reach the stars!' I would sigh and read the new fellow's work. Nine times out of ten it would be hopeless. Yet Faust insisted on the checks going out anyhow."

John Schoolcraft confirmed Faust's expansive generosity to young writers: "He functioned with them as a kind of one-man father-confessor, literary counselor and relief agency. He'd often be sending them money to pay their bills when he didn't have enough to pay his own."

One of Faust's notebooks contains an entry directly related to his way of life: "Never hold back. Give every man, woman and child the best you have in you, for we gain a true place in life only by giving our best to others."

Never a man to do things by half measure, his money was further depleted by his incredible library in Italy. It could have graced a palace, a treasure unto itself.

"All of the major English, French, German, Italian, Spanish, Russian and other European classics were represented," reports Easton. "There were scores of books on the Middle Ages and on the Renaissance. . . . Leather bindings were often worked with gold. Cost was no object. One invoice from Faust's London bookbinder ran to more than $10,000!"

Faust's hospitality with guests was also on the grand scale, and Brandt recalled that "those who tried to pay for anything when he was in the party had a fight on their hands. In Europe, he lived like a prince, and his hospitality stemmed directly from the Golden Age of Italy. Faust was a modern

Lorenzo in his villa, which fitted him as the glove fits the hand. The preparation of food was a ceremony. He loved fine wines, special salads, cheese with ripe pears, figs from his own trees — and he *knew* food, from the world's best to the simplest peasant dish, and he made you know it too when you were with him. Each meal was an occasion!"

Almost any encounter with Faust was memorable. Harper president Cass Canfield's account of an afternoon with him is typical: "His range of knowledge and understanding seemed to me extraordinary. He discussed the classics as one would the writings of contemporaries. He made the great men of Greece so vivid they seemed personal friends. At the end of this day with Faust I had been refreshed by his vitality and his vast appetite for life."

By 1938, the man who was Max Brand had moved to Hollywood, turning his manic energy loose on a multitude of film projects. He created the celebrated Doctor Kildare series for MGM, wrote adventure scripts at Warners for Errol Flynn, and returned to the western genre one final time with *The Desperadoes* in 1943, starring Glenn Ford as "Cheyenne" Rogers in "an original screen story by Max Brand" for Columbia.

In 1944, bored with his $3,000-a-week film chores and fired by the idea of covering World War II from the front lines, Faust talked his way into representing *Harper's Magazine* and shipped off for his beloved Italy at the beginning of the Italian offensive.

He had begun his writing career as a reporter in Honolulu; now he was repeating the pattern. The King of the Pulps had become a war correspondent.

There was a difference, however, between Faust the young reporter and Faust the veteran fictioneer: his damaged heart was acting up, and late into his fifty-first year he was overage for battle conditions. But life, to Frederick Faust, was an adventure, and he was eager for this new opportunity to test the limits of his strength and courage. As his Hollywood pal Steve Fisher expressed it: "He was a romantic, a true soldier of fortune, and going into war at his age was more wild dream than sensible idea. But he lived on dreams and by them. He was the only writer I've ever known who was exactly like the characters he wrote about, as fabulous and magic and gallant as any of them."

When he arrived at Fifth Army headquarters, Faust asked to be sent across the

Garigliano River to the front lines with the forward attack force (Company E, of the 351st Infantry), but was told that this would be extremely dangerous, and that he would be much wiser to wait with the other correspondents until the main offensive was launched. The troops were going up against heavily manned German positions under the expert command of Field Marshal von Kesselring.

Faust wouldn't listen. He insisted that he had to be "in the thick of things" to write his story. "I want to know how these men feel when they're pinned down by mortar fire — what their reactions are, what they say and do in battle. All my life, I've written fiction, but this is fact and these men are in a tight spot I didn't invent. I want to see how they get out of it, and I want to be there with them when they do."

D-Day was set for the night of May 11, 1944. Abiding by the rules of the Geneva Convention, which forbade correspondents to bear deadly weapons, Faust carried a "walking stick" (cut from an olive tree by one of the soldiers) as he charged up the slope with the front-running troops.

Objective: the small hillside village of Santa Maria Infante, near Minturno, a key

German stronghold in the Gustav Line. The darkness exploded into raw light under a fierce German barrage and the Americans suffered severe losses in the hail of shells.

"That's when he got hit," reported Sergeant Jack Delaney, who was in the charge with Faust. "Halfway up the slope. Shell fragment in the chest. We went to help him, but he waved us back, told us to take care of the two wounded boys next to him. 'They're worse off than I am,' he said. When they finally carried him back to the drift line he was talking, said he wasn't in any pain, and would be all right. But that's when he died . . . and we went on to take Santa Maria."

One cannot know what Frederick Faust was thinking in those final minutes of his life — but he was a man who had never feared death. In his first professionally printed poem, at the beginning of his career in 1917, he had written:

And all at once I knew death is a thing
    That stoops down, whispering
A dear, forgotten secret in your ear
    Such as the winds can sing,
And then you sleep, and dream, and have
    no fear.

Nearly thirty-eight years have passed since that fateful night in Italy and the books of Max Brand are more popular than ever. A hundred of his western novels are in print, and critic Malcolm Cowley has pointed out that "more of Faust's books have been translated into more languages than those of any other American writer except Upton Sinclair." More than fifty-five films have been made from his works; his characters have been featured in magazines, on radio, on the stage, in comic books, newspapers and on television — and "new" Max Brand books continue to appear each season.

It gives me great personal satisfaction to bring the best of his shorter western tales together in this volume, closing a full circle in my life as reader and writer.

The world of Max Brand was very real to me. The reading memories of my teen years glow with his fighting heroes, his great horses, his greater villains, in the dreaming days when I fought beside John Saxon to defeat the Solitaire . . . crossed the Rio Grande with the Montana Kid . . . stood fast with Jim Silver against the guns of Barry Christian . . . rode the vengeance trail with Harry Destry . . . and followed the cry of wild geese into darkness with Whistlin' Dan Barry.

Now, almost four decades later, I close the circle. Let me finally, then, list them, the Faust westerns I remember best, abrim with wondrous deeds, miraculous escapes, blazing with action, poetry, beauty and strength. Let their titles strike sparks from the mind: *Destry Rides Again, The Untamed, Silvertip, The Border Kid, Brothers on the Trail, The Seventh Man, Twenty Notches, Fightin' Fool, Pillar Mountain, Montana Rides!, The Rancher's Revenge.* . . . They form a rich legacy, bright threads from the vast tapestry of adventure he left us.

And still I hear the music of his singing guns.

Woodland Hills,   WILLIAM F. NOLAN
California

WINE ON THE DESERT

The classic "Wine on the Desert" is Max Brand's most popular short story. Since its original appearance in This Week, *some forty-five years ago, it has seldom been out of print. Many editors have selected this superbly taut, expertly written tale of the Old West for re-printing in anthologies and textbooks. Among them was Harry E. Maule, who included this story in his distinguished Modern Library collection,* Great Tales of the American West. *Maule wrote: "Bridging the gap between the leaders of the western story in the early 1900s and the present was the fabulous Max Brand. . . . His 'Wine on the Desert' blazes the trail toward the best of the western stories as we know them today — in which attention to characterization and literary finish replace the old emphasis on action."*

Certainly the outlaw Durante is a character to remember. Unlike the majority of Faust's good badmen, he has no redeeming qualities. Dick Durante lives by his wits and his gun, and Faust renders him in hard edges, without

34

sentiment or softness. This story is a product of the closing years of Faust's western writing career, fashioned with clarity and careful craftsmanship, demonstrating his total mastery of the genre he had, by 1935, made his own.

As sharply cut as a diamond, this glittering little tale of the desert remains fixed in the memory — and its final, bitterly poetic image permanently haunts the mind.

THERE WAS NO hurry, except for the thirst, like clotted salt, in the back of his throat, and Durante rode on slowly, rather enjoying the last moments of dryness before he reached the cold water in Tony's house. There was really no hurry at all. He had almost twenty-four hours' head start, for they would not find his dead man until this morning. After that, there would be perhaps several hours of delay before the sheriff gathered a sufficient posse and started on his trail. Or perhaps the sheriff would be fool enough to come alone.

Durante had been able to see the wheel and fan of Tony's windmill for more than an hour, but he could not make out the ten acres of the vineyard until he had topped the last rise, for the vines had been planted in a hollow. The lowness of the ground, Tony used to say, accounted for the water that gathered in the well during the wet season. The rains sank through the desert sand, through the gravels beneath, and gathered in a bowl of clay hardpan far below.

In the middle of the rainless season the well ran dry but, long before that, Tony had every drop of water pumped up into a score of tanks made of cheap corrugated iron. Slender pipelines carried the water from the tanks to the vines and from time to time let them sip enough life to keep them until the winter darkened overhead suddenly, one November day, and the rain came down, and all the earth made a great hushing sound as it drank. Durante had heard the whisper of drinking when he was here before; but he never had seen the place in the middle of the long drought.

The windmill looked like a sacred emblem to Durante, and the twenty stodgy, tar-painted tanks blessed his eyes; but a heavy sweat broke out at once from his body. For the air of the hollow, unstirred by wind, was hot and still as a bowl of soup. A reddish soup. The vines were powdered with thin red dust, also. They were wretched, dying things to look at, for the grapes had been gathered, the new wine had been made, and now the leaves hung in ragged tatters.

Durante rode up to the squat adobe house and right through the entrance into the patio. A flowering vine clothed three sides of the little court. Durante did not know the name of the plant, but it had large white blossoms with golden hearts that poured sweetness on the air. Durante hated the sweetness. It made him more thirsty.

He threw the reins of his mule and strode into the house. The water cooler stood in the hall outside the kitchen. There were two jars made of a porous stone, very ancient things, and the liquid which distilled through the pores kept the contents cool. The jar on the left held water; that on the right contained wine. There was a big tin dipper hanging on a peg beside each jar. Durante tossed off the cover of the vase on the left and plunged it in until the delicious coolness closed well above his wrist.

"Hey, Tony," he called. Out of his dusty throat the cry was a mere groaning. He drank and called again, clearly, "Tony!"

A voice pealed from the distance.

Durante, pouring down the second dipper of water, smelled the alkali dust which had shaken off his own clothes. It seemed to him that heat was radiating like light from his clothes, from his body, and the cool dimness of the house was soaking it up. He heard the wooden leg of Tony bumping on the ground, and Durante grinned; then Tony came in with that hitch and sideswing with which he accommodated the stiffness of his artificial leg. His brown face shone with sweat as though a special ray of light were focused on it.

"Ah, Dick!" he said. "Good old Dick! . . . How long since you came last! . . . Wouldn't Julia be glad! Wouldn't she be glad!"

"Ain't she here?" asked Durante, jerking his head suddenly away from the dripping dipper.

"She's away at Nogalez," said Tony. "It gets so hot. I said, 'You go up to Nogalez, Julia, where the wind don't forget to blow.' She cried, but I made her go."

"Did she cry?" asked Durante.

"Julia . . . that's a good girl," said Tony.

"Yeah. You bet she's good," said Durante. He put the dipper quickly to his lips but did not swallow for a moment; he was grinning too widely. Afterward he said: "You wouldn't throw some water into that mule of mine, would you, Tony?"

Tony went out with his wooden leg clumping loud on the wooden floor, softly in the patio dust. Durante found the hammock in the corner of the patio. He lay down in it and watched the color of sunset flush the mists of desert dust that rose to the zenith. The water was soaking through his body; hunger began, and then the rattling of pans in the kitchen and the cheerful cry of Tony's voice:

"What you want, Dick? I got some pork. You don't want pork. I'll make you some good Mexican beans. Hot. Ah ha, I know that old Dick. I have plenty of good wine for you, Dick. Tortillas. Even Julia can't make tortillas like me. . . . And what about a nice young rabbit?"

"All blowed full of buckshot?" growled Durante.

"No, no, I kill them with the rifle."

"You kill rabbits with a rifle?" repeated Durante, with a quick interest.

"It's the only gun I have," said Tony. "If I catch them in the sights, they are dead. . . . A wooden leg cannot walk very far. . . . I must kill them quick. You see?

They come close to the house about sunrise and flop their ears. I shoot through the head."

"Yeah? Yeah?" muttered Durante. "Through the head?" He relaxed, scowling. He passed his hand over his face, over his head.

Then Tony began to bring the food out into the patio and lay it on a small wooden table; a lantern hanging against the wall of the house included the table in a dim half circle of light. They sat there and ate. Tony had scrubbed himself for the meal. His hair was soaked in water and sleeked back over his round skull. A man in the desert might be willing to pay five dollars for as much water as went to the soaking of that hair.

Everything was good. Tony knew how to cook, and he knew how to keep the glasses filled with his wine.

"This is old wine. This is my father's wine. Eleven years old," said Tony. "You look at the light through it. You see that brown in the red? That's the soft that time puts in good wine, my father always said."

"What killed your father?" asked Durante.

Tony lifted his hand as though he were

listening or as though he were pointing out a thought.

"The desert killed him. I found his mule. It was dead, too. There was a leak in the canteen. My father was only five miles away when the buzzards showed him to me."

"Five miles? Just an hour. . . . Good Lord!" said Durante. He stared with big eyes. "Just dropped down and died?" he asked.

"No," said Tony. "When you die of thirst, you always die just one way. . . . First you tear off your shirt, then your undershirt. That's to be cooler. . . . And the sun comes and cooks your bare skin. . . . And then you think . . . there is water everywhere, if you dig down far enough. You begin to dig. The dust comes up your nose. You start screaming. You break your nails in the sand. You wear the flesh off the tips of your fingers, to the bone." He took a quick swallow of wine.

"Without you seen a man die of thirst, how d'you know they start to screaming?" asked Durante.

"They got a screaming look when you find them," said Tony. "Take some more wine. The desert never can get to you here. My father showed me the way to keep the

41

desert away from the hollow. We live pretty good here? No?"

"Yeah," said Durante, loosening his shirt collar. "Yeah, pretty good."

Afterward he slept well in the hammock until the report of a rifle waked him and he saw the color of dawn in the sky. It was such a great, round bowl that for a moment he felt as though he were above, looking down into it.

He got up and saw Tony coming in holding a rabbit by the ears, the rifle in his other hand.

"You see?" said Tony. "Breakfast came and called on us!" He laughed.

Durante examined the rabbit with care. It was nice and fat and it had been shot through the head. Through the middle of the head. Such a shudder went down the back of Durante that he washed gingerly before breakfast; he felt that his blood was cooled for the entire day.

It was a good breakfast, too, with flapjacks and stewed rabbit with green peppers, and a quart of strong coffee. Before they had finished, the sun struck through the east window and started them sweating.

"Gimme a look at that rifle of yours,

Tony, will you?" Durante asked.

"You take a look at my rifle, but don't you steal the luck that's in it," laughed Tony. He brought the fifteen-shot Winchester.

"Loaded right to the brim?" asked Durante.

"I always load it full the minute I get back home," said Tony.

"Tony, come outside with me," commanded Durante.

They went out from the house. The sun turned the sweat of Durante to hot water and then dried his skin so that his clothes felt transparent.

"Tony, I gotta be damn mean," said Durante. "Stand right there where I can see you. Don't try to get close. . . . Now listen. . . . The sheriff's gunna be along this trail some time today, looking for me. He'll load up himself and all his gang with water out of your tanks. Then he'll follow my sign across the desert. Get me? He'll follow if he finds water on the place. But he's not gunna find water."

"What you done, poor Dick?" said Tony. "Now look. . . . I could hide you in the old wine cellar where nobody . . . ."

"The sheriff's not gunna find any water,"

said Durante. "It's gunna be like this."

He put the rifle to his shoulder, aimed, fired. The shot struck the base of the nearest tank, ranging down through the bottom. A semicircle of darkness began to stain the soil near the edge of the iron wall.

Tony fell on his knees. "No, no, Dick! Good Dick!" he said. "Look! All the vineyard. It will die. It will turn into old, dead wood. Dick . . ."

"Shut your face," said Durante. "Now I've started, I kinda like the job."

Tony fell on his face and put his hands over his ears. Durante drilled a bullet hole through the tanks, one after another. Afterward, he leaned on the rifle.

"Take my canteen and go in and fill it with water out of the cooling jar," he said. "Snap to it, Tony!"

Tony got up. He raised the canteen, and looked round him, not at the tanks from which the water was pouring so that the noise of the earth drinking was audible, but at the rows of his vineyard. Then he went into the house.

Durante mounted his mule. He shifted the rifle to his left hand and drew out the heavy Colt from its holster. Tony came dragging back to him, his head down. Durante watched Tony with a careful revolver but he gave up the canteen without lifting his eyes.

"The trouble with you, Tony," said Durante, "is you're yellow. I'd of fought a tribe of wildcats with my bare hands, before I'd let 'em do what I'm doin' to you. But you sit back and take it."

Tony did not seem to hear. He stretched out his hands to the vines.

"Ah, my God," said Tony. "Will you let them all die?"

Durante shrugged his shoulders. He shook the canteen to make sure that it was full. It was so brimming that there was hardly room for the liquid to make a sloshing sound. Then he turned the mule and kicked it into a dogtrot.

Half a mile from the house of Tony, he threw the empty rifle to the ground. There was no sense packing that useless weight, and Tony with his peg leg would hardly come this far.

Durante looked back, a mile or so later, and saw the little image of Tony picking up the rifle from the dust, then staring earnestly after his guest. Durante remembered the neat little hole clipped through

45

the head of the rabbit. Wherever he went, his trail never could return again to the vineyard in the desert. But then, commencing to picture to himself the arrival of the sweating sheriff and his posse at the house of Tony, Durante laughed heartily.

The sheriff's posse could get plenty of wine, of course, but without water a man could not hope to make the desert voyage, even with a mule or a horse to help him on the way. Durante patted the full, rounding side of his canteen. He might even now begin with the first sip but it was a luxury to postpone pleasure until desire became greater.

He raised his eyes along the trail. Close by, it was merely dotted with occasional bones, but distance joined the dots into an unbroken chalk line which wavered with a strange leisure across the Apache Desert, pointing toward the cool blue promise of the mountains. The next morning he would be among them.

A coyote whisked out of a gully and ran like a gray puff of dust on the wind. His tongue hung out like a little red rag from the side of his mouth; and suddenly Durante was dry to the marrow. He uncorked and lifted his canteen. It had a slightly sour smell; perhaps the sacking which covered it had grown a trifle old. And then he poured a great mouthful of lukewarm liquid. He had swallowed it before his senses could give him warning.

It was wine!

He looked first of all toward the mountains. They were as calmly blue, as distant as when he had started that morning. Twenty-four hours not on water, but on wine!

"I deserve it," said Durante. "I trusted him to fill the canteen. . . . I deserve it. Curse him!" With a mighty resolution, he quieted the panic in his soul. He would not touch the stuff until noon. Then he would take one discreet sip. He would win through.

Hours went by. He looked at his watch and found it was only ten o'clock. And he had thought that it was on the verge of noon! He uncorked the wine and drank freely and, corking the canteen, felt almost as though he needed a drink of water more than before. He sloshed the contents of the canteen. Already it was horribly light.

Once, he turned the mule and considered the return trip; but he could remember the head of the rabbit too clearly, drilled right through the center. The vineyard, the rows of old twisted, gnarled little trunks with the bark peeling off . . . every vine was to Tony like a human life. And Durante had condemned them all to death!

He faced the blue of the mountains again. His heart raced in his breast with terror. Perhaps it was fear and not the suction of that dry and deadly air that made his tongue cleave to the roof of his mouth.

The day grew old. Nausea began to work in his stomach, nausea alternating with sharp pains. When he looked down, he saw that there was blood on his boots. He had been spurring the mule until the red ran down from its flanks. It went with a curious stagger, like a rocking horse with a broken rocker; and Durante grew aware that he had been keeping the mule at a gallop for a long time. He pulled it to a halt. It stood with wide-braced legs. Its head was down. When he leaned from the saddle, he saw that its mouth was open.

"It's gunna die," said Durante. "It's gunna die . . . what a fool I been . . ."

The mule did not die until after sunset. Durante left everything except his revolver. He packed the weight of that for an hour and discarded it, in turn. His knees were growing weak. When he looked up at the stars they shone white and clear for a moment only, and then whirled into little racing circles and scrawls of red.

He lay down. He kept his eyes closed and waited for the shaking to go out of his body, but it would not stop. And every breath of darkness was like an inhalation of black dust.

He got up and went on, staggering. Sometimes he found himself running.

Before you die of thirst, you go mad. He kept remembering that. His tongue had swollen big. Before it choked him, if he lanced it with his knife the blood would help him; he would be able to swallow. Then he remembered that the taste of blood is salty.

Once, in his boyhood, he had ridden through a pass with his father and they had looked down on the sapphire of a mountain lake, a hundred thousand million tons of water as cold as snow . . .

When he looked up, now, there were no stars; and this frightened him terribly. He never had seen a desert night so dark. His eyes were failing, he was being blinded. When the morning came, he would not be able to see the mountains, and he would

49

walk around and around in a circle until he dropped and died.

No stars, no wind; the air as still as the waters of a stale pool, and he in the dregs at the bottom . . .

He seized his shirt at the throat and tore it away so that it hung in two rags from his hips.

He could see the earth only well enough to stumble on the rocks. But there were no stars in the heavens. He was blind: he had no more hope than a rat in a well. Ah, but Italian devils know how to put poison in wine that will steal all the senses or any one of them: and Tony had chosen to blind Durante.

He heard a sound like water. It was the swishing of the soft deep sand through which he was treading; sand so soft that a man could dig it away with his bare hands. . . .

Afterward, after many hours, out of the blind face of that sky the rain began to fall. It made first a whispering and then a delicate murmur like voices conversing, but after that, just at the dawn, it roared like the hoofs of ten thousand charging horses. Even through that thundering confusion the big birds with naked heads and red, raw necks found their way down to one place in the Apache Desert.

VIRGINIA CREEPER

From time to time, as a fiction writer, Faust would dig into his own past and produce a story closer to reality, less remote, stemming from his personal life experiences. "Virginia Creeper" is one of these; it is clearly autobiographical, set in the San Joaquin Valley of central California where young Faust worked as a boy. Like the hero of this story, he labored on a hay press from dawn to dusk, on hire to various ranchers, and guided high-piled horse-drawn haywagons along the Mariposa Road, east of Stockton. Steve Tucker's stern, demanding father in this story is based on Faust's often painful memories of his own father, who left him an impoverished orphan at thirteen. Even the story's title is derived from life. Faust's son-in-law, Robert Easton, has written: "The Ampelopsis vine, or Virginia Creeper, is based directly on one Faust planted at his villa in Italy. The vine grew to cover the entire south wall."

This superb character study of early California is a fine example of Frederick Faust's abil-

ity to bring genuine depth and compassion to a printed page.

STEVE TUCKER PITCHED on; old Champ, the hired man, did the loading. Tucker's back was too narrow and his legs were too long for the neat handling of sacked wheat or baled hay, but his very length gave him a greater leverage on a pitchfork. They were getting in the last of the hay crop on the land John Tucker had rented from the Mullihans. It had been planted for wheat but the crop had suffered for the lack of spring rains. The growth had been cut for hay which ran about a ton and a half to the acre. Now the sun was still high, but Steve Tucker hurried his work because there was a three-mile haul to the home barn and all the chores to do before dark. He leaned well over the shocks of hay and drove his fork straight down until the tines grated on the hard dobe soil; then he swayed back, got the end of the fork under his leg, and made a final heave. Sometimes, though he almost sat down to his work, the shock would only be staggered by the first effort; but the second one would bring it up, though his left arm shook like a wire in the wind and his knees turned sick with weakness.

The great forkful, rising high above him, crushed down on top of the wagon load where Champ walked back and forth, building the sides as straight and true as though he were constructing a stack to stand out all winter. He had a knack for doing this.

They got the last shock aboard and the tines of the fork shivered and sang as Tucker raked together the last wisps of the hay and tossed it up.

"I seen Dago Joe when he was good, and Jump Watterson, too, but all I gotta say is you sure can pitch hay," said Champ.

"Go on," protested Tucker. "Anybody with two hands and a back can pitch hay, but a stacker is born, not made. You've got three tons and a half on top of that old rack."

He looked with admiration up the straight, shimmering sides of the load; then he climbed up to the driver's seat, stepping on the tongue of the wagon, then on the croup of the near wheeler, and so to the high seat. Champ, with a pitchfork on each side of him, already had sunk down on the crest of the load. That was why Champ had not got on in the world. His brain stopped as soon as his hands had finished working.

The four horses looked absurdly inadequate for starting such a mountain of hay. The forward thrust of the load hid half the length of the wheelers.

"Hey, boys. Gittup!" called Steve. "Hey, Charlie, Prince! Hey — *Queen!*"

He always saved her name for the last. The old bay mare on the off wheel needed a moment for digging her hoofs into the ground and stretching her long, low body. The other three already had their traces taut and their hipstraps lifting, but the wagon was not budged until Queen came into her collar. As she made her lift, the near wheeler came back a little, fairly pulled out of place by her surge; then the wagon lurched ahead.

It was a stiff pull because the wheels were cutting well down through the surface of the dobe. The horses leaned forward, stamping to get firmer foothold. Tucker could hear the breathing of the off leader, Charlie, who was a bit touched in the wind; he could hear the crinkling of the sun-whitened hay stubble under the wheels. The hay load jounced over the bumps,

55

throwing up a sweet breath.

They passed the shack, the staggered corral, the broken-backed barn of the old Stimson place where that family had lived until the last generation, when the banks got them. The banks got everything, sooner or later. Two bad crops in a row would make the most provident farmer go borrowing and after that life was poisoned. The Stimson place, like a gloomy prophecy, was soon out of sight, but never out of mind. But now they came from the field toward the road. From the height of the field there was a big dip and a sharp rise to the top of the grade. Tucker sang out loudly, cracked the long lash of his whip, and got the team into a trot on the downslope. The wagon rolled easily almost to the crest, but there was a need for Queen's sturdy pulling to get them safely out on the top. It was always an exciting moment, that descent from the field and rise to the road, with the running gear crackling, and the load atwist and asway. Once on the broad back of the highway, the horses could rest, for though the surface was rutted and the ruts poured full of the white dust, the wheels bit through easily and found a hard under-surface. One ton in the soft of a field was as hard on a horse as two and a half tons on the road.

They were barely out on the Mariposa Road when Mildred Vincent came by on her bay mare and a fellow beside her in real riding togs. His boots shone through the layer of dobe dust with an aristocratic glimmer, it seemed to Tucker.

"Steve!" called the girl, waving. "Oh, I'm glad to see you. Jerome, it's Steve Tucker. Jerome Bartlett, Steve. Can you come over after supper?"

"Yeah. I'd like to come. Thanks," said Tucker.

He had taken off his hat and the hot sweat rolled down over his face and turned cool in the stir of the wind. He never was asked out for meals because he had to stay home to look after his bedridden father. Now the two galloped ahead, the stranger sitting well down into his saddle. He looked strong and straight and his tan had been built up on athletic fields and beaches; it was not the dark mahogany which comes out of work in hay and harvest fields. He rode not like a Californian, but holding the reins in both hands with his elbows close to his ribs.

"That feller if he had some gold lace on

him would look like a general," said Champ, from amidst the rustling of the hay. "Wonder if Millie is gunna take him? Maybe he's a millionaire from San Francisco. She's come to the marryin' age, all right. There was a time when I thought you was gunna have her, Steve, but what with all that college education under her belt, I guess she'll look pretty high."

Five years ago Steve Tucker had given up his entrance into college in order to spend one year on the ranch. His father had pointed out that one good year would make everything easier and, besides, he had gone so far in higher mathematics that he could do the four-year engineering course in three, without trouble. So Tucker had remained on the ranch, while one year lengthened to five and loss matched profit with every crop. Mildred, who had been with him in the country school and who had been two years behind him at Stockton High School, would be a college senior that fall. She was the symbol and indicator of the distance he had been left behind by life which flows so softly and travels so far.

He roused himself from that thought to find that the team was picking up speed; in fact, they were nearing the home corral and the roof of the little house showed beyond the top of the fig tree. Now they swept from the crest of the road into the corral; the side of the hayload made a rushing sound against the barn and he jammed on the long, iron-handled brake when the center of the wagon was just beneath the door of the mow.

The sun was growing large in the west, now. "We'll pitch off the hay in the morning," he said to Champ. "You take care of the team and I'll get the cows milked. Put some salve on the shoulder of Queen. Dig out the padding so the collar won't press on the sore tomorrow."

"She oughta be laid up till that shoulder heals," said Champ. He was always solicitous of Queen's well-being.

"I know she should, but what can we do?"

The cows were already waiting at the pasture gate. Old Red was lowing with impatience, and Whitey was dripping milk into the dust. She must lose two or three quarts a day. Steve pulled the creaking gate open and watched the five cows, the three heifers, the four knock-kneed calves come hurrying for water. The youngsters galloped, the cows went with a long wallowing shamble.

Tucker walked to the house, scrubbed his hands with yellow soap, got the milking stool and two three-gallon buckets. They rattled together as he went back down the boardwalk to the corral.

"Stevie!" called his father's voice from the upstairs window.

"Hey, Dad," he called.

But his face did not light until he noticed the green pattern of the Virginia Creeper which was opening a beautiful green fan along the unpainted side of the shack.

"Hurry it up!" called John Tucker.

"Yeah — hurrying," said Steve, and went on in a gloom.

The weighted rope slammed the gate to the corral behind him and sent a long, mournful echo through his heart. Over at the Vincent place Millie and that neat young fellow, Jerome Bartlett, would be sitting out on the green of the lawn, laughing and talking.

It seemed to Tucker five years at least since he had laughed.

The cows had finished drinking. They stood about switching their tails at flies or streaking their sides with saliva as they

60

reached back to lick away the itch.

"So-o-o, Boss!" called Tucker. "So-o-o, Red! Old Red! Come, girl! Come on, damn you! So-o-o, Red!"

The old cow waddled out of the mud near the watering trough and ambled towards him. She looked like the model of some fat-bellied merchant tub with a queer figurehead carved at one end and the hafts of four slender oars at work out of all time with one another. After her drifted the other cows, stopping to kick at flies and then forgetting what they had been about. But at last they were all gathered in a lower corner of the corral. He milked old Whitey first because she was losing in a steady trickle. Under the big grip of his hands, it gushed out of her. It ran as if from two faucets. He held the pail between his feet and he could feel the vibration of the tin as the heavy streams thumped against it. They made loud, chiming sounds. Even when the pail was almost full, the milk plumped through the inches of froth with a resonant pulsation. And a steaming sweetness rose into the face of Tucker.

The roan-colored two-year-old heifer was the hardest and the most fidgety to handle. She held up her milk. He had to squeeze so hard that it hurt her and she kept lifting a hind foot and kicking out behind her. Steve's hands and forearms were aching when he finished with her and carried the two brimming buckets back toward the house. The sun was a great red face over the blue of the Coast Range; in the eastern sky the twilight color was gathering before the sunset.

He strained the milk into wide-mouthed gallon tins which he placed in the cooler outside the house. It was a tall frame of shelves with burlap nailed about it and water siphoning over it day and night from a big pan on top. The evaporation kept butter fairly firm even when the temperature was a hundred degrees in the shade.

He started the fire in the kitchen stove, put on the kettle of water, and heard his father calling, "Steve! Oh, Steve!"

He went upstairs and entered the room. It was the best in the house but that was not saying a great deal. Rain seepage had stained the roses of the wallpaper and the ceiling had never been plastered. One looked through the crisscross of the laths up to the slanting rafters of the roof. The window, which faced west, was filled with the brilliance of the sunset and one little branch of a green translucence had crawled a foot or so across the screen.

"Look at this. It just came this afternoon," said John Tucker, heaving himself up in the bed. Sometimes he seemed to Steve stronger than ever above the hips but below them his legs were dead, whitened shanks with the feet like great deformities at the ends of them. He held out a letter in a hand that had grown so white that the veins across the back of it showed as blue as ink.

Steve read:

Mr. John Tucker
R. F. D. No. 4,
Box 188.

Dear Sir:
We beg to confirm our letter dated 18 May and regret that we have had no reply to our request.

While we beg to remit you herewith enclosed your bill up to the end of May, we again ask you the favor to remit us cheque in settlement of same, as we cannot at all, wait no longer for this payment on account of great difficulties we are crossing in trade.

Trusting to be favored and to save us further corrispondence on this matter, we beg to remain

Yours obedient.

THE FIVE MILE STORE
Baccigalupi and Baccigalupi
(Signed)
Joseph Baccigalupi.

As Steve lifted his eyes, his father growled through his beard, "There's no Dago as bad as a damned Portuguese Dago." He smoothed the sleek of his bald head with one hand and added, "They want to be saved further correspondence in this matter, eh? They can all be damned!"

"They're better to deal with than a bank," answered the son. "The interest is no higher and they don't stick a gun under your nose when the money comes due. The Baccigalupis are all right."

"Don't tell me what's right!" exclaimed John Tucker. "I can remember back when there were *business* people to deal with in California. I can remember when I could go into Stockton and have any bank in the damned town glad to give me five thousand dollars. Why? Because my name was good.

64

That's why. They loaned money to *men*, in those days. Now they lend it to machines and dirt."

"I'll go down tomorrow and see Joe Baccigalupi, but —" said Steve. He clipped his teeth together.

"What were you going to say?"

"Nothing," said Steve.

"No, you'd rather go down in the kitchen and snarl behind my back, wouldn't you? Why don't you come out with what you've got to say?"

"I haven't anything to say," said Steve, swallowing hard.

"That's a lie," said his father. "But before you go, pull the screen open and tear the vine off. What is it, anyway?"

Steve went to the window and looked down at the tender shoot.

"It's a Virginia Creeper," he said. "I planted it the autumn before last — and look where it is already!"

"You planted a creeper? Want to fill the house with dampness and bugs? Want to give us all malaria and rheumatism? Haven't I told you that I'd never have vines growing on my house?" shouted John Tucker.

He banged his hand on the table beside

his bed so that the lamp jingled and his pile of books shook over aslant.

"Yes, I've heard you say that," admitted Steve.

"Then what in hell do you mean? Do I have to drag myself out of the house and go around spying on you? Tear that damned vine off the screen now; and dig it up by the roots tomorrow."

Steve tapped his fingers against the screen. It gave back a dull chiming, a flat note without resonance.

"I'd as soon —" he murmured.

"You'd what?" barked his father.

"I'd as soon," said Steve, "tear out a handful of hair."

"What are you talking about?"

Steve walked to the door.

"Come back here and tell me what the devil you mean!" roared John Tucker.

"I'd better not talk," said Steve. "I'm worn out, like the ground. Barley and wheat, wheat and barley for sixty years. Now nothing but tar weed and wild oats — I'd better not talk."

"Speak up what you mean. You talk like you're drunk!"

"I'll go down and cook dinner."

"Dinner can wait and be damned. What

are you driving at? Worn out like the ground?"

"Worn out," said Steve. "That's what I mean. Tired out like the soil. All it gives us is trouble, now. And if I talk, all I'll give you will be trouble, tonight."

"You will, will you? Let me hear what kind of trouble you can give me. But the first thing is — tear that damned vine off my window!"

Steve walked through the doorway and down the hall.

"Come back here — by God!" cried John Tucker. The bed creaked. There was a thumping and trailing sound across the floor, but it did not issue into the hallway as Steve went down the stairs.

He fried thin beefsteak and boiled potatoes with their jackets on. Some corn pone he had made that morning he broke into roughly triangular shapes and piled on a platter. There were mustard greens which he had picked in the field though the season of their tenderness had passed, and he had some clabber cheese. Part of this food he put on the table for Champ and himself; the rest he arranged on a tray and carried up the stairs as he had done every night for four years.

When he came into the room, the lamp was lighted. It was not as bright as the glare in the eyes of John Tucker. He cleared the table and put the tray on it.

"Now I'm going to hear you apologize."

"For what?" said Steve, and looked straight into the electric gray of John Tucker's eyes.

It was the first time in his life, he realized, that he had dared to face that glance; but there was a hard wall of anger in him that shielded him from fear.

"The time has come," said his father, "when there's got to be a showdown. There can't be two captains on one ship. You'll be the boss or I'll be the boss, and as long as I own this ranch, by God, I'll do the running of it."

Steve said nothing. He could not have unlocked his jaws for speech.

"If you don't like my way, get out!" shouted John Tucker.

"Aunt Sarah," said Steve, slowly, "has always wanted to come over and take care of you, and Champ will do the work on the place pretty well."

"I'd rather have vinegar poured into milk than Sarah's face poured into my days!"

"You'll have to have somebody to look out for you."

"You're going, are you?"

"I'm going," said Steve.

"Sell the place tomorrow and take your share and get out, then!"

"I own Queen and Bess and the Jackson buck," said Steve. "That's what I'll take. I don't want a share of this place. I want to forget it."

"Forget me, too, then! Get out of my sight and out of my life!"

Steve went down to the table and found Champ halfway through his meal.

"Old man kind of mad?" asked Champ.

"Kind of," said Steve.

"When he gets to raring, he sure can go," said Champ. "I ever tell you about that time up at Angel's Camp when a couple of Dutchmen jumped him in Wilson's Bar?"

"Yeah, you told me about that," said Steve.

"Aw, did I?" murmured Champ.

He became depressed and silent, while Steve finished eating and started the dishes. Steve went upstairs into his father's room and found that the supper tray had not been touched. John Tucker lay in bed with his big fists gripped, his eyes glaring at some terrible nothingness.

"Done?" asked Steve.

John Tucker said nothing, so Steve left the tray and went out again. He finished the dishes. Champ, who would have despised such woman's work, remained in the dining room smoking. It was his big time of the day.

"You stay on and take charge of things, Champ," said Steve. "Father will tell you whatever you want to know. I'm leaving in the morning."

He put some hot water into a laundry tub on the back porch, undressed, scrubbed himself down, and went up to his room. He put on a blue serge suit, a high, hard collar that hurt his throat, and a pair of seven-dollar shoes that made his feet feel light. The softness and snugness of them comforted his soul. Then he walked up the road to the Vincent place. A great grove surrounded that big, square, white house and there was a lawn under the trees. In the distance a pair of windmills were clanking musically; and sprinklers whirred on the lawn, filling the air with a noise like a spring wind through trees.

A piano was rousing up a tune in the

front room; a lot of young voices took up the air. There was always music in the Vincent house because there was always money in the Vincent bank account.

The front door jerked open.

"Left it out here. Be back in a moment!" cried the voice of Mildred Vincent.

She left the door a bit ajar and a shaft of light followed her, bobbing on the gold of her hair.

"Hello," said Steve.

"Hai — Steve! You gave me a start. Come on in — just a minute while I find —"

"I can't come in," said Steve.

"What's the matter? Is your father ill tonight?"

"No, he's the same. But I have some things to do tonight. I'm leaving in the morning."

"Are you taking a trip? You ought to, Steve. You ought to have more fun."

"I'm going for good."

"Not leaving your father! Not that! But I've always said it was the most wonderful — I've always thought —"

"I'm taking a team and a Jackson buck down to the Islands. They always need men and teams down there in the haying.

I can make enough to see me through most of a college year, between now and August."

"But your father, Steve?"

"We've agreed to it. Aunt Sarah will come over and take care of him."

"But your Aunt Sarah —"

"So I came over to say goodbye and to tell you —"

A sudden stroke of emotion stopped his voice.

"Well, goodbye," said the girl.

She held out her hand in a certain way that stopped all talk. He barely touched it and went quickly.

It was three miles across to Aunt Sarah's place but he was glad of the chance to stretch his legs and start breathing again. By leaving home, it was plain that he was leaving Mildred Vincent farther than he had thought. Since those old days when she had been his girl, he had thought that a world of difference had opened between them, but now he could see that they had been almost hand in hand compared with the cold distance that had come between them now. Did she expect that he was to lay down all the years of his life in the service of John Tucker?

72

He reached the old house of Aunt Sarah and talked to her in the bareness of the front hall with the gleam of the hatrack mirror beside him and the sheen of balusters climbing dimly up the stairs into darkness. The house was as empty as Aunt Sarah's life.

He said, "Father and I have disagreed. If you'll come over to take care of him, I'll be glad."

She looked at him for a long moment before she began to nod her gray head. She had something of the look of her brother, the same grimness on a smaller scale.

"He's drove everybody else out of his life; and now he's drove you, eh?" she said. "I'll come right over."

The parting was brief, the next morning. Steve held out his hand and said goodbye.

His father looked at the hand and then at him.

"Get out of my sight!" he said.

Down on the Islands, where the alluvial soil is deeper than wells are dug, where the drinking water is yellow and has a sweetish taste, where the ground is so rich that sometimes a fire will start it burning, where twenty sack crops of wheat are known and where triennial floods wash away the profits of the farmers, Steve Tucker found it easy to get work with his Jackson buck. He got two dollars a day for his own share, two for the machine, and a dollar a head for the horses, with keep thrown in, of course. That made a monthly net profit of a hundred and eighty dollars, minus what he spent for cigarette tobacco and brown wheat-straw paper.

The hours were long and the work was hard. The dust that flew in the Islands stained the skin and hurt the eyes. The most cheerful men began to grow silent after a few days in that country, but Steve was silent by nature and he had set himself to a long and hard purpose.

The haypress which hired him was run by a big Scotchman with a bush of red hair on his head.

"You a Tucker that's any relation of John Tucker?" said this giant.

"I'm his son," said Steve, and stuck out his jaw a little. No man in the world had so many enemies as his father.

The Scotchman turned to his partner.

"This here John Tucker, the kid's father," he said, "I seen him on Main Street in Stockton, four years back, run out a snatch a kid off the tracks from in front of a streetcar. And the car ran on and smashed him against the rear end of a dray. Your father ever get well, Tucker?"

"He's still laid up," said Steve.

"He is, eh? Well, we'll hire you." Then he added to his partner, "John Tucker was as big a man as me. And he got his hips all smashed in."

When work begins at five in the morning and ends with the coming of twilight, men are too tired to think. All that Steve recalled out of the past, during a month, was the bobbing, golden head of the girl as she had run down the steps that night, and the clenched fists and the glaring gray eyes of his father. If the work of the others was hard, his task was still more bitter, because long after they were in bed, he was shaping two by fours to take the place of the long, wooden teeth which he had broken on the Jackson buck during the day. He was thin and hollow-eyed that evening at dinner in the cookhouse when a telegram was brought to him by the owner of the farm.

It said:

YOUR FATHER VERY ILL.
PLEASE COME BACK.
                    MILDRED

Steve returned the next day.

A southeast wind had darkened the sky with a continual march of clouds and he told himself that John Tucker must be about to die. When he reached the house, the windmill was whirling furiously in the storm, the wheel veering from side to side, and he could hear the rapid plumping of the stream into a half-empty tank. That was a sad music fit for death scenes, he thought.

The picture of the veteran lying with gripped fists, silent in his bed, was filling his mind as a mountain fills the sky.

When he pulled open the kitchen door, it was not Aunt Sarah that he saw, but Mildred Vincent in a calico apron. He stood there with the door propped open against his rigid arm and the wind entering behind him. The room had been changed and the cookery was not stale and sour but a light fragrance through the house. He knew these things as he took in a great breath of astonishment.

76

"Steve!" she cried out. "You *have* come!"

"How is he?" asked Tucker, pushing the door shut at last.

"He's changed, and thin, and he's set his will like iron. It's going to be a shock when you see him."

"I'll go on up."

"Just a moment. Champ is up there now, getting orders about the place."

"Does the doctor say anything?"

"I can't get him to see a doctor. He wouldn't have your Aunt Sarah in the house. He won't let Champ come nearer than the door of his room. We got a nurse but he wouldn't let her come near him. He doesn't seem to mind having me around, so I come over every day."

"Why?" asked Tucker.

"You know why, Steve — because every drop of blood in every Vincent should be willing to die for John Tucker."

"They should?" he repeated, staring.

"You don't know? Do you mean to say that your father never told you the story?"

"Never."

She drew in a great breath. "He wouldn't!" she murmured. "That's how great his soul is! But when my father was alive — long ago when he was a wild-headed youngster — he and another man got into trouble with a single miner — and the miner beat them, guns and all. Nearly killed father — but then the miner spent a month nursing him back to life — it was John Tucker who did that!"

A thousand moments out of his own life came back to Steve.

"Yes," he said at last, "he could do that. And that was why you were nice to a great gawk like me?"

"No, I liked you for your own sake. Steve, is it possible he never told you — and we such close neighbors all these years?"

Steve shook his head. An ache that had begun in his heart the day before began to stifle him.

"Has he a fever?" he asked.

"Yes. Not a high one. He won't eat — hardly anything —"

A heavy, slow step on the stairs. Steve, moving into the hall, saw Champ come down. The hired man, turning his hat between his hands, glanced up once and then walked on, blinded by his thoughts.

"I haven't told your father you were coming. I didn't dare confess I'd sent the telegram."

"Has he mentioned me?"

"No, Steve, not once."

She came halfway up the stairs with him.

"God bless you for coming so quickly. He's terribly changed. Be gentle with him, please."

When Steve Tucker entered his father's room it was strangely dim as though a shade had been drawn down. Then he saw that the Virginia Creeper had grown clear across the screen, the one tendril reinforced by many. From the clouded sky, only a green gloom entered through the leaves.

"What in hell are you doing here?" asked John Tucker.

"I've come back," said Steve.

"Who asked you back?"

"Nobody," said Steve.

"Then get out of my sight."

Steve said, "I'll stay out of your sight as long as you please, but I'm keeping on the place."

"I'll be damned before I'll have you on my land!" shouted John Tucker.

"All right, then. You'll have to be damned."

The gray glare of the eyes fascinated him. He turned from them and went to the window. He opened the screen and ripped the little clinging feet of the ampelopsis away from the wire.

"Let that be!" cried John Tucker. "What you mean?"

"It shuts out the light and the air," said Steve. "Why did you let it grow?"

"Because it damn well pleased me to let it grow. What d'you mean by — by God, I'm going to —"

He had heaved himself up on his elbows. Now that more light entered the room Steve saw how great the wastage had been. The square, jowled face was covered with lank furrows.

"What did you mean by it?" demanded Steve, pointing his finger. "What did you mean by letting that vine cover the window and spoil your reading light?"

His father started to speak; his lips remained parted but made no utterance.

Steve sat down in the chair beside the bed.

"I've been mighty unhappy while I was away," he said. "It was lonely never hearing you growl."

"There can't be two captains on one ship!" declared John Tucker.

"You're the captain," said Steve.

"And what I say has got to go!"

80

"It goes with me," said Steve.

"Does it?" said John Tucker. He let himself sink suddenly back into the pillows. He was breathing hard.

"I'm going to have a change of air," he said.

"All right," said Steve. "I'll take good care of the place."

"You'll come with me!"

"All right," said Steve, "I'll come with you, then."

The eyes of John Tucker opened; they were the mildest blue in the world.

"Where do we go?" asked Steve.

"Down to the Bay," said John Tucker. "Air's brisker, down there. Down to Berkeley — get a house up there in the hills — up there near the University —"

Realization poured over Steve in floods of cold happiness.

John Tucker said, "I waited five years for you to grow up. I waited so long that when you *did* grow up the other day, I didn't understand. But you're only a young brat still. Five years is nothing, now that you're a man. You can make up the time."

"We both can," said Steve.

When he left the room, a flash of something across the floor made him turn at the door. The tendrils of the ampelopsis, waving like ragged, green flags, framed a sky in which a changing wind had piled the clouds into white heaps that began to blow away like dust. The brightness on the floor had been one sudden pouring from the sun.

He found Mildred Vincent still halfway up the stairs, crying. She made a hushing sign and tiptoed down before him.

Only when she had closed the kitchen door behind them, and then in a stifled voice, did she dare to say, "I heard everything, and it was beautiful, Steve. I know he'll get well now. But what did you do to the vines on the window? I tried to clear them away every day, and he never would let me."

"Well, I did it," said Steve.

"No wonder he was in a fury! Why did you do it?"

"I needed to let in some light," said Steve. "It's an odd thing. I can't explain it. But he and I understand. We both gave in."

"It makes me feel like an outsider," she told him.

"After you've brought all this about?"

He made a gesture of wonder which she seemed to understand, for she put her hand in his, and then she was in his arms, his lips on hers, his arms crushing her, never to let go.

MACDONALD'S DREAM

No Max Brand collection would be complete without an action pulp tale from Western Story Magazine, *which carried the bulk of Faust's western fiction from late 1920 into early 1935.*

During these peak years of production, Faust hammered out more than 5,000 pages annually for this voracious weekly magazine under Frank Blackwell's editorship, often appearing three times, under as many names, in a single issue. A cover would proudly announce: "Top-Notch Western Tales by Max Brand, John Frederick and George Owen Baxter!" It was under the Baxter by-line, early in 1923, that Western Story *printed the novelette "Macdonald's Dream" (under its Blackwell-assigned title of "Sunset Wins").*

Here, in the colorful personage of Gordon "Red" Macdonald, is the quintessential Max Brand outlaw gunfighter in full stride, a larger-than-life myth figure possessed of uncanny strength and magic abilities with a six-gun. Yet, while he is totally characteristic of Faust's hero gunmen, Macdonald is also a figure of dark mystery, riding a fateful trail, seeking a woman who is alive to him only in his dreams.

In the Max Brand canon, "Macdonald's Dream" is a strange, disturbing and unique tale. Galloping through it is one of Faust's great wonder horses, the red stallion called Sunset, who fears no man and who carries Macdonald into a land of dreaming danger, to an ultimate and shocking confrontation with his greatest enemies.

"The source of all my fiction," Faust wrote to a friend in 1942, "has been an escape from reality — into a bright and blue and golden world. The words flow as automatic writing, like the material of a dream."

Here, then, the dreams of Frederick Faust are shaped to those of his legendary hero Gordon Macdonald, mythic into mystic. The tale he spins for us is impossible to forget, sweeping us along a dark trail to a stunning gunpowder climax — in the best tradition of Max Brand's full-bodied pulp adventure fiction.

I

HIS FATHER WAS a Macdonald of that old strain which once claimed the proud title of Lord of the Isles. His mother was a Connell of that very family which had once owned Connell Castle. At the terrible slaughter of the Connells at the Boyne, those who were left of the race fled to the Colonies. After the Macdonalds had followed Bonny Prince Charlie into England in that luckless year, 1715, the remnants of the proscribed race waited for vengeance among the Highlands, or else followed the Connells across the Atlantic.

The Connells were great black men, with hands which could crush flagons or break heads. The Macdonalds were red-headed giants, with heaven-blue eyes and a hunger for battle. But the passing of generations changed them. They became city dwellers, in part, and those who dwelt in cities shrank in stature and diminished in numbers. They became merchants, shrewd dealers, capable of sharp practice. They lived by their wits and not by the strength of their hands. They gave corporals and raw-handed sergeants to the war of the Revolution; to the

Civil War, nearly four generations later, they gave majors and colonels and generals. Their minds were growing, and their bodies were shrinking.

And so at last a Mary Connell, small, slim-throated, silken black of hair, wedded a Gordon Macdonald, with shadowy red hair and mild, patient, blue eyes. They were little people. He was a scant five feet six inches in height, and yet he seemed big and burly when he stood by the side of his wife. What manner of children should they have?

For five years there was no child at all, and then Mary died in giving birth to a son. He was born shrieking rage at the world, with his tiny hands doubled into fat balls of flesh, and his blue eyes staring up with fury, and he was born with red hair gleaming upon his head. His father looked down upon him in sadness and bewilderment. Surely this was no true son of his!

His wonder grew with the years. At thirteen, young Gordon Macdonald was taller than his father and heavier. He had great, long-fingered, bony hands and huge wrists, from which the tendons stood out, as though begging for the muscles which were to come. And his joy was not in his books and his tutor. His pleasure was in the streets. When the door was locked upon him, he stole out of his bed at night and climbed down from the window of his room, like a young pirate, and went abroad in search of adventure. He would come back again two days later with his clothes in rags, his face purpled and swollen with blows, and his knuckles raw. They sent him to a school famous for Latin and broken heads. He prostrated two masters within three months with nervous break-downs, and he was expelled from the school bruised, but triumphant.

"Force is the thing for him then," said his weary-minded parent. "Let us discipline his body and pray God that time may bring him mildness. Labor was the curse laid on Adam. Let his shoulders now feel its weight!"

So Gordon's father made him an apprentice in a factory, at the ripe age of fifteen, to bow his six feet two of bones and sinews with heavy weights of iron and to callous his hands around the rough handles of sledge hammers.

But though he came home at night staggering, he came home singing. And if he grew lean with the anguish of labor in the first month, he began to grow fat on it in the second. His father cut off his allowance. But on Saturday nights Gordon began to disappear; money rolled into his pockets, and he dressed like a dandy. Presently his father read in one paper of a rising young light heavyweight who was crushing old and experienced pugilists in the first and second rounds under the weight of wildcat onslaught; and in a second paper he saw a picture of this "Red Jack" and discovered that he was his own and only son!

After that he prayed for guidance, and he received an inspiration to send his boy away from the wiles of the wicked city for a year and a day. So he signed young Macdonald on a sailing ship bound for Australia. He bade his boy farewell, gave him a blessing, and died the next month, his mind shattered by a financial crash. But he had accomplished one thing at least with his son — Gordon Macdonald came back to Manhattan no more.

In the port of Sydney, far from his homeland, Gordon celebrated his seventeenth birthday with a drunken carousal, and the next day he insulted the first mate, broke his jaw with a pile-driving jab, and was thrown into the hold in irons. He filed through his chains that night, went above, threw the watch into the sea, dived in after him, and swam ashore.

Macdonald was hotly pursued. He stole a horse to help him on his flight. He was cornered at the end of the seventh day, starved, but lionlike. With his bare hands he attacked six armed men. He smashed a rib of one, the jaw of another, and fractured the skull of the third before he was brought down spouting crimson from a half-dozen bullet wounds.

The nursing he received was not tender, but he recovered with a speed that dazed the doctor. Then he was promptly clapped into prison for resisting arrest, for theft, and for assaulting officers of the law.

For three months he observed the cross section of the world of crime which was presented to him in prison. Then, when he was weary of being immersed in the shadows of this world, he knocked down a guard, climbed a wall, tore a rifle from the hands of another guard, and stunned the fellow with a blow across the head, sprang down on the farther side, dodged away through a fusillade of bullets, reached the desert land, lived there like a hunted wild beast for six months, with a horse for companion, a rifle for a wife, and a revolver for a chosen friend. At last he reached a seaport and took ship again on free blue waters.

When the ship touched at Bombay, the hand of the law seized him again. He broke away the next night, reached the Himalayas after three months of wild adventure, plunged into the wastes of Tibet, joined a caravan which carried him into central Asia, came to St. Petersburg a year later, shipped to Brazil, rounded the Horn on a tramp freighter, and deserted at a Mexican port.

At the age of nineteen Gordon Macdonald rode across the border into Texas for the first time. He stood six feet two and a half inches in his bare feet. He weighed two hundred pounds stripped to the buff. He knew guns and fighting tricks, as a saint knows the Bible, and his whole soul ached every day to find some man or men capable of giving him battle which would truly test his gigantic strength.

But on his long pilgrimage he had learned a great truth: No matter how a man defies his fellows, he must not defy the law. For the law reaches ten thousand miles as easily as a man reaches across a table. And the law has fingers of steel. Imagine the mind of a fox planted in the body of a Bengal tiger, a beast of royal power and a brain of devilish cunning. Such was Gordon Macdonald. He looked like a lion, he thought like a fox, and he fought like ten devils, shoulder to shoulder.

First he joined the rangers, not for the glory of suppressing crime, but for the glory of the dangers to be encountered in that wild service. He gained ten commendations in as many months for fearless work; in the eleventh month he was requested to resign. The Texas rangers prefer to capture living criminals rather than dead ones.

So Gordon Macdonald resigned and rode again on his friendless way. He rode for ten years through a thousand adventures, and in ten years no man's eye lighted to see him come, no woman smiled when he was near her, no child laughed and took his hand. Dogs snarled at him and shrank from his path. But Macdonald cared for none of these things. A thunderbolt does not hope for applause from the world it is about to strike. No more cared Gordon Macdonald. For he was awake to one thing only, and that was the hope of battle. Speed, as in the wrist of a cat; strength, as in the paw of a grizzly; wisdom, as in the soul of a wolf — these were his treasures. Through all the years he fought his battles in such a way that the other man first drew his gun. Therefore the law passed Macdonald by unscathed. And all the years he followed, with a sort of rapturous intentness, a ghost of hope that someday he would meet a man who would be his equal, some giant of force, with the speed of a curling whiplash and the malignity of a demon. He lived for the day he might match himself against such a great devastator, an incarnate spirit of evil.

Such was "Red" Macdonald at the age of thirty. He was as striking in face as in body. That arched and cruel nose, that long stern chin, that fiery hair, and, above all, his blue eyes stopped the thoughts and hearts of men. One felt the endless stirring impulse in him. To look into his eyes was like looking on the swift changes of color which run down the cooling iron toward the point. It was impossible to imagine this man sleeping. It was impossible to conceive this man for an instant inactive of mind, for he seemed to be created to forge wily schemes and plan wild deeds.

He had crowded the events of a dozen lives into his short span of years. And still, insatiable of action, he kept on the trail which has only one ending.

Such was Macdonald in his thirtieth year when he first encountered the great stallion, Sunset.

II

When the brilliant colors at the end of day begin to fade from the clouds, when they are shimmering with a rusty red, such was the tint of the hide of this splendid animal, and yet the mane and the tail and the four stockings of the stallion were jet black. It was this rich, strange crimson that first startled Gordon Macdonald and held his mind. Like thick blood with light striking across it, he thought, and that grim simile stayed in his mind. There was something of fate in this meeting, he felt. A strange surety grew up in him that his destiny was inextricably entangled with the big red stallion. And equal surety came to him that if he had this horse, evil would come of it, and yet the horse he must have!

He rode closer to the edge of the corral and examined the stallion in detail. It was not color alone in which Sunset was glorious.

94

He was one of those rare freaks of horseflesh in which size is combined with exquisite proportion. It is rare to find a tall man whose legs are not too long, or whose arms are not too lean; there are sure to be flaws and weaknesses when a man stands over six feet in height. And, rare as it is to find a big man who conforms to the Greek canons, it is rarer still to find a tall horse neither too long nor too short coupled, with bone to support his bulk, but not lumpy and heavy in the joints, and with a straight, strong back. So exact, indeed, were Sunset's proportions, that it might have seemed with the first survey that he was too lean and gangling of legs; but, when one drew closer one noted the great depth of body where the girth ran, the wide, square quarters, rich in driving power, the flat and ample bone, the round hoofs, black as ink, the powerful sweep of the long shoulders, dimpled over and rippling with muscles like the tangled lashes of a thousand whips. He stood a scant inch under seventeen hands, but he was made with the scrupulous exactness of a fifteen-hand thoroughbred, one of those incredible carvings of nature that dance like kings about the turf at a horse show, or take the jumps as though winged with fire.

The heart of Macdonald contracted with yearning. He looked down with disgust to the nag which bore him. Big-headed, long-eared, squat and shapeless of build, the gelding had only one commendable quality, and that was an immense strength which was capable of supporting even the solid bulk of Red Macdonald, with a jog trot that might last from morning to night. But on such a steed he was easy prey; a swift riding posse might swoop down and overtake him in a half hour's run.

He looked up to the ragged sides of the mountains. The rider of such a horse as Sunset could make his home among those peaks. From those impracticable heights he could sweep down like a hawk on the wing and take toll from the groveling men of the plains — strike — ravage — destroy — beat down enemies — award justice for past injuries — and then away on wings again — wings strong enough to sweep him up the slopes and back to safety, while the sweating posse labored and puffed and cursed and moiled vainly in the dust far behind him!

No wonder that Macdonald looked back from those distant heights to the dark red stallion with a heart on fire with eagerness. Yonder stood the giant horse nosing the hand of a man who was talking softly to him and stroking his sleek neck. Macdonald dismounted. He stepped closer to the pair.

He had one gracious quality, a soft and deep bass voice. He used it with more effect because in all his travels he had picked up no slang; he spoke the same pure tongue which he had learned in his boyhood.

"I wonder," he said to the stranger, "if you're the man who owns this horse?"

He was a tall and slenderly built youth, with long tawny hair, a brown, weather-marked face with calm gray eyes looking out at Macdonald. "Yep," he said. "I own Sunset."

"Sunset?" echoed Macdonald, and looked back at the stallion. It was an appropriate name, and he said so. It was doubly appropriate now, as the big horse turned and a wave of crimson sun rippled along his flank, like a highlight traveling over bright silk.

At the deep, quiet sound of Macdonald's voice, Sunset came closer, snorted softly, then reached out with bright and mischievous eyes and nibbled at the brown back of Macdonald's hand.

"He doesn't seem to be afraid of me," said Macdonald.

The teeth of the stallion caught up a fold of skin on the back of Macdonald's hand and pinched it very gently. Playfully, the red horse started away, tossing and shaking his mane. He came back again slowly. Once more he sniffed at the stranger, thrusting out his beautiful head. Wonder of wonders, he permitted that great, strong hand of Macdonald to reach and touch his velvet muzzle. He permitted the tips of those terrible fingers to rub his forehead, to touch his silken ears, to stray along his throat. Eyes gleaming, he reached high, caught the brim of Macdonald's hat, twitched it off, and then, wheeling like a dog playing a game, bolted across the field, whipping the hat from side to side and flashing his heels in the air.

"Hey!" yelled the youth. "Come back here, Sunset!" He turned, flushing, toward Macdonald. "Say, now, I'm mighty sorry that happened!"

But Macdonald was staring after the fleeing horse, like one enchanted by a dream of beauty. The long sweep of that gallop made him dizzy with delight. His lips parted to the tenderest of smiles. On the farther side of the field Sunset dropped the sombrero and dashed his hoofs upon it. Then he picked up the hat again and came back at full gallop, the fragments dangling from his teeth, his head thrust out, his ears flattened, his mane flying like the plumes above a Grecian helmet, swift as an arrow loosed from a string, the ground shivering under the impact of his bearing hoofs. Like red flash of danger, he shot at them, then threw himself back and slid to a halt of stiffly braced legs, while his hoofs plowed up long strips of the turf. At the very feet of Macdonald he dropped the tattered sombrero.

"Like he expected a lump of sugar for spoiling my hat!" said Macdonald, grinning. "And look at this! He comes right back to my hand again! Man, man, there's only one horse in the world — there's no other like him!"

Sunset reached out to catch a lock of Macdonald's red hair in his teeth. Perhaps a mother feeling the tugging hands of an infant could understand how Macdonald's heart ached with joy to see this magnificent dumb creature defy him without malice and tease him as though he were some harmless child.

"What have you done to him?" growled the young owner. "Never saw Sunset play up like this to any other man."

It was wine of purest delight to Macdonald.

"He doesn't take up with strangers, then?"

"Takes them with his heels, if he can!"

"Well," said Macdonald, "I guess he knows I mean him no harm." He turned to the youth. "What's your name?"

"Rory Moore."

"Moore, is your horse for sale?"

"Nope."

"I've got five hundred dollars in my pocket."

"Sunset's not for sale. I raised him from a colt!"

"Five hundred is a lot of money. It takes a long time for a cowpuncher to save that much."

"No use, stranger!" declared Moore.

"Six hundred then!"

"Not if you made it six thousand!"

"Moore, here's nine hundred and eighty dollars. It's yours. Give me the horse!"

"Like I told you, mister, he's just plain not for sale."

Moore recoiled a bit, for the expression

of Gordon Macdonald had changed. His lips had stiffened. His body trembled. There was even a change in the hand which had been stroking the neck of the stallion, for the horse suddenly drew back and sniffed suspiciously at the bony fingers. But if there had been a glimpse of danger in the face of Red Macdonald, he smoothed it away quickly enough and managed to smile.

"No way in the world you'd give up that horse — couldn't be taken from you?

"Not unless the luck was against me!"

"Luck?"

"I mean I've never backed down at dice for any man!" Rory Moore was laughing at the thought. "Look here, I've got a pair with me. Your nine hundred against Sunset — one roll."

Macdonald reached for the little cubes, then drew his hand back.

"I never gamble," he said.

"What?" cried the other, as though the sun had vanished from the heavens. "Never gamble?"

"No." He turned, took one last, long look at Sunset, who had pressed his breast against the fence, as though eager to follow. Then Macdonald stepped to his gelding.

"What name'll I remember you by?" asked Moore.

But Macdonald did not answer. Mounting quickly, he spurred the gelding toward the town, whose roofs were already visible above the trees.

III

"Busted? *You!*" said Gordon Macdonald, shaking his head in disbelief. "You can make the cards do everything but talk! I've watched you practice with the dice and call your throw nine times out of ten, even bouncing them against a wall!"

The gambler lifted his wan, lean face, nodded wearily. "Yeah," he said, "I can do that. And I had my big game planted, Macdonald. There was a fortune in sight — a hundred thousand if there was a cent in that game! I had the cards stacked. Gent started betting against me. He had two aces and two jacks. I'd given him the ace of spades and the ace of hearts and the jack of spades and the jack of diamonds. He opened on the jacks, and I gave him the aces on the draw. The fifth card I dealt him ought to have been the seven of clubs.

102

Well, damn my eyes, it wasn't the seven but the ace of clubs that I'd given him — the first mistake I'd made in a hundred deals, and how I made it I dunno! An ace full on jacks is what he hands me, and with three measly deuces! That's why I'm busted, Macdonald!"

"Just watch that name, will you?" said Gordon Macdonald.

"They don't know you here?"

"No, it's new country for me."

"Me, too, and bad country it is. What name d'you want? I call myself 'Jenkins'!"

"Call me Red."

"All right . . . Red. You ain't fixed to stake me, are you?"

"What do you mean?"

"I meant, to stake me a couple of square meals. Ain't eaten since I can remember!"

Macdonald rubbed his knuckles slowly across his chin. "Suppose I *do* stake you."

"Why, then I'll sure pay you back, partner, the minute —"

"Suppose I stake you to five hundred dollars?"

"Five hundred!" Jenkins whispered. "What can I do for you? You know I ain't any hand with a gun or —"

"I want you to gamble for me."

"You mean, I'm to split with you after —"

"I want no split," Macdonald said. "If you win you win, and you keep the coin you make!"

Jenkins swallowed with difficulty, and his haunted eyes clung to the face of Gordon Macdonald.

"There's a youngster in town. His name is Moore."

"Rory Moore!"

"You know him?"

"Everybody in town knows him. The Moores used to own most of this here country. Look across the street!"

Macdonald looked across to the lofty, gabled front of the hotel — a spacious building, set far back from the street in deep grounds, in which all the garden growth had perished.

"That used to be the Moore house," said Jenkins.

"What happened?"

"Rory's father blew the whole wad of coin. He was a hot spender. Paris was his speed! Come back with a mighty small jingle in his purse and a funny accent. All his kids got was his empty purse!" And Jenkins laughed with a malicious satisfaction. "If he wanted to throw his coin away, why wasn't poker right here in Texas as good as Monte Carlo? Down with a gent that don't patronize home folks, I say!" His thin lips writhed into a snarl.

"This Moore — he likes to play pretty well?"

"Sure he does. And he usually wins. That's how he made enough money to start his ranch. He's got the devil's own luck with dice and cards. *Too* much luck, I'd say!"

"You mean, he's crooked?"

There was an expressive shrug of the shoulders.

"I ain't *seen* him crook the cards," Jenkins confessed. "But he's a bad one — a fighter." He stopped short, watching Macdonald.

"A fighter, you say? Neat with a gun, eh?"

"Quick and certain — which is what counts most!"

"Would you have the nerve to sit in with Rory Moore at a game and beat him?"

Jenkins turned white.

"What if I made a slip — and he seen? I'd be ready for planting, right there!"

"And what if you didn't make a slip?"

"Then I'd clean him out!" He twisted

his bony hands together in glee at the prospect.

"You figure Moore's the sort that would bet down to his last dollar?"

"He'd bet the boots he rides in," declared Jenkins. "And, if he stuck by the game, a talented gent could clean him out of his ranch — out of everything! But what's the use of talking like that. I ain't got a stake to start a game, have I?" He fixed upon Macdonald the eyes of a ferret.

"Five hundred dollars, Jenkins. I'll stake you as high as that."

"And how do we split?"

"He has a horse —"

"Sunset, you mean?"

"That's the name. Jenkins, I want that horse. When you break him, he'll stake Sunset. I want Sunset. You can keep the cash!"

For a time they were both silent, the lips of Jenkins tight, his eyes fired with an inner hunger.

"Well, I figger a man has to die some-time," said the gambler at last. "And ain't it better to die flush than broke?"

"No doubt about that!"

"I'll take you up, Red! Gimme the coin, and I'll lay for him! I'll get him tonight. I been broke so long that this looks like heaven! You trust me?"

Macdonald handed Jenkins the money with a tight smile. "I trust you."

"Sure you do! Sure you do!" murmured Jenkins. "I guess there ain't many west of the Mississippi that would try a crooked play with you." He squinted at Macdonald. "One thing I never could make out about you, Red."

"What's that?"

"You can do anything that any other man can do and better than most! But you always stay shut of cards. Don't seem to want to take chances that way. With your nerve, you'd get by fine. *Real* fine!"

"Has an honest gambler a chance of winning?"

"Honest gambler!" sneered Jenkins. "There ain't any such bird!"

"That's why I don't gamble," said Macdonald.

"But, look here," argued Jenkins, "do you think that I'm going to play square with Rory Moore?"

Macdonald scowled upon his confederate.

"I offered Moore a lot of money for that horse. He was a fool not to take it, and you're a worse fool, Jenkins, to ask questions!"

IV

Gordon Macdonald left Jenkins and stalked off across the street to the hotel. Since he had not slept in forty-eight hours, he could barely keep his eyes open long enough to finish a bedside cigarette. He squinted through the shadows of the room at the old photographs and paintings along the walls. These might all be members of the Moore clan — kinsmen, relations, supporters of the old power in the days when it was great, when this hotel was like a castle in the midst of a little principality.

Macdonald finished the cigarette, turned on his side, and was instantly asleep. It was a sleep filled with visions.

It seemed to Gordon Macdonald that he was mounted at last upon the great red beauty, Sunset, and that he was galloping over the mountain desert like a dry leaf soaring on a wind. A dizziness of joy swept into his brain, with the sway and swing of that gallop. There was perfect accord between the red stallion and himself. A pressure of his knee was as good as a twist of the reins, and his voice was both bit and spur.

They came to a river twisting among the hills, a swift, straight stream, save where it now and then dodged the knees of a hill and plunged on again. Macdonald looked upon that river with a careful eye, but he could not remember having seen in before.

He went on along its bank, glorying in the brown rushing of the waters with streaks and riffles of yellow foam upon the surface. On either side the banks were being gouged away. Here and there trees were toppling on the edges, with half their roots torn away. And even the hills of rock, which the stream dodged, were rudely assaulted and carved by the currents.

And, just as this dashing, thundering torrent was different from other peaceful rivers full of quiet, of pauses, and stars, was not he, also, equally different from other men? Did he not strike down those who opposed him? A thousand crimes might be laid to his account, but who was strong enough or cunning enough to call him to a reckoning?

At length he came to a turn of the river, so that its main body was removed some distance from him as he drove on straight up the valley, and, as the waters were withdrawn, it seemed to Macdonald that their voice was gathered in great, thick accents: "Turn back! Turn back! Turn back!"

So startling was the clearness of that phrase that he shook his head and boomed out a fragment of song to thrust the thought from him, but, when he listened to the river again, it was calling as clearly as ever: "Turn back! Turn back! Turn back!"

He halted Sunset and looked about him. Now, it seemed to Macdonald that he had indeed seen this river before. He could recall no single landmark, but he remembered the whole effect, as one remembers the sound of a human voice without being able to identify it.

Now he followed the stream again, as it dwindled swiftly. He crossed a fork, where another creek joined it. He went on, and in another half mile arrived at the big spring which gave the river birth. A little farther on he came to the divide, a ragged crest which overlooked to the east a rich plain, dotted with trees, spotted here and there with houses, and in the distance the gathered roofs of a town with a few clusters of spires above them. And, as he paused, the wind blew to him faintly the lowing of cattle made musical with distance. Another sound was forming behind him, the small voice of the creek, and again it seemed to be building words: "Turn back! Turn back! Turn back!"

Macdonald grew cold in his sleep. A heaviness of foreboding depressed him. Again, he looked upon the plain below. It was still bright with sun.

There could be nothing to fear in this, he told himself, and straightway he gave Sunset the rein. Down the slope they clattered in a wild gallop. They started across the fields, with Sunset jumping the fences like a bird on the wing. And so they came suddenly to a long avenue of black walnut trees, immense and wide-spreading, trees that interlaced their branches above the head of Macdonald.

He stopped Sunset. It was more than familiar, this long double file of trees. He had seen it before. He closed his eyes. He told himself that if he turned his head he would see a section behind him, where three trees had died, and where three smaller and younger trees had been planted. He turned his head, he looked, and it was

111

exactly as he had guessed.

This was very mysterious. He had never seen the plain before, he told himself, and yet here he was remembering exact detail. Macdonald looked hastily around him. There was nothing to justify that warning voice from the river. There was only the whisper of the wind among the branches above him, and the continual shifting and interplay of shadows on the white road, and fat, lazy cows in the neighboring fields. Nothing could be less alarming — unless the rattle of approaching hoofbeats bore some unsuspected danger toward him.

In a moment a rider was in view, swinging around a bend in the road, a girl of eighteen or twenty on a speedy bay mare, borne backward in the saddle a bit by the rate of the gallop, laughing her delight at the boughs of the walnut trees and the deep blue sky beyond them.

As her face grew clear to him, Macdonald turned cold indeed! He knew that he had never seen her, yet her face was more familiar to him than his own! He had come into a ghostly land, with voices speaking from rivers and with roads on which familiar strangers journeyed.

She came straight on, clad in a tightly

fitted jacket, with long sleeves bunched up at the shoulders, and she was perched gracefully in a side saddle, with the skirt of her riding habit sweeping well down past the stirrup.

When she saw him she raised a slim hand in greeting, and he heard her cry out in a high, sweet voice that went through and through him. The bay mare came to a halt with half a dozen stiff-legged jumps, then busied herself touching noses with Sunset. The girl in the side saddle was laughing, but her eyes were filled with tears.

"Oh," she cried, "I've been waiting so long — and here you are at last! I thought my heart would break with the long waiting, Gordon, but now it's breaking with happiness!"

"Do I know you then?" Macdonald was asking her. "Have I really met you before?"

"Don't you remember?"

"I try to remember, but there's a door shut in my mind, and I can't open it."

"We have met in our dreams, Gordon. Don't you remember now?"

"I almost remember. But your name is just around the corner away from me."

"I've never had a name — for you," she

said. And then her face clouded. "But, if I *should* tell you my name, it would spoil everything."

"How can a name spoil anything?"

"If I showed you my father's house you would understand."

He shook his head.

"If I lost you, how could I find you again, since I don't know your name?"

"Find the river, and the river will always bring you to me. But now, we must ride fast! They'll never overtake us, once we get to the hills and ride down the valley road beside the river, just the way you came."

"I've never run from any man!" he answered sternly. "How can I run now? Who will follow?"

"My father and all his men. Have you forgotten?"

It was from this, then, that the river voice had bidden him turn back. But Macdonald did not turn back; on he went, with the girl riding close beside him, beseeching him to stop.

When they came to the end of the great avenue of walnut trees, they entered a village and passed through it until they came into a deep garden and straight under the facade of a lofty house, one of the largest he had ever seen, with great wooden turrets and gables. To Macdonald it looked like a castle.

"Is this your father's house, where he lives with all his men?" he asked of the girl.

But no voice answered him, and when he turned she was gone.

"They've stolen her away from me," he thought to himself. "They have taken her into the house, and if I follow her there, they will kill me; but if I do not follow her I shall never see her again." And it seemed to Macdonald that, if he never saw her again, it would be worse, far worse than death. For the sound of her voice he would have crossed the wildest sea. And there was a slenderness to her, like that of a child, that took hold on his heart.

He dismounted, and strode up the wide steps, but when he came to the door of the house, though he had not heard a sound of a footfall following him, a strong hand clutched him by the shoulder.

Swiftly he spun around, but there was nothing behind him save empty air, yet the ghost fingers held him by the shoulder, biting into the bone like a hand of fire.

Macdonald awoke. There *was* a hand

upon his shoulder, and over his bed a dim figure was leaning. Instantly he struck out with his fist, and the figure fell back.

"For Lord's sake," groaned a voice from the floor, "it's only *me* — Jenkins!"

V

So vivid had been the dream, so bright the sunshine which he had seen in it, so clear the flowers and the trees and the shrubs in that great garden and the looming house above him, that for a moment the black darkness in the room seemed unreal.

Macdonald pulled the groveling Jenkins to his feet.

"A dangerous thing to wake a man up like that — in the middle of the night," he growled. "Wait till I light a lamp."

"No!" panted the gambler. "Somebody might be watching — somebody might guess —"

"Guess what?"

"That you put me up to the work."

"What work?"

"Playing with Rory Moore and breaking him."

The whole story rolled back upon the

mind of Red Macdonald, and for the moment the face of the girl in his dream grew dim.

"Ah, yes," he said. "Tell me what happened?"

"Moore played like a crazy man. I won so fast it had me dizzy. Finally he was broke. He put up his watch, he put up everything he had."

"Even the stallion — Sunset?"

"Yeah, Sunset. You'd have thought that he was staking his wife on them cards. And when he lost he put his head between his hands and groaned like a sick kid."

"But you got the horse, Jenkins?"

"It's in the stable behind the hotel. I'm leaving first thing in the morning. I'll tell them at the stable that I sold that hoss to you. Then I'll light out for Canada."

"Why run?"

"Moore may find out what I am, that some folks figger I don't always play square with the cards. And if he thinks that he's been cheated out of that hoss, he'll kill me, Macdonald! He'd be sure to sink a bullet into me."

Macdonald's face darkened with scorn. "You card-juggling rat! I've used you, and I'm done with you. You have the money, and I have the horse. Now get out!"

He could feel Jenkins shrinking away from him through the darkness, and from the door he heard the stealthy whisper of the gambler.

"I dunno that I'm any worse than you. You put me up to this game. I dunno that I'm any worse than you."

"Damn you!" sneered the big man. "Get out!" Then the door shut quickly behind Jenkins.

After the gambler had gone, the strangeness of the dream returned. Gordon Macdonald lighted a lamp and sat down with his face between his hands, but he found that his heart was still beating wildly, and the face and the form of the girl were fixed in his thoughts. He could remember the very texture of the sleeve of her riding habit. He could remember the way a wisp of hair, blown loose from beneath her stiff black hat, swayed across her cheek. He could remember how her bay mare had danced and sidled, coming down the avenue of walnut trees. And, above all, he still held the quality of her voice in his ear. How she had pleaded with him not to approach that house behind the garden! And how mysteriously she had disappeared. What might have happened had he not persisted in going on? And what was the pull and the lure which drove him so irresistibly ahead?

He stared around the room. It seemed to Macdonald that, if he could rest his eyes on some familiar object, his nerves would quiet. But what his glance first encountered was the dark and faded portrait of an old gentleman with a white muffler around his throat, and one hand thrust pompously into the bosom of his coat. The old man was smiling, and the smile was a grotesque caricature done in cracked paint. The blue of his eyes was dim with time.

The whole room exuded a musty aroma of the past. Macdonald told himself that this was no more than an old family mansion long used as a hotel — every room occupied many times in the course of each year. But the more he used his reason the more it failed him.

Fear was growing in him, and it was an unsettling sensation. Fear was a stranger to Red Macdonald. He recalled the day when five men had cornered him in an Australian desert and held him, more dead than living, in a group of rocks for forty-eight hours, without water — and not even in the worst of those hours had he felt this clammy thing called fear. Yet now there was a weakness in his stomach and in his throat. Driven by a powerful curiosity, Macdonald forced himself to go to the mirror. What he saw there seemed to be the face of another man. The pupils of his eyes were dilated. His lips were drawn. His bronzed cheeks had turned to a sickly yellow, and his forehead was glistening with perspiration. He glanced quickly over his shoulder to the window, for it seemed to him as though a pair of eyes, a moment before, had been watching him from its black rectangle, with the high light from the lamp thrown across it, blurring the outer dark.

He consulted his watch. It was half past two, and at this hour he certainly could not start his day's journey. But the very thought of remaining longer in that room was unspeakably horrible to Gordon Macdonald.

He dressed at once. There was Sunset, at least, waiting for him in the stable. At that thought half of the nightmare fears left him. He hurried through the packing of his bedroll, then left the room.

On the desk in the deserted little lobby Macdonald left more than enough to pay his bill. Then he started out for the stable.

It was deserted. Even this stable, which

the Moores had built behind their home, was lofty and mansionlike, finished at the top with sky-reaching gables and adorned at the upper rim of the roof with an elaborate cornice of carved wood, half of whose figures had cracked away with the passage of the years.

As Macdonald stepped through the great arch of the central door, he found a single lamp burning behind a chimney black with smoke. He took this lamp, carried it over to the stalls. He examined the horses. There were five, kept there for the night. Others were in the corrals behind the building.

In the first of these corrals he found Sunset.

The stallion had been placed by himself, and the moment the light from the lamp struck on him, he came straight for the bearer, his big eyes as bright as two burning disks, with the lamplight running along the silk of his red flanks.

Macdonald uttered a faint exclamation of delight. It was the first time in his wild life that he had secured anything through fraud. Treachery had never been one of his faults of character. But, as the horse nosed at his shoulder and whinnied softly, as though they had been friends for many a year,

Macdonald's heart leaped. Every man, he had always felt, will commit one crime before his life ends, and this must be the crime of Macdonald: He had gone behind another man's back, and cheated him with hired trickery!

He was revolted at the thought of Jenkins and the part he had played in partnership with the cowardly little gambler. But he would use Sunset as tenderly as any master could use him. That, at least, was certain.

In five minutes his saddle was on the back of the stallion, his roll was strapped to it, and he had vaulted into the stirrups and jogged out onto the main street of the town. All was quiet. The town slept the sleep of the mountains, black and stirless. The stars were bright above Red Macdonald. And under him the stallion was dancing with eagerness, playing lightly against the bit.

He spoke gently, and Sunset swept into a breathtaking gallop, no pitch and pound, as of the range mustang, but a long and sweeping stride, as though the beat of invisible wings bore him up and floated him over the ground.

Now the blackness of the plain lay before them, and Sunset was settling to his work.

A horse? No, it was like sitting on the back of an eagle. The cold of the nightmare left Macdonald, and it seemed that, if he turned, he would see the girl of his vision cantering beside him, laughing up to him!

Would he ever see her again?

One thing was clear. He must find action — action which would employ him to the full. He must fight against odds. He must plunge into danger, as into cleansing waters, and these would wash the memory of the girl from his mind.

So at least it seemed to Red Macdonald, as he rode on into the night. He searched his mind for an objective. It was no longer easy to find the danger which was the breath of his nostrils. Time was when a shrug of a shoulder or a careless word would plunge him into battle. But those days had passed. His reputation had spread wide before him, and men now stood back from Red Macdonald.

Then the inspiration came to him. Five years before, in the town of Sudeth, he had killed young Bill Gregory, and the Gregorys one and all had sworn revenge. What could be more perfect? Macdonald had only to ride into the town and take a room at the hotel. The next move would be up to the

Gregorys. And they were not the type of men to forget past oaths.

VI

The tidings of Red Macdonald's coming went out on wings, and that night the Gregorys assembled. In the course of two generations a large family had multiplied and become a clan, of which the head was old Charles Gregory. It was at his ranch house, a mile from the town of Sudeth, that the assembly gathered. The elders sat around a large oak table. The younger men, the fighting van of the Gregory family, were ranged around the wall, smoking cigarettes, speaking rarely. For it was felt in the Gregory family that age had its rights and its wisdom, and that young men might listen with profit.

Old Charles Gregory himself sat at the head of the table. Time had withered, but not faded, him. His arms and hands were shrunk like the hands of a mummy, but his thin cheek still held a healthful glow, and his eyes were as bright as the eyes of a youth.

"We all know why we're here," he said.

"The hound has come back. It wasn't enough that we didn't follow him and finish him after he murdered poor Bill. We kept the law and stayed quiet. But being quiet only made him figure that he could walk right over us. So he's back here sitting easy at the hotel and waiting for us to do something. The question is: What are we going to do?"

The elders around the table neither stirred nor spoke, but there was a slight and uneasy shifting of feet near the wall and a soft jingling of spurs.

"There's been a lot of talk about how Bill died," said old Gregory. "There's been five years for talk to grow, and talk grows faster than any weed on the range! So for you that don't know the facts clear, I'll tell you, because, come my time of life, the longer ago a thing happens the clearer it is in my mind."

He paused, and for the moment looked like a weary mask of death. Again his eyes looked out from the steep shadow of his brows, and he went on: "It started over nothing, the way most shooting scrapes start. Bill comes riding into town one day and goes up on the veranda and sits down in a chair. Pretty soon Abe Sawyer comes up and says to him: 'You know who that chair belongs to?'

" 'I dunno,' says Bill.

" 'Red Macdonald has been sitting in it,' says Abe.

" 'Who's Macdonald?' says Bill.

" 'A nacheral born man-killer,' says Abe, 'the worst man with a gun that ever was born.'

"Bill sits and thinks a minute.

" 'I dunno how much of a gunfighter he is,' says Bill, 'but he sure enough ain't got this chair mortgaged.'

"Abe didn't say no more about it. He went off and sat down to watch, and pretty soon Macdonald comes out through the door of the hotel and taps Bill on the shoulder.

" 'Excuse me, partner,' he says, 'but this is my chair!'

"Bill answers without turning his head, 'D'you think that you can hold down a chair all day by just sitting in it once?'

" 'I was fixing my spurs,' says he, 'and I left one of 'em lying on each side of the chair. That makes it mine.'

"Bill looks down, and sees the spurs for the first time. He looks up to the face of Macdonald, and he said later that it was like looking into the face of a lion. His nerve sort of faded out of him.

" 'Maybe you're right,' says he and gets up and takes another chair. But, while he's sitting in the other chair, he sees half a dozen of the gents, them that have watched the whole thing, sort of looking at him and then at one another smiling. He's got half a mind to go over and pick a fight with Macdonald right there, to show that he has nerve enough to suit any man. But then he remembers that he's going to marry poor Jenny inside of a week, and he decides that he ain't got no right to take on a gunman.

"He goes on home. As soon as he sits down to the supper table in comes cousin Jack, who starts joking with Bill because he'd give up his chair to Macdonald. Bill don't say a word to nobody. He gets up from the table and goes out and saddles a hoss and starts for Sudeth town. He looks up this Macdonald at the hotel, and starts in cussing him, with his hand on the butt of his gun. He says that Macdonald must have started talking about him and calling him yellow. But Macdonald speaks back to him plumb soft and says that he don't want no trouble, and that the matter of the chair don't mean nothing. But Bill won't back down. He goes up and punches Macdonald on the jaw. Macdonald knocks him down. While Bill's on the floor he pulls his gun, and Macdonald waits till he sees the steel flash, then he pulls his own Colt, quick as a snake, and kills poor Bill."

Charles Gregory paused, looking at his withered hands, clasped above the table. There was no sound in the room.

"That's the straight of it. But since then we've heard a lot about Red Macdonald. He lives on murder! We've traced him a ways, and we've planted twenty dead men to his credit! Now, boys, this Macdonald is the man we told to get out of Sudeth and never come back, and here he is in our town again, bold as brass! I seen the sheriff today. All he said was that he had a long trip to make and was leaving pronto, which was the same as saying that he knew that Macdonald was a plumb bad one, and that he wouldn't dislike having us wipe him out. Ain't I right? The only question is: How are we going to do it?"

There was a small, respectful pause at the conclusion of this speech, and finally Henry Gregory, a wide-shouldered, gray-headed man, spoke from the end of the table. No man in the room was more respected.

"I've had my storms," he said, "and I've done my fighting. But the older I get the more I figure that no good can come out the muzzle of a Colt. I say no more fighting! Let Macdonald stay. Poor Bill is dead. It's done and over! There ain't no doubt that this Macdonald is a professional, and before we could get rid of him, a couple of our boys are sure to go down. I say — hands off."

"There'd be a lot of talk!" exclaimed another at the table.

"Nobody but a fool would accuse us Gregorys of being cowards," said Henry. "What fools say don't bother me none. We can let 'em chatter!"

From the wall, young Jack Gregory moved forward through the drift of cigarette smoke. "I got something to say that needs saying pretty bad. It was me joking Bill that sent him into town to fight. God knows I didn't mean no harm. Me and Bill was always pals. But it was me that got him killed, so what I got to say is this: Let me go in and face Macdonald and try my luck. It's *my* business!"

There was a hum of dissent.

"No," said old Charles Gregory, "we've passed our word that Macdonald should never come back to Sudeth, and he's done it. Right or wrong, we've passed our word. It ain't the business of Jack here. It's the business of all of us! Speaking personal, I say it'd be suicide to send only one man. We need two. Macdonald is a lion! We'll draw lots to see who goes."

In another moment they were busy preparing the lots and then making the draw. By weird chance it fell upon both the sons of the family peacemaker, Henry Gregory. Steve and Joe were his only sons, great-boned, silent fellows, as swarthy of skin as Indians and as terrible as twin wildcats in a fight. Certainly the choice could not have fallen upon two more formidable men.

"But it ain't right," protested Jack. "I sure ought to have a hand. If Steve and Joe are hurt, the blame of it will come back on me!"

"Shut up!" snarled his father. "You're playing the fool, son. Are you wiser than the lot of us?"

So Jack was shouted down, but his mind was not put at rest. He heard it decided that the attack on Macdonald should be made in the morning. He heard the farewells, as the meeting broke up. And, witnessing all these things through a mist, all he saw clearly was the stern face of Henry Gregory, now wan with sorrow for his sons. Jack Gregory rode out with the others, fell to the rear, and presently had turned down a path and started for the town of Sudeth.

VII

At the hotel, Macdonald waited, turning over the danger in his mind, as a connoisseur turns over the thought of an expected feast. He had put his head into the jaws of the lion. How those jaws would close was the fascinating puzzle. The Gregorys might attack him by surprise, or in a crowd, or they might wait for the night, when they would have a better fighting chance.

Such surmise filled his mind all the late morning. In the early afternoon he fell asleep.

The instant he closed his eyes, he was once more traveling up the river in the mountains, with the voice forming out of the sounding current: "Turn back! Turn back! Turn back!" Once more he climbed to the headwaters of the stream, crossed the divide, and saw before him the same sunny plain, exactly as it had been before . . .

He wakened suddenly; and that afternoon he slept no more, but went down into the lobby of the hotel, onto the veranda in front, and waited.

The evening came, and still there was no sign of the Gregorys. But word was brought to him that the sheriff had left town. And then new word came that the Gregorys were meeting that evening. Wherever Macdonald went, though he had no friends and no companions, there was always a certain number of men, like jackals who follow the king of beasts, ready to carry information to the great man. He treated them with cool contempt; but on occasion they were invaluable to him. It was one of these fellows who brought word of Rory Moore.

"What about him?" asked Macdonald sharply. "What the devil do you know about Moore?"

"Nothing but what everybody will know soon enough. Rory Moore is telling folks that you stole Sunset."

It brought a growl from Macdonald. He

dropped his cigarette to the floor and smashed it with his heel.

"It's a lie! I bought Moore's horse from a man named Jenkins who won it from him in a gambling game."

"Moore swears it was a frame-up. He says he's found out that Jenkins was a professional gambler, a crooked player whose real name is Vincent."

"Go on," said Macdonald coldly, "tell me the rest of it."

"Seems that this Jenkins, as he was calling himself, started right out of town after he'd cleaned Rory Moore up at cards. Early the next morning Moore got on Jenkins's trail. By noon he'd run him down. He put a gun on Jenkins, and the hound got down and crawled and confessed everything."

"Which *was?*"

"Jenkins said you'd come to him and offered to stake him to five hundred dollars, if he'd use it to clean out Moore and make him put up his horse at the end of the game. The horse was what you wanted. And the scheme worked. Moore, anyway, got all his money back from Jenkins, and now he's looking to find you and Sunset.

I'm wondering if he'll have a hard time of it?"

Here the speaker laughed softly — and Macdonald joined in the laughter. Of all the men he had faced in the past half dozen years, there had been none to compare with Rory Moore in dash and spirit. He had not the slightest doubt that the young rancher was a true warrior. A battle against him would be a pleasure. After this Gregory business at Sudeth, he would return to Moore's home town and await him there in the hotel. What could be better than that? Fresh danger to stir the blood!

Now it was evening — and Macdonald was in the lobby of the hotel when a silence fell over the room. The babel of voices died away. There was a soft and sudden shifting of positions. Red Macdonald, looking into a small mirror hanging on the wall in front of him, saw a big fellow striding through the door. The pale, drawn face, the glaring eyes, the jaw set hard and thrust out a little, were the features of a man on the verge of meeting death itself.

"Macdonald!" called the stranger.

Gordon Macdonald turned slowly to face the young cowman.

"Calling me?" he asked.

"I'm calling you, Macdonald. My name's Jack Gregory!"

And, as he spoke, his right hand trembled near his holstered gun. With the blandest of smiles, Macdonald held out his hand.

"Very glad to meet you, Gregory," he said.

The gesture was disregarded.

"I want to talk with you outside."

"Certainly."

They passed through the door and descended the steps. Instantly the door of the hotel was packed with a blur of white faces, watching eagerly. Macdonald looked about him with infinite satisfaction. It was a moonless night, to be sure. But the sky was clear, and the stars were shining. Certainly there was light enough for Macdonald to shoot almost as straight as by daylight. He had fought a score of times by the light of the stars.

"I've come to beg you to leave the town," said Jack Gregory.

"*Beg* me to leave it?" asked Macdonald.

"Just that."

"And if I don't leave?"

"We fight!"

"I'm sorry to hear that," said Macdonald,

135

and in the starshine he smiled upon Jack Gregory.

"Macdonald," pleaded the other, "it was fool joking of mine that drove Bill to come and have it out with you. I got his death on my conscience. Now some of the others are coming for you, but it ain't their business. It's mine and I'm askin' you to leave. Everybody knows you're a brave man. If you leave town nobody'll think any the worse of you."

"You'd get a big reputation cheap," said Gordon Macdonald. "But what would I get?"

"A cold thousand. I've saved that much, and —"

"You fool!"

"Listen to me! I'm desperate! I know that I can't stand up to you, but if you won't go by persuasion, I got to try my gun!"

It was a situation unique in the experience of Red Macdonald, and he hesitated. But what cause had he to love the world, or trust or pity any man in it? From the very first his life had been a battle.

"If I gave way," he said coldly, "the story would go that you'd bluffed me, Gregory. I'd rather be dead than shamed."

There was a groan from Jack Gregory.

"You cold-hearted devil!" he cried. "If there's no other way —"

He reached for his Colt.

Macdonald saw Jack's gun flash up. It was shooting at ten paces, and even a poor shot was not apt to miss at this range. He dropped his right hand on the butt of his gun, making it swing up, holster and all. At the same instant, he pulled the trigger. Jack Gregory spun and dropped.

He had been shot squarely between the eyes.

VIII

No doubt, when all was said and done, it was as fair a fight as had ever been seen in the town of Sudeth. Yet there was a roar of anger from the spectators when they saw young Gregory fall.

They poured out through the doorway in a rush, and every man had a drawn gun in his hand.

One section of the mob spilled out toward the body of Gregory, lying face down in the dust. The other section swarmed toward the slayer.

"Finish the murdering dog!" cried one.

"No. Hold him for the sheriff!" shouted another.

"And see him get free on self-defense? We'll be our own law! Macdonald, put up your hands!"

There had been no chance to run. In that clear starlight with a dozen guns covering him, Macdonald knew that he could not get away. Therefore, he stood his ground, and at the order he obediently raised his arms above his head, not straining them high up, as men in fear will do, but holding them only a trifle above the height of his shoulders, standing at ease and facing the rush of the mob.

"Get iron on his wrists."

"No irons! A rope! Where's a rope?"

"Here's one!"

"Put down your hands real slow, one at a time," commanded the man with the rope. "Jab a gun into his middle a couple of you, and kill him if he tries to move!"

Macdonald smiled. Perhaps this was a little more than he had bargained for, but it was not at all unpleasant. The joy in peril, which he had found so early in life and loved so long, was singing in him now. They had his life upon the triggers of a dozen guns, yet if he could strike suddenly enough, their very numbers —

Macdonald had been lowering his right hand slowly, to show that he intended no sudden move toward escape. Now he jerked it down and knocked away the two revolvers which had been thrust against his body. One of them exploded. At the same instant Macdonald drove forward into the crowd, crouching low, as a football player charges a line. They tumbled away before him like snow before a plow. Who could fire, when the bullet, nine chances out of ten, would find the body of a friend?

Two men loomed ahead of Macdonald. He smote one on the side of the head, saw the head rebound, as though broken at the neck, as the man went down. Macdonald's shoulder crashed against the breast of the other, and the man fell back with a gasp. There was now a way open before him, and he went down it, like a racing fox with the cry of the hounds behind.

They were firing at him, but the bullets flew wild. Macdonald reached the corner of the hotel and whipped around it. He headed down the side of the building, then darted for the corrals, with the mob still in fierce pursuit.

He found Sunset and vaulted into the saddle. It seemed that the fine animal knew what was expected of him. A tap on the side of the neck turned him around, and a word started him away at a gallop. Sunset took the fence with a wide leap that brought a yell of despair and rage from the pursuers — and in another moment man and horse had vanished into the blackness of the night.

Macdonald had galloped less than half a mile before he turned Sunset, and headed boldly straight back for the hotel. He stole quietly up the back stairs to his room. No one had yet touched his belongings. He packed, returned down the stairs, went out to Sunset, and galloped once again into darkness.

As for the town of Sudeth, it passed through a sudden and violent transition. For two hours the townsfolk raved against the cool-handed murderer and swore that they would run him to earth — until a committee went up to investigate the belongings of Macdonald and found them gone. On the plaster wall was scrawled: "Thanks, gents, for a very pleasant party."

A storm of wonder and then of appreciation. For there was something almost supernatural in the courage of a man who could return on the heels of the very mob hunting his life. The townsmen lost their taste for the hunt. That would be left to the Gregorys.

IX

Macdonald knew that the Gregorys would never stop hunting him until they had clashed in final battle — yet he had no desire to put a great distance between himself and his pursuers. First the score with Rory Moore was to be settled. And he let Sunset run like a homing bird straight across the hills toward home.

They reached the town nearly a day later, in the red time of twilight, with the streets hushed and peaceful.

Distantly, he heard a dog barking. Otherwise, the area seemed dead. It was like riding into a ghost town.

Of course this was easily explainable, Macdonald told himself. The people were at table, and since they all kept the same hour for supper, they were off the streets. Yet this conclusion did not entirely satisfy him. There was a solemnity about this place, with the far off wailing of the dog, that warned him back like the voice of the river in his dream.

At the hotel Macdonald found the same sleepy atmosphere as he stood in front of the desk and asked for lodging.

Incredibly, he was assigned the *same* room he had occupied the last time — when he had left so suddenly in the middle of the night. Macdonald wanted to protest, but was kept quiet by the very violence of his feelings. How could he declare that this was the last place on earth in which he wished to spend another night?

Still, he could not force himself to walk upstairs to the room. Not yet. Instead, he left the hotel to seek out Sunset at the stables.

The tall stallion was digesting a liberal feed of sweet-smelling hay. Half a dozen hungry chickens, roaming abroad in search of forage, had clustered around the outskirts of the hay, scratching into it and picking busily at the heads of grain. But the big stallion kept on steadily at his meal, merely cocking one sharp ear when the beak of a hen picked a little too close to his soft muzzle.

Macdonald leaned on the corral fence,

watching quietly, until the gathering shadows drove even those hungry chickens away from the hay and back toward their roosting places.

"Yep," said a voice to the side, "that's a plumb easy-going hoss, I'd say."

Macdonald looked around with a scowl. What he found was a little old man, so bent that his head was thrust far in front of his body. He balanced himself with a round-headed cane on which his brown hands rested. He had a short-stemmed pipe between his gums and puffed noisily at it.

"This here's a famous hoss," said the old man. "Belongs to Red Macdonald!"

"Never heard the name," said Macdonald.

"I come here to have me a look at him before Macdonald rides him away again. I disremember when I seen a finer hoss than Sunset! Makes me right sorry to think about him being wasted on a man-killing, law-spoiling hound like Macdonald."

"Is he as bad as all that?" asked Macdonald slowly.

"He's worse," said the other, and he removed his pipe from his mouth so that he might speak with more vehemence. Macdonald saw that the stem was wound with string to give a better grip to the gums of the old man. "What would you say about a gent that kills just for the sake of the killing?"

"I think that depends on how he kills," said Macdonald. "Every man is a hunter, if you come down to it. If this Macdonald takes as big a chance as the next man, what's so wrong in that?"

"Suppose he killed with poison?"

"Are you saying he does *that?*" cried Macdonald.

"Just as bad. He's such a good shot, and his nerves are so plumb steady, that he knows he ain't running no real risk when he faces another man. There ain't one chance in a hundred that he'll get so much as scratched. That's why I say he might as well use poison for his killings. And to think that a hoss like Sunset —"

But Macdonald had heard enough. He turned away, walked back into the hotel, and slowly climbed the stairs to his room.

On the way he fought over the truth about himself. Just how much chance *did* the other fellow have, when matched against the practiced hand and quick gun of Red Macdonald?

His body bore many scars. He had been

wounded almost as often as he had wounded others. But that was only in the early days. How long had it been now, since an enemy had wounded him in a face-to-face gunfight?

The old man at the corral had been right! He might as well have killed by poison.

Macdonald lowered himself to the bed, and, staring into the darkness, thought about the men who had fallen before him in his life of violence. He closed his eyes — and in another moment was riding up the river among the mountains — the river whose voice gathered into human words: "Turn back! Turn back! Turn back!"

X

It was all as it had been before. Macdonald rode to the top of the divide, where the water dwindled to a little spring. He looked over the plain, across a sweep of sunshine and shadow. The faint lowing of cattle was blown to him upon the height. And, as before, a sudden chill passed into the heart of Gordon Macdonald. For the voice of the river could not be wrong. He felt he was on the verge of a revelation.

Yet he could not turn back. A nameless

eagerness filled him, far overbalancing his fear. Down the hill he swept and over the meadow at the long-reaching gallop of the red stallion. He came in time to the same avenue of walnut trees, and along that avenue he rode, with growing dread.

Now he came again to the town, all quiet under the sun, and stood once more before the great castle of a house where the girl had disappeared.

Slowly he mounted the steps, and the tall house before him was deeply silent. Macdonald knocked at the door. It was opened so quickly that it was obvious his approach had been noted.

At first he saw no one inside the dark, high hall of the place. He stepped in. The moment he did so Macdonald discovered who had opened the door for him. He could never forget that pale face — the face of Anthony Legrange, as he had been on that night eight years before, when he died in Cheyenne with a bullet from the gun of Red Macdonald in his heart.

Legrange was smiling, a calm smile of mockery and scorn.

Macdonald stared at him. "I thought you were dead. But I'm a thousand times glad to see that I was wrong! A thousand times glad, old fellow!"

The pale man said nothing. He turned, beckoned to Macdonald.

They passed through several shadowed rooms, down a long corridor, into a wide banquet hall. At a huge table, the largest Macdonald had ever seen, men were seated. Some were eating, some were drinking, and some were smoking, so that the air was blue with smoke. Yet Macdonald could detect no taint of tobacco, and though the men were laughing and talking, they were making no sound; also, the fall of knives and forks upon the plates was soundless!

Here, assembled in this great hall, were men from a dozen nations, and every one was a man Red Macdonald had slain!

Just before him in the first chair, was young Jack Gregory, with no mark of the bullet upon his forehead. And at the side of Gregory sat a great Negro, a giant of his kind, naked to the waist, just as he had been on that night, so many years before, when he had grappled with Gordon Macdonald in the fire room of a tramp freighter. Their battle rushed back clean and clear upon the mind of Macdonald. He saw the Negro, blood streaming down his face, snatch up a great bar of iron. He saw himself catch up a lump of coal and with a true aim knock down the big stoker. He saw them grapple again, as his strong hands found a firm grip upon the throat of the giant black man. The man's life had fled away under Macdonald's killing fingers. . . .

Next to the stoker sat a hideous Malay, with a split upper lip, rolling his wild eyes as he talked. That was the human devil who had leaped upon him from a Bombay alley. Macdonald's knife had found the Malay's throat.

And there, the burly English mate who had enforced obedience with the weight of his fists. They had grappled and gone over the rail together. Macdonald had come up, but the mate had not.

Finally, sitting side by side, yellow of skin and dark of eyes, were the "Arizona Kid" and his three brothers. Macdonald had trailed them in Texas, when he was a ranger, and had killed them all in one glorious, bloody battle. Now the Arizona Kid pointed to Macdonald, and gave him a wide, yellow smile. The Kid's three brothers began to laugh at Macdonald, and, indeed, all the others along the table were silently laughing and pointing, until cold sweat rolled down the face of Red Macdonald.

"You fools!" he shouted. "What's the joke? I've sent you to damnation, every one of you, and I'd send you there again and think nothing of it! I had no fear of you living, and do you think for an instant that I'm afraid of you because you come back after death to gibber at me?"

The silent laughter continued, as Macdonald raged at them. "I've fought every man of you fairly, face to face! I took no advantage. I never struck a man that wasn't fighting back! I never harmed a man that asked for mercy. Why do you laugh at me? Why?"

But they gave him no answer — and the maddening shadow-laughter drove Macdonald from the room.

At the threshold of the next he was greeted by the delicate sweetness of flowers, and as he entered he saw that they were banked everywhere about the room. Wild flowers and crimson roses, and great purple violets. The air was alive with their fragrance.

The room was utterly silent.

In its center stood an open coffin on a flower-draped pedestal, and in that coffin lay a dead man. Macdonald leaned forward to make out his face. It was Moore — Rory Moore, dead before he had been struck!

And, suddenly, the girl was there! — the lady of the vision, still in her riding costume. Her lips trembled, but no sound came from them. Tears streamed steadily down her face and, staring at her, Macdonald realized now that the face of the girl and the face of Rory Moore were incredibly alike. What was drawn on a large and manly scale in Rory's dead face was made small and exquisitely beautiful in the living face of the girl.

"I'm innocent of his death!" cried Macdonald. "I swear to you that I have not touched him!"

At his voice the girl looked up; there was horror and hatred in her eyes.

"No! *No!*" shouted Macdonald — and wakened to find himself on his knees in the darkness of the room, with his arms stretched out before him, and his voice moaning vague words.

XI

In that room, where the dream had possessed him, he looked sharply around, and it was as though scales had fallen from his eyes. He could see it all now. Mystery? There was none at all! What he had half seen and left unnoted by his conscious mind, he was now keenly aware of, for here was all the substance of his dream. With new eyes, he examined those faded paintings along the walls. There was the narrow, rushing river streaking down from those ragged hills which rolled back against the sky. And here, too, was the sweeping bird's-eye view of the sunlit plain. But where was the girl?

He had only to turn to the opposite wall to see her, just as she had ridden into his dream, sitting lightly on the side saddle and riding down a long avenue of walnut trees.

Macdonald had lived for two days in what he considered an exquisite torment. But now he began to wonder if the torment into which he was passing might not be worse. For there had lingered in his mind during all those hours the hope that some day he would find her, just as she had been when she rode in his dream. And if all the terror of the dream had gone, all the beauty of it was gone, too!

The girl had lived only in his dream, no more than a figure on painted canvas. He could never find her now.

There was a light rap at the door, and Macdonald took up his Colt. He eased upon the door. A dusty, barefoot boy was there, with a letter in his hand, his wide, frightened eyes fixed upon the face of Red Macdonald, as though upon an evil spirit. The boy ran off the instant the big man took the envelope. Macdonald tore it open and found within the shortest and the most eloquent of notes: "I am waiting for you. Rory Moore."

Macdonald sat down on the bed, still holding the Colt. Again, he examined the painting of the girl. What he had seen in the dream was true; she *was* the very image of Rory Moore!

XII

Like all great events which become a part of history, what happened that day was remembered even to the smallest details. Gordon Macdonald had been carefully observed as he walked from the hotel, dressed with unusual care, a red bandanna around his throat, a sombrero decorated with silver medallions upon his head, and with his boots shined until they were like twin mirrors. One might have thought that he was going to be the best man at a wedding, or the groom himself. But everyone knew that he was going out to take a life. For the rumor had passed through the length and breadth of the town that Rory Moore was waiting in front of the blacksmith shop, and that he had sent a message to the terrible Macdonald.

So scores of eyes were watching as the big man walked down the single street of the village. He had never seemed taller. He had never seemed more grand. He carried with him that unconscious air of calmness and reserve which goes with men who have done great deeds.

He paused at the corral. There he leaned against the fence and called. And the big red stallion came running to the voice of his master. Later in the telling of the tale, a dozen men swore that they saw Gordon Macdonald pass his arms around the neck of the horse and put his cheek against the head of Sunset.

Then he went on again with as light a stride as ever. When the watchers thought of Rory Moore, their hearts shrank within them. For it seemed impossible that such a force as Red Macdonald could be stopped by any man.

Macdonald reached the general merchandise store, and paused there to speak to an old Mexican woman who came with a toothless whine to ask for money. He was seen to take out a wad of rustling bills and drop it into her hand. She poured out a volley of blessings. But her benefactor went on without a glance behind him.

And finally he had come in sight of the blacksmith shop. A cluster of men fell back. One or two lingered beside Rory Moore, begging him to the last minute not to throw away his life. But he pushed them aside, and strode well out into the street, where the fierce white sun beat down upon him.

"Macdonald!" cried Rory Moore in a wild, hoarse voice.

"Well, Rory," answered the smooth man-killer, standing tall and careless in the shimmering noon heat, "are you ready?"

"I've waited for you, Macdonald — and now I mean to kill you!"

"Then go for your gun and be damned!"

And Moore, waiting for no second invitation, reached for his Colt.

Carelessly, it seemed, Gordon Macdonald reached for his own weapon. Yet such was the consummate speed of motion that his gun had flashed free before the revolver of Rory Moore was half out of its holster.

But Macdonald did not fire. Instead, he smiled thinly at young Rory Moore.

Moore triggered the heavy Colt, and his bullet knocked up a little fountain of dust at the feet of the giant. He fired again, and Macdonald fell backward into the dust of the street. The big sombrero dropped from his head, and he lay with his long red hair spread like blood across the dust.

So incredible was it to all who watched that Macdonald should indeed have fallen, that there was a long pause before the townspeople, moving slowly, closed around the big man, like wolves around a dead lion.

Perkins, the storekeeper, gingerly picked up Macdonald's gun where it had fallen into the dust. The storekeeper held it toward the sun, turning it slowly, examining it as one might have examined the sword of Achilles, after the arrow had struck his heel, and the venom had done its work.

Perkins broke the gun open.

It was empty.

"There ain't but one way of looking at it," said the sheriff, when he came into the town that evening. "Macdonald didn't want to kill young Moore. But he had to face him, or be called a coward. And there you have it! He'd been a hound all his life, but he died a hero!"

The story of Gordon Macdonald was not yet done. It was Mrs. Charles Moore who felt compelled to visit the dead man's room, and with her went her niece, the sister of Rory Moore. They found the room undisturbed. There was Macdonald's rifle, his other revolver, his slicker, and his bed roll.

They began to look around the room itself.

Six shining bullets were scattered on the floor under the painting of the girl from Macdonald's dream.

"It's a picture of my Aunt Mary," said the sister of Rory Moore.

"Yes," nodded Mrs. Moore. "Poor dead soul! And, child, child, how astonishingly you've grown to be like her! I've never seen such a likeness — just in the last year you've sprouted up and grown into the very shadow of her!"

The girl's head was lowered; she was silent.

"Heavens child, you're weeping!"

"I saw him when they carried him in from the street," said Mary softly. "And even in death he seemed a greater man than I'll ever know!"

And faintly, in the muted light of the room, tears ran and glittered along the soft pink curve of her cheeks.

PARTNERS

When American Magazine printed "Partners" in their January, 1938, issue they called it a "storiette" — meaning a very short story. It is not, however, short on content. Faust managed to pack a great deal of plot and conflict into these few dynamic pages, proving that his talent as a major storyteller was not always dependent upon a wide canvas.

The excitement and power of his best western writing is here compacted into an emotional time bomb which he sets ticking in the opening paragraph. The climactic meeting in the snows of Caldwell Pass between Banning and Huntingdon grips and surprises the reader.

From the beginning of his career, Frederick Faust reserved the main use of his real name for verse. Only ten pieces of fiction appeared under his true by-line during his lifetime. "Partners" was one of the ten, proving his pride in this story.

That pride was justified, and this taut little excursion into suspense surely deserves a place in a collection of his best western tales.

AFTER SEPTEMBER, NO one takes Caldwell Pass, because although it is the shortest way west from Bisby, it is so high, so threatened with avalanches of snow and rubble. It has a bad name, also, for the northwest wind, which, once it sights its way down the ravine, can blow frost even into the heart of a mountain sheep.

This was a December day, but Banning was spending the early afternoon in Caldwell Pass, sitting behind a stone with his rifle across his knees. Once a bird shadow slid over him. As it moved beside the rock it touched Banning with a finger of ice and forced him to shift his position. But he waited with the patience of a good hunter until he heard the footfall come down the pass toward him. Then he slid the rifle out into the crevice of the rock.

He waited till he could hear the man's breathing. Then he said, "Hands up, Jack!"

Huntingdon turned his back sharply. Seen from behind there was no trace of middle age about him. He looked as trim and powerful as a young athlete.

The echo in the ravine had fooled him.

159

"Well, Harry?" he was saying.

"Keep your hands up. You'll get it straight through the back of the head if you don't," said Banning to the big man.

He went out and laid the muzzle of the rifle against the base of Huntingdon's skull. He held the gun under his right arm and patted the clothes of his partner with his left hand. He found the fat lump which the wallet made, and drew it out. There was no weapon. "All right, Jack. Turn around."

Huntingdon turned. He was a bit white on each cheek, below the cheekbone. He kept on smiling.

"How much did you take?" asked Banning, with his gun still threatening.

"I cleaned out the safe."

"You left me flat?"

"I left you the house, the office, and the good will," said Huntingdon.

"I had the house and the office and the good will before you came," said Banning.

"You had a mortgage on the house; nobody ever came to your office; and where was the good will?"

Banning frowned. He had been telling himself that he was the mere executor of justice; but he might have known that the tongue of Huntingdon would turn this execution into murder.

"Kind of surprised to find me here, aren't you?" asked Banning.

"I'm surprised — a little."

"Why, I've always seen through you," said Banning. "I knew about you and Molly right from the first."

He laughed, without letting the laughter shake his body or the gun in his hands.

"You never knew a wrong thing between us."

"Maybe there wasn't anything wrong enough to get a divorce for," said Banning.

"Molly's dead," said Huntingdon. "For God's sake, Harry . . . she's dead!"

Banning licked his lips. It pleased him to see the pain in Huntingdon's eyes.

"There's more things than bedtime stories in the world," he persisted. "There's a sneaking into a man's life and taking his wife away from him. There's a holding together of eyes, when the hands don't touch. There's a way of just kind of silently enduring the poor damned fool of a husband. There's —!"

He got out of breath and took a deep inhalation through his teeth.

"I wish she could see you here, with the stolen money!" said Banning.

161

Huntingdon smiled, "I think you're going to kill me."

Banning looked at that handsome face with a dreadful amazement; for he saw that his partner was not afraid.

"Before you put the bullet into me, though" said Huntingdon, "I want to speak about the money. I've worked for ten years for you. You called me a junior partner. But I was only a slave. At the end of that time, I had nothing."

"You know the kind of expenses . . ." began Banning.

"At the end of the ten years," said Huntingdon, "I find eighteen hundred dollars in the safe, and I take it. It's the only way I'll ever get a share. I take the money and get out. I thought I was going ten thousand miles to have elbowroom between us. . . . But this way is about as good. It will put the greatest possible distance between us."

"Now, what in hell d'you mean by that?"

"You couldn't understand."

"It's too high for me to understand? It's above me, maybe?" All at once Banning screamed, "Take this, then! And this!"

He fired as he was shouting. And the rifle went crazy in his hands. It missed

162

twice. The third bullet hit Huntingdon between the knee and the hip. He sank slowly to the ground. The blood came up in a welter of dark red. It soaked his trouser leg at once and began to trickle down over the rock.

"You're too high for me, are you?" yelled Banning. "Well, what you think now? . . . Another thing, damn you, and you listen hard to it. What did you ever do with your life before you hooked up with me in the partnership? Just a bum. Just a rambling bum. Never did a thing. Isn't that true? Speak out!"

"It's true," said Huntingdon.

"Never a damn' bit of good to yourself or anybody else till you hooked up with me," said Banning.

Huntingdon nodded. "In a sense, I suppose, we needed each other; in a sense, perhaps we were ideal partners."

Banning began to laugh, and then a chill gust of wind stopped his breath, quickly, like a handstroke. It was not a mere breath of wind. It was the true northwester which had found the ravine and was sighting down it as down a gun barrel.

He withdrew himself from his passion and, looking about him, saw that the sun was about to set. It was more than time for him to start home. In spite of his fleece-lined coat, his teeth would be chattering long before he got out of the pass. He turned with the rifle toward Huntingdon. His face was blue with cold. Banning had lifted the gun butt to his shoulder, but now he lowered it again.

"I've got to leave you, Jack," he said. "But it'll be thirty below in half an hour, with plenty of wind to drive the cold through you. You're going to have a few minutes to think things over, and then — you'll get sleepy!"

He saw Huntingdon's eyes widen; and then he was calm again.

"Good-by, then," said Huntingdon.

"Ah, to hell with you!" snarled Banning.

He whirled, determined to run the entire distance down the pass in order to keep from freezing, but with his first springing step his feet shot from beneath him, because he had stepped in the blood that ran from Huntingdon. He came down heavily on his right knee, and heard the bone crunch like old wood.

For an instant the pain leaped out of the broken bone and ached behind his eyes; then he forgot all about it because he realized that he was about to die. The northwest wind pitched its song an octave higher, and right through the heavy, fleece-lined coat it laid its invisible hand on the naked flesh of Banning.

Huntingdon's voice said, cheerfully, "If you finish me off now, and take my clothes, the warmth of them will do you less good than the warmth of my body. . . . But if we haul to the windward of that rock and lie down close together . . . Sam Hillier comes through the pass tomorrow morning with his pack mules. We might last it out."

"Lie close together? You and me?" said Banning in a sort of horror. And then he saw that it was the only way.

Moving was bitterest agony, but both he and Huntingdon got to the shelter of the big rock, and the salvation from the wind was like a promise of heaven that they still might live. Banning lay flat on his back, his teeth set, with a scream working up higher and higher in his throat. The cut of the wind grew less. He opened his eyes and saw that Huntingdon was piling smaller rocks on each side of the boulder so that the icy eddyings of the gale might not get at them.

Afterward, Huntingdon lay down beside

him, gathered him close.

"What chance is there?" asked Banning. "What chance, Jack?"

"One in fifty," said Huntingdon. And then, as he felt the shudder pass through Banning's body, he added, "Yes, or one in five. The thing to do is to keep on hoping, and talking."

"Ay, and we've things to talk about," said Banning.

"We have," answered Huntingdon.

The warmth of Huntingdon's body began to strike through Banning's clothes. He blessed God for it.

"But, man, man," said Banning, "what a fool you were to come up into Caldwell's Pass on a December day without a heavy coat! Take this fleece-lined thing off me and put it over us both. And hope, Jack. It's hope that keeps the heart warm!"

DUST ACROSS THE RANGE

This 35,000-word short novel, written in the spring of 1937, was printed as a four-part serial in American Magazine. *It was Faust's last major western, and closed his twenty years in the genre which began in late 1917 when his fiction career was launched in* All-Story Weekly. *Although he was to publish a handful of shorter tales into mid-1938,* Dust Across the Range *was his western farewell. Not only does it rank with his finest prose fiction, but it is unique among all of his genre tales in its overt celebration of the western rangeland. Although Faust had been raised in the West, he had always chosen to use it as a mythic stage, across which to parade his knight-gunfighters, wedding Homeric saga to Old West legend. However, in his final short novel, myth gives way to hard-edged reality — as Faust delineates a land in flux. He paints a true word-portrait of the American West in the Depression years of the 1930s, when President Franklin*

D. Roosevelt sent out masses of eager young men to the forests and rangelands of the nation under the government-sponsored banner of the CCC (Civilian Conservation Corps.) They had a vital mission: to save the land from destruction. Projects were established to instruct farmers in contour plowing, the building of check dams, crop rotation, and other important methods of soil conservation.

Unchecked floods and dust storms were eating away three million tons of topsoil each year, and countless acres of valuable rangeland had been stripped bare by unrestricted grazing.

These were the terrible years of the Oklahoma Dust Bowl migrations, when the soil blew away on winds of agony, and thousands lost their homes and land to the ravages of storm.

It is against this realistic background that Faust sets his story of Harry Mortimer, a man dedicated to soil instead of six-guns, to the land he fights to save — and to Louise Miller, the stubborn rancher's daughter he learns to love.

There is surely no lack of action in Max Brand's last, truly mature western novel. While this was a West of telephones and tractors and trucks, it was still a land of men who did not hesitate to take up arms to protect the range their ancestors had settled. There is raw conflict *here. Colts still flash fire; horses are ridden at full battle gallop — and brawn still counts as much as brain in a story encompassing saloon punchouts and brutal boxing encounters. (Faust's lifelong passion for fistic sports finds full expression!)*

Capping it all, the author creates a veritable king of storms, so real you can taste the dust between your teeth and feel the rush of killing winds. Greater and more powerful than any outlaw villain, the storm itself becomes a living foe, against which Faust pits the strength and courage of Harry Mortimer.

At last in book form, Max Brand's final epic novel takes its place among the true classics of the American West.

OFF THE HIGH, level plateau of the range, cattle trails dip like crooked runlets of white water into the valley of the Chappany. Louise Miller, bound for home on her best horse, came off the level like a ski jumper from the take-off mound. She had the brown skin and the eye-flash and the tough sinew of an Indian, though there was no more red man in her than there was mustang in her thoroughbred.

She had come back to the ranch to celebrate her twenty-first birthday and take over the management of the 40,000-acre spread, while her father embarked on a two-year drifting voyage through the Old World. She had brought home in her pocket, so to speak, two specimens of man between whom she was to select a husband, because, as her father warned her, "ranch days can be kind of long," and she had ridden out alone on this day to think over the two of them and make her choice. She had made her decision and, having arrived at it, she was homebound, hell-bent, to tell big Frederick Wilson that in the pinch he was man enough to suit her.

That was why she took the second downward bend of the trail so fast that Hampton skidded under her. Then danger flashed in her eyes in the form of a three-stranded barbed-wire fence, as new and bright as a sword out of a sheath. She sat Hampton down on his hocks and skidded him to a halt a yard or so from the wire.

A hundred yards away nine men were building a second line of fence, stretching and nailing wire, or tamping new posts in place, or screwing augers into the hard ground. Eight of them were CCC men, she knew, donated by the government to help make the Hancock ranch an example of soil-conservation methods to the entire range. The ninth man, pinch-bellied and gaunt-ribbed from labor, was undoubtedly the fellow to blame for this pair of insane fences which cut the old trail like knives. He worked with a thirty-pound crowbar, breaking the hardpan.

That was Harry Mortimer, who for two years had been at work trying to make the Hancock place pay real money. He had a one-third share in the property and came out of the East with a brain crammed full of college-bred agricultural theory and a missionary desire to teach the ranchers new ways with the old range.

His family had spent long generations wearing down the soil of a New England farm until the bones of the earth showed through. Mortimer's father left the farm, went into business that prospered, but left in his son the old yearning to return to the soil. That was why agriculture had been his study in college, but when he looked for a sphere to work in after graduation, the rocky little New England farms seemed too small a field. That was why he had gone to the West to exploit his inherited share in the Hancock place.

Whatever the bookish idiocy that had suggested this pair of fences, Louise Miller wanted to get to him fast and tell him what she thought of the idea. So she hurried Hampton around the lower end of the fence. But here the ground chopped into an ugly "badlands" of little gullies and gravel ridges. Hampton began to go up and down over them like a small boat in a choppy sea. He slipped on loose soil. And the next instant Louise Miller was sailing toward the far horizon.

It never would have happened except that she was thinking about steering the chestnut, not keeping her seat. Damn everything, including her own folly and Harry Mortimer! Then she was sitting up, with the landscape settling back from a dizzy whirl. Sweating men were lifting her by the armpits, but Harry Mortimer was not among them. He had let this chip fall where it might while he climbed on one of the mules that grazed near the wagonload of posts and wire, and trotted off in pursuit of Hampton.

Vaguely she heard the CCC men speaking words of concern and comfort and felt their hands brushing her off carefully, but she was mainly concerned with wishing that Hampton would kick a pair of holes through Mortimer. Instead, the thoroughbred stood near the fence like a lamb and allowed himself to be caught and brought back at the mildest of dogtrots. Harry Mortimer dismounted from his mule and handed the girl the reins.

"I thought for a minute that you might have a long walk home," he said.

It was hard for her to answer, so she looked him over and pretended to be catching her breath. He worked stripped to the waist, with a rag of old straw sombrero on his head. The sun had bronzed him; sweat had polished the bronze. He had the light stance of a sprinter, but around his shoulders the strength was layered and drawn down in long fingers over his arms. The pain of labor and the edge of many responsibilities seamed his face, but above all he had the look of one who knows how to endure, and then strike hard.

At last she was able to speak, "Sorry you ran out of places where fences are needed. This is just some practice work for you and your men, I suppose? Or did you think it would be fun to block the trail and cut up the livestock on your barbed wire?"

He picked up the thirty-pound crowbar and tossed it lightly from hand to hand.

"While you're thinking up an answer," said Louise Miller, "I'd suggest that there's lots of fence to put up on my place, and where it will do good. . . . Where does the fun come in, Harry? Digging the holes or seeing the pretty wire flash in the sun?"

The CCC men laughed. She had understood that they lived in almost religious awe of their boss, but they stood back and laughed with deep enjoyment.

"Talk it up to her, Chief," they called. "Don't lay down in the first round."

"You have to give a lady the first hold, boys," said Mortimer, grinning at them. Then he added, "Any sore places from that fall, or are you just feeling sour?"

"Not at all," said the girl. "I'm simply asking a few questions."

"Want me to answer pretty Lou Miller?" he asked. "Or am I talking to the manager of the John Miller ranch?"

"I'm going to manage it, all right," she nodded.

"D'you know enough to?" he demanded. . . . "You fellows get back to that fence-line."

They departed, their grinning faces turned

to watch the comedy.

"Every Miller that ever was born knows enough to run a cattle ranch," she answered.

"By divine right, or something like that?" said Mortimer. "Then why don't you know why I'm running these fences?"

"I do know. It's for exercise, isn't it?"

He jabbed the crowbar into the ground and leaned on it, smiling. But she knew that if she had been a man his fist would have been in her face.

"How long has the trail run over this ground?" he asked.

"Two or three years," she said.

"Where was it before?"

"Over there," she answered, proud of her exact knowledge. "Over there where those gullies are opening up."

"Was there a trail before that one?"

"Yes. It traveled along that big arroyo."

"What made the gullies and what started the big arroyo washing?" he asked her.

"Why, God, I suppose," said the girl. "God, and the rain He sent. What else?"

"It was the trail," said Mortimer. "It wore down through the grass and down through the topsoil till it was a trench, and the first heavy rains began to wash the trench deeper. I'm building these fences to turn the downdrift and the updrift of the cattle from the tanks. I'm making them wear new trails."

She saw the justice of what he said. She saw it so deeply that she was angered to the heart because she could find no good retort.

"The point is that the old range and the old range ways aren't good enough for you, Harry. Isn't that the point?"

She waved her hand across the valley of the Chappany to the house of her father and the green lake of trees that washed around it, and to the miles of level ground that spread beyond.

"The other generations didn't know. Is that it?" she asked, sharpening her malice with a smile.

He considered her for a moment, as though he doubted the value of making an answer. Then he pointed.

"See the edge of that thousand acres of hay your father planted?" he asked. "And, spilling into the valley below it, you see the silt that's flowed onto the low ground? That silt spoils fifty acres of good river-bottom that's fit for the plow. Know how it comes to be there?"

"Wash from a heavy rain, I suppose?"

"Yes. Your father ripped up a thousand acres of virgin rangeland. His plow cut through the roots of grass of the topsoil that's been accumulating for a million years. The rain came on the loose ground and washed the cream of it away. The first dry season and hard wind that comes along, and that thousand acres will blow away like feathers; and the earth will have a million years of work to do all over again."

"Father had to have extra hay," said the girl. "That's why he planted. What else was he to do?"

"Look down the Chappany along the Hancock land," said Mortimer.

"It looks like a crazy quilt," she answered.

"Because it's strip-plowed to leave a percentage of holding grass; and it's contour-plowed in other places to keep the soil from washing. Those brush tangles in the gullies are dams that will keep the gullies from deepening. Every slope of more than twenty percent is planted to trees; every slope of more than twelve goes to permanent grass. In another year or so I'll have every acre of the Hancock place buttoned down to the ground with grass or trees, so that it *can't* blow."

"Do you happen to know," she said,

"that there's never been a dust storm on this range?"

"There *will* be, and soon," he answered. "Look at the mountains, yonder. That blowing mist isn't clouds. It's dust. It's ten thousand acres going to hell this minute!"

She stared toward the horizon and, above the blue of the mountains, saw a smudging darkness in the air. Mortimer was saying, "That's the Curtis Valley blowing up in smoke. A dry season and a strong wind. . . . Here's the dry season though it's only May. Realize that? Only May, and the range is bone dry."

She glanced down the slope at the lakes in the bottom of the valley. There were five of them extended by old dams. Three lay on her land; two belonged to the Hancock place. As a rule the Chappany ran for eleven months in the year, only ceasing in August, and during that month the cattle came in from miles off the dry back of the range. This year, to be sure, was very different, for as the little river ceased flowing, the water holes on the farther range also were drying up and the cows had already commenced to voyage to the valley for drink. Little wind-puffs of white spotted the tableland and drifted down into the valley as parched cattle came at a trot for the water. Scores of them even now stood shoulder deep in the lakes, and throngs were lying on the dry shore waiting to drink again, and again, before they started the trek toward the back country and the better grass.

Mortimer was pointing. "A dry season, and a hard wind," he said. "That thousand acres your father plowed is a gun pointed at the head of the entire county. If that starts blowing, the topsoil all over the range is apt to peel off like skin. . . . I tell you, every plow furrow on the range is like a knife cut; it may let out the life and leave you worthless dry bones. The whole range — beautiful damned miles of it — may go up in smoke. My land lies right under the gun."

Her brain rocked as she listened and she felt conviction strike her as with hands. If she could not argue, at least she could hate. Her father hated this man, and she would have felt herself untrue to her name if she did not hate him in turn.

"And that was why you tried to stab Father in the back?" she asked.

"I complained to the government and the soil-conservation authorities," he said. "I did that after I'd tried a thousand times to talk sense to John Miller. . . . And they would have *made* him toe the line, except that he knew the right political wires to pull."

She laughed through her teeth. "Wire-pulling? That's better than rope-pulling, Harry!" she said.

"You mean that your father would like to see me lynched?" he answered. "I suppose he would . . . he hates me. I despise him . . . But I'll tell you what I'd do. If I thought I could change his mind, I'd crawl a hundred miles on my hands and knees and I'd sit up and beg like a dog . . . because he's the king of the range and, until he wakes up, the whole range will remain asleep . . . and one night it'll blow away."

She swung suddenly into the saddle. This strange, savage humility troubled and stirred her so that it was hard to find in her heart the chord of hatred she sought. The only answer was to say, "Why not try him again, Harry? This evening, for instance. There's going to be a barbecue, and perhaps he'd be glad to see you. I'm sure the *boys* would be glad. And so would I!" She laughed again, put some of her anger into her spurs, and made beautiful Hampton race like a long-gaited rabbit, scurrying down the slope. . . .

Mortimer loaded his eight men into the wagon at noon and drove it back to the Hancock ranch house. He had been a fool, he told himself, to talk to the girl with a frank sternness, as though she were a man. He could not force a young wildcat like her to see the truth, but he might have tried to flatter her into a new point of view.

A dangerous expedient suggested itself to him now, and in that light of danger he began to see again the faces and the souls of the eight men in the wagon behind him. Every one of them had been with him at least a year and a half. Every man of them was like another right hand to Mortimer. They had come to him as a surly, unwilling, random collection which he had begged, borrowed, and stolen from the CCC camp at Poplar Springs, justified by his intention of making the Hancock ranch an exemplar in soil conservation to the entire range; but the eight had remained like members of a family. He gave them his time and they gave him back their ungrudging affection. He knew the worst that was in them and they understood his affection. They understood his ultimate purpose, also, which was far more than simply to put the Hancock ranch on a high-paying basis: He wanted to reform the ranching methods of the entire range and widen the margin of security which old-fashioned methods constantly diminished.

Each one of the eight had some useful quality, some weakness. Baldy Inman was the most docile of all, but when he went on a binge, once a month, Mortimer sat with him night after night and brought him home again to sobriety. Bud McGee loved battle, and twice Mortimer had dragged him out of saloon brawls at the risk of both their necks. George Masters loved poker and knew all too well how to deal. Chip Ellis and Dink Waller were always about to start for the gold lands of Alaska and talked up the beauties of far countries till the rest of the boys were on edge. Lefty Parkman had been in the ring and he helped on Sundays teaching the boys to box. He had beaten Mortimer, in spite of his lighter weight, Sunday after Sunday, until sheer dint of pain taught Mortimer the science and gave him a deadly left of his own. Pudge Major supplied music and noisy jokes.

Jan Erickson, the giant of the crew, had once broken away and followed the old call of the underworld as far as Denver, where Mortimer overtook him and brought him home again. Mortimer returned from that journey with an eye which changed gradually from black to purple to green, and Erickson's face was swollen for a month, but they never referred to what happened in Denver and remained as brothers together in the times of need.

It was while he thought of his crew, one by one, that the determination to take the great chance came strongly home in Mortimer. He stopped the wagon in front of the big shed which had been turned into a barracks for the CCC workers. Shorty, the cook, was already in the doorway banging a tin pan and yelling to them to come and get it. Mortimer, instead of going in with them to sit at the long table, passed into the Hancock house.

As usual, he found Charlie Hancock stretched on the couch in the parlor with the limes, the sugar, the Jamaica rum, and the hot-water jug conveniently on the table beside him. Because of the heat of the day he was dressed in trunks and slippers only, and he had a volume of Boswell's *Johnson* propped on the fat of his paunch. His glasses, his prematurely aged face, and his short gray mustache gave him the air of a country gentleman reposing in a Turkish bath.

This posture of reading had become hardly more than a posture recently, for, since Mortimer had appeared and was willing to take charge of the ranch, Charles Hancock had sunk into a long decline. A fine education had given edge to one of the clearest minds Mortimer had ever met; it was also the most vicious brain he knew. The main direction of the ranch work had been left to Mortimer, but there still remained on the place half a dozen haphazard cowpunchers whom Hancock had picked up, not so much because they knew cows as because they shot straight and were devoted to him. Aside from rum and books, guns were the main preoccupation of Hancock. If he left his rum bottle, it was generally to go hunting with some of his harum-scarum hired men. They did not mix with the CCC men.

"Wang!" called Hancock. "Bring another glass for Mr. Mortimer, and some more hot water."

The Chinaman appeared in the kitchen

doorway, bowed, and trotted off.

"I'm not drinking," said Mortimer.

"Still a slave to conscience, Harry?" said Hancock.

Mortimer began to pace the room, on one side staring out a window that looked up the valley of the Chappany where he had worked so hard during the two years, on the other looking vacantly at the photograph of old Jim Hancock, who had retired from the ranch to live in a cottage in Poplar Springs. On $50 a month he kept himself happy with frijoles and whiskey and let the world wag on its way. The literal arrangement was that the income from the ranch should be split three ways, one to old Jim, one to his son Charles, one to Mortimer; but as a matter of fact Charlie managed to use most of his father's portion besides his own.

"Yes," said Charles Hancock, answering his own question, "a slave to the conscience that forces you to make the world a better place to live in. You see nothing but green, Harry. You want nothing but green on it. What is there you wouldn't do for it?"

"I've been wondering," said Mortimer, vague with thought.

"Grass for cows, grass for cows!" said

Hancock, laughing, "You'd die to give it to 'em."

"It's something else," answered Mortimer, shaking his head. "It's the idea of a living country instead of a dying one. . . . Tell me, Charlie: What would happen if I showed my face at the Miller barbecue this evening?"

Hancock sat bolt upright, then slowly lowered himself back to the prone position. He took a deep swallow of punch. "Nothing," he said. "Nothing. . . . at first."

"And then?" asked Mortimer.

"At first," said Hancock, smiling as he enlarged his thought, "there would be a dash of surprise. Old John Miller wouldn't faint, but he'd come close to it. And his cowpunchers would have to remember that the whole range has been asked to see Lou Miller's twenty-first birthday. . . . Afterward, when the drink began to soak through their systems and got into their brains . . . that would be different. I don't know just how it would happen. Someone would stumble against you, or trip over your foot, or find you laughing in his face and take a word for an insult, or misunderstand the way you lifted an eyebrow . . . and presently you'd be stuck full of knives and drilled full of bullet holes!"

"You think Miller wants me dead as badly as that?" asked Mortimer.

"Think? I know! You bring down a damned commission on top of him. It rides over his land. It finds that the great John Miller had been overstocking his acres, destroying the grass with too many hoofs. The commission is about to put a supervisor in charge of the Miller ranch and cause all the Millers to rise in their graves. Only by getting a governor and a couple of senators out of bed in the middle of the night is he able to stop the commission. . . . And he owes all that trouble to you. Trouble, shame, and all. Wants you dead? Why, John Miller's father would have gone gunning for you in person, with a grudge like that. And John Miller's grandfather would simply have sent half a dozen of his Mexican cowboys to cut your throat. These Millers have been kings, Harry, and don't forget it."

"Kings . . . kings," said Mortimer absently. "The girl will be running the place in a few days. And she's as hard as her father."

"Soften her, then," said Hancock.

"She challenged me to come to the

barbecue," said Mortimer. "If I come . . . will that soften her?"

"Of course it will," answered Hancock. "And the guns will soften *you*, later on. Are you going to be fool enough to go?"

"If I win her over," said Mortimer, "I win over the whole range. If the Miller place uses my ideas, all the small fellows will follow along. If I go to the silly barbecue, maybe it will make her think I'm half a man, at least. You don't hate a thing you can even partly respect."

"Ah," said Hancock. "He's a noble fellow. Ready to die for his cause, and all that. . . . You bore me, Harry. Mind leaving me to my rum punch?"

Mortimer went out into the shed that housed the CCC men and passed through the room where the eight sat with a platter of thin fried steaks.

"Hi, Chief," said Pudge Major. "Are you giving me your share?"

"He can't eat . . . the Miller gal fed him up to the teeth," suggested Chip Ellis.

"He's lovesick," shouted Bud McGee. "You can't eat when you're lovesick!"

They all were shouting with laughter as he passed them and entered the kitchen, where Shorty was stubbing about on his wooden leg, laying out his own meal on a table covered with heavy white oilcloth.

"Hi, Chief," he said. "Can't you chew a way through one of those steaks?"

"What's the lowest a man can be?" asked Mortimer, sitting on the window sill.

"Cabin boy on a South Seas tramp," answered Shorty instantly.

"How about a man who tells a girl he loves her? Makes love and doesn't mean it?"

"You take it with gals, and the rules are all different," said Shorty. "Now, over there in Japan. . . ."

"A girl here, Shorty, as straight as a ruled line, even if she's as mean as a cat."

"Why, if a gal is straight and a gent makes her crooked . . . why, they got a special place in hell for them, Chief," said Shorty.

"Reasons wouldn't count, would they, Shorty?" asked Mortimer.

"There ain't any reasons for spoiling a clean deck of cards," said Shorty.

Mortimer went back into the dining room and took his place at the head of the table. He speared a steak and dropped it on his plate. "There's no work this afternoon," he said.

"Quit it, Chief!" protested huge Jan Erickson. "You mean you declare a holiday?"

"I'm going to a party, myself," said Mortimer, "and I've never asked you to work when I was off playing, have I?"

"Where's the party?" asked Pudge.

"Over the hills and far away," said Mortimer.

He spent the early afternoon preparing himself with a scrubbing in cold water; then he dressed in rather battered whites, climbed into the one-ton truck, and prepared to deliver himself at the barbecue.

Charles Hancock appeared unexpectedly in the doorway of the ranch house, a fat, red, wavering figure. He called out, "If you want to take that Miller girl into camp, you'd better slick yourself up with a five-thousand-dollar automobile. You can't go fast enough in that contraption. She'll keep seeing your dust."

Mortimer looked at his partner for a moment in silent disgust, then drove off through the white heat of the afternoon.

When he bumped across the bridge and

finally rolled up the trail onto Miller land, he felt that he had crossed the most important Rubicon of his life. Others were coming in swaying automobiles, in carts and buggies, and above all on mustangs which had cruised from the farthest limits of the range, but he knew that he would be the most unexpected guest at the carnival. Halfway up the slope the swinging music of a band reached him. He felt like a soldier going into battle as he reached the great arch of evergreens which had been built over the entrance to the Miller grounds.

Sam Pearson, the Miller foreman, ranged up and down by the gate giving the first welcome to the new arrivals, and the first drink out of a huge punchbowl which was cooled in a packing of dry ice. When he saw Mortimer, the foreman came to a pause on a ready-made speech of welcome and stood agape with the dripping glass of punch in his hand. Then he came slowly up to the side of the truck and narrowed his eyes at Mortimer as though he were searching for game in a distant horizon.

"What kind of legs have you got to stand on, Mortimer?" he asked. "What you think is gunna hold you up all through the day?"

"Beginner's luck," said Mortimer.

The foreman suddenly held out the glass. "Have this on me," he said. "You got so much nerve I wish I liked you."

Mortimer drove on into the space reserved for parking, between the corrals behind the house. There he climbed slowly down to the ground and went on toward the Miller residence, with a sense that his last bridge, his last way of retreat had been broken behind him.

The crowd gave him some comfort in the feeling that he might lose himself among the numbers who drifted beneath the trees surrounding the ranch house. Throngs of colored lanterns swung from the lower branches and the gala atmosphere helped his sense of security. But he was noticed at once. A whisper spread, and heads were continually turning, amazed eyes were staring at him.

He put on an air of unconcern, but the weight of a man-sized automatic under his coat was the sort of companionship he wanted then.

It was Louise Miller whom he kept an eye for as he wandered casually through the crowd. He went down by the big open-air dance floor, where the band played and where a ring had been built for the wrestling and boxing which were to be part of the entertainment; but she was not there. He passed back to the open glade, where a huge steer was turning on a great spit against a backing of burning logs. For three generations the Millers had barbecued their meat in this manner for their friends, but roast beef was only one dish among many, for in enormous iron pots chickens and ducks were simmering, and in scores of Dutch ovens there were geese, saddles of venison, and young pigs roasting. There were kegs of beer and ale, kegs of whisky, incredible bowls of rosy punch, and such an air of plenty as Mortimer had never looked on before.

He lingered in the central scene of the barbecue too long and as he turned away he saw a pair of big cowpunchers solidly barring his way and offering fight as clearly as boys ever offered it in a schoolyard. Mortimer sidestepped them without shame, and went on, with their insulting laughter in his ears. He knew without turning his head that they were following him. Men began to be aware of him from both sides and from in front. He heard derisive voices calling out: "The dirt doctor!" "Give him a start home!" "Help him on his way!"

He shrugged his shoulders to get the chill out of his spinal marrow. He made himself walk slowly to maintain a casual dignity, but he felt his neck muscles stiffening. When he stumbled on an uneven place, an instant guffaw sounded behind him, and he felt as though a great beast were breathing at his shoulder. It was in the crisis of that moment that he saw Louise Miller come swiftly through the crowd, panting with haste as she came up to him.

"Are you crazy — coming here?" she demanded.

"I thought you asked me," said Mortimer.

"Come back to the house with me. I've got to talk with you and get you away," she said. "I've never heard of anything so idiotic. Didn't you see them closing in around you like wolves for a kill?"

"Just a lot of big, harmless, happy boys," said Mortimer, and she glanced up sharply to see the irony of his smile.

They came through the trees to the wide front of the old house, and then through the Spanish patio, under the clumsy arches, and so into the house. She led him into a library. A vague, undecipherable murmur of voices sounded through the wall from the next room, but the girl was too intent on him to notice the sound.

"Sit down here," she commanded. "I'll walk around. I can't sit still. . . . Harry Mortimer, listen to me!"

He lighted a cigarette as he leaned back in the chair and watched her.

"It isn't my fault that you've come, is it?" she asked. "You know it wasn't a real invitation, didn't you? Ask you up here into a den of wildcats? You knew that I didn't intend that!"

"What *did* you intend, then?" he asked.

She pulled up a chair opposite him, suddenly, and sat down on it, with her chin on her fist, staring at him. The billowing skirt of her dress slowly settled around her. "You know," she said, "Those fences . . . the silly fall I took . . . and then I wasn't making very good sense when I argued; and it was a sort of crazy malice, to have the last word, and leave a challenge behind me. Ah, but I'm sorry!"

The lowering and softening of her voice let him look at her deeply for an instant.

"I'm not sorry," he told her. "D'you see? I'm here in the castle of the baron — right in the middle of his life. Perhaps he'll listen to reason now."

"Because he can see that you're ready to

die for your cause? No, he'll never listen! He's as set as an old army mule, and as savage as a hungry grizzly. He's in there now, Harry, and I've got to get you away before he —"

Here the door at the side of the room opened and the deep, booming voice of John Miller sounded through the room, saying, "We'll announce Lou's engagement to you before the evening's over, Fred."

"But, Mr. Miller, if we hurry her . . ." said a big, handsome fellow in the doorway, as blond as Norway and built like a football tackle.

"She's made up her mind, and that's enough for me," declared John Miller, leading the way into the library.

His daughter and Mortimer were already on their feet. In her first panic she had touched his arm to draw him away, but he refused to avoid the issue; the two of them stood now as though to face gunfire. It opened at once. John Miller, when he made out the face of Mortimer, ran a hand back through the silver of his long hair and grew inches taller with rage. He actually made a quick step or two toward Mortimer before another thought stopped him and he remembered that no matter who the man might be, he was a guest in the Miller house. He had the blue eyes of a boy and they were shining like bright, twin devils when he came up and took the hand of Mortimer.

"Mr. Frederick Wilson, Mr. Mortimer," he said. "I am happy . . . a day when everyone . . . I see, in fact, that you and my daughter are old friends?"

He was in a sweat of white anger, though he kept himself smiling. Frederick Wilson, who could not help seeing that something was very wrong, looked quizzically from his fiancée to Mortimer.

"I'm sorry that I was here when you wanted to be private," said Mortimer, withdrawing.

"Ah, about that!" exclaimed Miller, "But I can trust you not to spread the word in the crowd? I want to save it as a surprise."

Mortimer was already close to the door and, as he turned to go through it, he heard the girl exclaiming, "But an announcement!"

"Have you two minds or one?" answered her father. "If you have only one, it's already made up. . . . Now, what in the devil is the meaning of Mortimer here in my house, when the poisonous rat has been doing everything he can to . . ."

Mortimer was already out of earshot and walking slowly down the hall, through the patio, and once more into the woods of the carnival, with the music of the band roaring in his ear.

He was not noticed immediately, and he tried to interest himself in the variety of the people who had come to the barbecue, for they included every type, from tough old-timers whose overalls were grease-hardened around the knees, to roaring cowpunchers from all over the range and first-class citizens of Poplar Springs.

Near the glade where the roasting ox hissed and spat above the fire, he saw a compacted group that moved through the crowd like a boat through the sea, and a moment later he recognized the lofty, blond head of Jan Erickson! They were there, all eight of them, and they gathered around him now with a shout and a rush.

He took Pudge Major by the lapels of his coat and shook him. "You're behind this, Pudge," he said. "You're the only one who could have guessed where I was going. Now, you take the rest of 'em and get out of here. D'you know that every man jack in this crowd is heeled? And if trouble starts they'll shoot you boys into fertilizer."

"And what about you?" asked Pudge.

"I'm having a little game," said Mortimer.

"Yeah, and when you're tagged, you'll stay 'it,'" answered Dink Waller. "We'll just hang around and make a kind of a background so's people will be able to see you better."

"Listen to me. I'm ordering you back to the Hancock place," commanded Mortimer.

This seemed to end the argument. They were looking wistfully at their chief when George Masters exclaimed, "This is time off. Your orders ain't worth a damn this afternoon, Chief. We're where we want to be, and we're going to stay."

With a half-grinning and a half-guilty resolution they confronted Mortimer, and he surrendered the struggle with a shrug of his shoulders; but already he felt, suddenly, as though he had walked with eight sticks of dynamite into the center of a fire.

A thundering loudspeaker called the guests to the platform entertainment, a moment later, and that invitation called off the dogs of war from Mortimer and his men. They drifted with the others toward the dance floor, and from the convenient slope Mortimer looked on with anxious, half-seeing eyes at dancers doing the buck and wing, at a competition in rope tricks, at a pair of slick magicians, at wrestlers, at a flashy bit of lightweight boxing, at an old fellow who demonstrated how Colts with their triggers filed off were handled in the old days. And still he was wondering how he could roll his eight sticks of dynamite out of the fire, when a huge, black-chested cowpuncher got into the ring to box three rounds with a fellow almost as tall and robed from head to foot with a beautiful coverage of muscles. The blond head of the second man meant something to Mortimer and, when the fellow turned, he recognized the handsome face of Frederick Wilson, smiling and at ease with the world.

The reason for his confidence appeared as soon as the gong was struck and the two went into action.

"He's got a left, is what that Wilson's got," said Lefty Parkman. "He's got an educated left, and look at him tie it onto Blackie's whiskers!"

The big cowpuncher, full of the best will in the world, rushed in to use both hands, as he had done many a time in saloon brawls, only to bump his face against a snapping jab. When he stood still to think the matter over, he lowered his guard a trifle, and through the opening Frederick Wilson cracked a hammer-hard right hand that sagged the knees of the man from the range.

"What a right!" said Lefty Parkman, rubbing his greedy hands together. "But Blackie don't know how to fall!"

The cowboy, though his brains were adrift, still tried to fight, while Frederick Wilson, with a cruelly smiling patience, followed him, measured him, and then flattened him with a very accurate one-two that bumped the head of Blackie soundly against the canvas. Friends carried him away, while the crowd groaned loudly. Only a few applauded with vigor. Big John Miller, standing up from his chair on the special dais, with his silver hair blowing and shining, clapped his hands furiously; but Lou Miller merely smiled and waved, and then turned her head. That sort of fighting was not to her taste, it appeared.

Frederick Wilson, in the meantime, had discovered that the fight did not please the crowd, so he stood at the ropes and lifted a gloved hand for silence. When the quiet came, he called in a good, ringing bass voice: "My friends, I'm sorry that was over so soon. If anybody else will step up, I'll try to please you more the next time."

Some wit sang out, "Paging Jack Dempsey!" and the crowd roared.

Then Mortimer found himself getting to his feet.

Lefty Parkman tried to pull him back. "You're crazy," groaned Lefty. "He's got twenty pounds on you. You can fight, but he can *box*. He'll spear you like a salmon. He'll hold you off and murder you!"

But Mortimer gained his full height and waved to attract attention. He felt as naked as a bad dream, but a bell had struck in his mind that told him his chance had come to lay his hands on the entire range. They despised him for his bookishness. If they could respect him for his manhood the whole story might change. Their hostility was breaking out in the cries with which he was recognized. "It's the doctor! — It's the dirt doctor!" they shouted. "Eat him up! Give him the dirt he wants, Wilson!"

"I'll try to help you entertain," called Mortimer to Wilson, and hurried back to the dressing tent near the dance floor. He had a glimpse, on the way, of the puzzled face of Lou Miller and of John Miller fairly expanding with expectant pleasure. In the tent he rigged himself in togs that fitted well enough. Blackie sat slumped in a chair at one side, gradually recovering, his eyes still empty and a red drool running from a corner of his mouth.

"How'd it go, Blackie?" asked Parkman.

"I was doin' fine," said Blackie. "And then a barn door slammed on my face."

Lefty Parkman took his champion down through the crowd, and poured savage advice at him every step of the way. "Keep your left up," he cautioned. "Don't mind if he raises some bumps with his left. It's his right that rings all the bells. Don't give him a clean shot with it. Keep jabbing. Work in close, and hammer the body. And if you get a chance try the old one-two. Keep the one-two in your head like a song. . . . And God help you, Chief!"

The strained, anxious faces of the CCC men were the last pictures that Mortimer saw as he squared off with Wilson after the bell. Then a beautiful straight left flashed in his eyes. He ducked under it and dug both hands into the soft of Wilson's body. At least, it should have been the soft, but it was like punching rolls of India rubber.

They came out of the clinch with the crowd suddenly roaring applause for the dirt doctor, but Mortimer knew he had not hurt the big fellow. Wilson had stomach muscles like a double row of clenched fists. And he was smiling as he came in again behind the beautiful, reaching straight left. Mortimer remembered, with a sudden relief, that the rounds were only two minutes long. But merely to endure was not enough. He wanted to wipe Frederick Wilson out of the Miller mind.

He sidestepped the straight left and used his own. It landed neatly, but high on the face. As Wilson shifted in, Mortimer nailed him with the one-two in which Lefty Parkman had drilled him so hard during those remorseless Sundays at the ranch. It stopped Wilson like a wall, but the right hand had not found the button. Mortimer jumped in with a long, straight left to follow his advantage, and the wave of uproar behind him washed him forward. For there is an invincible sympathy with the underdog in the West, and even the dirt doctor got their cheers as he plunged at big Wilson.

What happened then, Mortimer could not exactly tell. He felt his left miss and slither over the shoulder of Wilson. Then a stick of dynamite exploded in his brain.

He had hurt his knees. That was the next

thing he knew. And his brain cleared to admit a tremendous noise of shouting people. He was on hands and knees on the floor of the ring, with the referee swaying an arm up and down beside his face, counting: "five . . . six . . . seven . . ."

Mortimer came to his feet. He saw Wilson stepping toward him like a giant crane, and the ready left hand was like the crane's beak aimed at a frog. He ducked under the two-handed attack. But the glancing weight of it carried him like a tide of water against the ropes. Head and body, alternately, the punches hammered him. He saw the tight-lipped smile of pleasure and effort as Wilson worked. The man loved his job; and a bursting rage gave Mortimer strength to fight out into the open.

His head was fairly clear, now. He gave as good as he was taking. He noticed that the gloves were soft and big. They might raise lumps, but only a flush hit was apt to break the skin. He threw another long left. And again he felt his arm glance harmlessly over the shoulder of Wilson. Again a blow struck him from nowhere and exploded a bomb of darkness in his brain. Something rapped sharply against the back of his head.

That was the canvas of the ring. He had

been knocked flat.

He seemed to be swimming out of a river of blackness with a current that shot him downstream toward disaster. Fiercely he struggled . . . and found himself turning on one side, while the swaying arm of the referee seemed to sound the seconds as upon a gong: "six . . . seven . . . eight . . ."

He got to his knees and saw through a dun-colored fog John Miller waving his arms in exultation; but Lou Miller's face was turned away.

That was why Mortimer got to his feet as the tenth count began. He ducked under the big arms of Wilson and held on. Then the bell rang the end of the round, and the savagely gripping hands of Lefty Parkman were dragging him to his corner.

The whole group of his eight men were piled around him, Erickson weeping with rage, while he and Pudge Major and Dink Waller swung towels to raise a breeze; Chip Ellis and George Masters were massaging his legs, while Bud McGee rubbed the loose of his stomach muscles to restore their normal tension, and Baldy Inman held the water bottle. But Lefty Parkman, clutching him with one arm, whispered or groaned instructions in his ear.

"Lefty, what's he hitting me with?" begged Mortimer.

"Listen, dummy!" said Parkman. "When you try the straight left he doesn't try to block it. He lets it come and sidesteps. He lets it go over his shoulder, and then he comes in with a right uppercut and nails you . . . You got no chance! He's killing you. Lemme say that you've broken your arm! He'll kill you, Chief; and if he does Jan Erickson is going to murder him, and there'll be hell all over the lot! . . . Lemme throw in the towel, and you can quit and . . ."

"If you throw in the towel . . ." said Mortimer through his teeth — but then the gong sounded and he stepped out, feeling as though he were wading against a stiff current of water.

Wilson came right in at him, fiddling with a confident left to make way for a right-hander that would finish the bout; and as the ears of Mortimer cleared he could hear the crowd stamping and shouting, "Sock him, Doc! . . . Break a hole in him! . . . Plow him up!"

Wilson dismissed this cheering for the underdog with a twitching grin and lowered his right to invite a left lead.

The wisdom of Lefty Parkman's observations remained in the brain of Mortimer as he saw the opening. It was only a long feint that he used. Instantly the device which Parkman had explained was apparent. Without attempting to block the punch, Wilson sidestepped to slip the blow and, dropping his right, stepped in for a lifting uppercut, his eyes pinched to a glint of white as he concentrated on the knockout wallop.

That was what Mortimer had hoped. The feint he held for an instant until his body almost swayed forward off balance. Then he used the one-two which Lefty had made him master. The right went to the chin no harder, say, than the tapping hammer of the master blacksmith. It gave the distance, the direction for the sledgehammer stroke of the left that followed, and through the soft, thick padding of the glove Mortimer felt his knuckles lodge against the bone of the jaw. He had hit with his full power and Wilson had stepped straight into the blow.

It buckled Wilson's knees. He covered up, instinctively, lurching forward to clinch, and over his shoulder Mortimer saw John Miller with his hands dangling limply, unable to applaud this startling change of fortune. But Lou Miller was on her feet, bent forward.

He saw this double picture. Then he lifted two blows to Wilson's head and sent him swaying back on his heels. There was the whole length of the body open to the next blow, and strained taut, as though a hand had stretched a throat for the butcher's knife. Mortimer plunged his right straight into that defenseless target and doubled it up like a jackknife.

He stepped back as Wilson fell to his knees, embracing his tormented body with one arm. The other hand gestured to the referee.

"Foul!" said the lips of Wilson.

"Get up and fight," ordered the referee, as he began his count. He was a tough fellow, this referee. He had done some fighting in his youth in Chicago and eastward. Now some of an unforgotten vocabulary flowed from his lips. First, with a wide gesture, he invited the scorn of the crowd and got a howling rejoinder. Then, as he counted, he dropped rare words between the numbers, as: ". . . three, you yellow skunk . . . four, for a four-flusher . . . five, a coyote is St. Patrick beside you . . . six, for a ring-tailed rat . . ."

Wilson struggled to one knee, making faces that indicated dreadful agony; and Mortimer saw John Miller shake both fists in the air and then turn his back in disgust. The interest of Mortimer in the fight ended at that moment. He hardly cared when the referee counted out Wilson the next moment. But, as he climbed through the ropes, the eight men reached up to clutch him with hands of congratulation.

Afterward, Lefty Parkman rejoiced in the dressing tent. "You got it just the way I wanted," he said. "You plastered the sucker just as he stepped in. Oh, baby, if you chuck this ranching, I'll make a light heavyweight champ out of you inside three years. Nothing but bacon three times a day, and eggs all day Sunday! . . . Say, Chief, will you throw in with me and make a try at it?"

Mortimer smiled vaguely at him. He had something of far greater importance to think about, for, as he remembered the enthusiastic voices that had applauded him as he left the ring, it seemed to him that he might have broken through the solid hedge of hostility which had hemmed him in for two years on the range. There remained one great step to take. If he could win over the girl, it would be the greatest evening of his life, and he had determined to play his cards like a crooked gambler if that was necessary to his winning.

"Start drifting around," he told Lefty. "Circulate a little and find out how John Miller took the fading of big Wilson. I'll see you later at the barbecue."

In his anxiety about further consequences he hardly knew what food he tasted when he found a place at one of the long tables in the barbecue glade, but he was keenly aware of favorable and critical eyes which kept studying him, and it was plain that while he had won over a large number of the crowd, his work was far from ended. Then Lefty Parkman leaned at his shoulder and murmured, "Miller is sour. He must have had a whole roll on that Wilson. When you dropped Wilson, Miller said he wished you'd never showed your face on the range."

That was serious enough; the grave face with which Lou Miller passed him a little later was even more to the point. She was drifting about among the tables to see that everyone had his choice, and when she passed Mortimer all recognition was dead in her eye. But when he turned his head to look after her, she made a slight gesture toward the trees. He waited only a moment before he left the table and went after her. Her pale figure led him through swaying lantern light that set the tree trunks wavering, and on through silver drippings of moonlight until she reached the edge of the woods.

When he came up, she said quietly, "You must leave at once. Some of the men here hate you, Harry. And my father won't believe that you beat Fred Wilson fairly. He thinks there must have been a foul blow, as Fred claims."

The hope of winning over John Miller vanished completely. But there remained the girl, and if she were to be placed in immediate charge of the ranch she would be gain enough.

"I can't leave," he said.

She came closer to him and laid a hand on his arm. The moonlight that slid through a gap in the leaves overhead made silver of her hair, her throat, and her hand. "You don't understand me," she said. "When I say that you ought to go now, I mean that there's really danger for you here."

"Is your father going to do me in?" he asked.

"He knows nothing about it," she answered, "but I know there are a hundred men who feel sure Father would be glad if you were run off the range. You have to go — now. I'll stay with you until you're off the place."

He was silent.

"Will you listen to me?" she repeated. "Harry, I know what you want. You want to open up the whole range to the new ideas. Maybe you're right about them, but none of us can believe it. Do what a wise man ought to do. Give up. Sell out. Try your luck in some other place where your brains will tell. You've poured in two years on this range. You can waste twenty more and never win."

"That's good man-talk," he said. "But, Lou, do you ever talk like a woman?"

She laughed a little and stepped back from him. "Well, what's to come now?" she asked.

"Some silly sentimentality," said Mortimer.

"Between you and me?" she asked, still laughing.

He drew a slow, deep breath, for he had

213

made up his mind that she was no more than a unit of the enemy to be beaten down or won over, but there seemed in her now such a free courage and frankness, and the moon touched her beauty with such a reverent hand that his heart was touched and he despised the thing he was about to attempt. That weakness lasted only a moment. He went on along the way which he had laid out for himself.

He said, "Has it ever seemed a little strange to you that I've given up two years of my life to soil conservation in a country where I'm damned before I start, and where I have to share profits and work under the thumb of a drunk like Charlie Hancock?"

"That doesn't sound like sentimentality," answered the girl. "It sounds the truth. No. I've never been able to understand you. I've thought you were a sort of metal monster."

"Well, can you think of anything except plain foolishness that would keep me at the work here?" he demanded.

"I'm trying to think," she answered.

"I'll help you," he said. "Remember two years ago? You were out here from school. Easter vacation. I was standing in front of the Hancock place. You rode Hampton —

zip over the edge of the hill and down the hollow, and then zooming away out of sight beside the ruins of the old wind-mills. And wings got hold of my heart and lifted me after you."

He took another breath after that lie. The girl was still as stone. The moonlight seemed to have frozen her and the airy lightness of her dress. She said nothing.

"What about the announcement of that engagement?" he asked harshly.

"There won't be any announcement. It's ended," she replied. "Harry, what are you trying to tell me? You've hardly looked twice at me in two years."

"I was being the romantic jackass," he said. "The stranger with the great vision and the strong hands. I was going to change the whole range, and then offer you my work in one hand and my heart in the other . . . I've been a fool, Lou, but don't laugh at me if you can help it."

"I won't laugh," she said.

He went on: "I thought that if I ruled out everything but the work, I'd get my reward. Instead of that I have people laughing at me. And I suppose I dreamed that you were receiving radio messages, so to speak, from the fool across the valley

215

who loved you."

"Love? Love?" said the girl.

"Before I get out of the country like a beaten dog, I had to tell you the truth," he lied. And yet as he looked at her he wondered if the lie were altogether perfect. "I don't expect you to do anything except laugh in my face."

A thudding of hoofbeats and a creaking of leather came through the trees behind them. She made a gesture, not to him, but to the ground, the world, the air around them.

"I can't laugh," she said. "I believe it all . . . My heart's going crazy, and I'm dizzy. It's the moonlight, isn't it? It's the crazy moonlight. You're not snapping your fingers and making me fall in love like this, are you?"

From the trees the riders came out softly, the hoofbeats deadened by the leaf mold. There were a thronging dozen of them, with sombreros pulled low and bandannas drawn up over their mouths to make efficient masks.

One of them sang out, "Stand back from him!" And as the girl sprang away, startled, something whistled in the air over Mortimer's head. The snaky shadow of the rope dropped across his vision, and then he was grappled by the noose, which cunningly pinned his arms against his sides.

Sam Pearson, the foreman of the huge Miller ranch, was on the saddle end of the rope with a hundred and ninety pounds of seasoned muscle and nearly forty years of range wisdom. He did not have direct orders from Miller, but the indirect suggestions were more than enough for Pearson. He felt, personally, that it was an affront to the entire Miller legend to have this hostile interloper on the ranch at the barbecue; and there was a virtuous thrill in his hand as he settled that noose around Mortimer's arms.

Sam's mount, which was his best cutting horse, spun like a top and took Mortimer in tow at a mild canter over the flat and then down the slope of the Chappany valley. The screaming protest of Lou Miller shrilled and died out far to the rear, quite drowned by the uproar of Pearson's cowpunchers. They had plenty of liquor under their belts; they all felt they were striking a good stroke for the best cause in the world; and the result was that their high spirits were unleashed like a pack of wolves. Like wolves they howled as they dashed back and forth around Pearson and his captive. And, as their delight grew, more than one quirt snapped in an expert hand to warm the seat of Mortimer's pants.

The Easterner ran well. Sam Pearson had to admit; he kept up a good sprint, which prevented him from falling on his face and being dragged, until they came over the edge of the level and dropped onto the slant ground, with the five Chappany lakes glimmering silver-bright in the hollow beneath them.

At that point Pearson's rope went slack, and he saw Mortimer spin head over heels like a huge ball of tumbleweed. It was so deliciously funny to Sam Pearson that he reeled in the saddle with hearty laughter. He was still howling with joy and the shrill cowboy yells were sticking needles in his ears when a very odd thing happened, for the whirling, topsy-turvy body of Mortimer regained footing and balance for an instant, while running with legs made doubly long by the pitch of the slope, and, like a great black, deformed cat he flung himself onto Monte McLean, who rode close to his side.

There was plenty of silver-clear moonlight to show Monte defending himself from that savage and unexpected attack. Monte was a good, two-handed fighter and he whanged the Easterner over the head and shoulders, not with the lash, but with the loaded butt of his quirt. However, in an instant Mortimer had swarmed up the side of the horse and wrapped Monte in his arms.

This was highly embarrassing to Pearson. If he yanked Mortimer off that mustang, he would bring Monte down to the ground with him. If he did not yank Mortimer out of the saddle, the Easterner would probably throttle Monte and get away. There was another thing that caused Pearson to groan and that was the realization that he had kept the tenderfoot on such a loose rope that he had been able to work his arms and hands up through the grip of the noose. He was held now like an organ-grinder's monkey, around the small of the waist.

Other trouble came on the run toward Sam Pearson. He saw a girl on a horse stretched in a dead gallop come tilting over the upper edge of the slope. That would be Lou Miller. She was a good girl and as Western as they come. But there is a sharp limit to the feminine sense of humor, and it was as likely as not that the girl thought this was a lynching party instead of a mere bit of Western justice and range discipline.

219

The idea was, in brief, to start Mortimer running toward the horizon and encourage him to keep on until he was out of sight.

Sam Pearson simply did not know what to do, and therefore he did the most instinctive thing, which was to give a good tug on the rope. To his horror, he saw both Monte and Mortimer slew sidewise from the saddle and spill to the ground.

They kept on rolling for a dozen yards, and then they lay still, one stretched beside the other. Big Sam Pearson got his horse to the place and dived for the spot where Monte lay. He picked up the fallen cow-puncher. The loose of the body spilled across his arm as he shouted, "Monte! Hey, Monte! A little spill like that didn't do nothing to you, did it? Hey, Monte, can't you hear me?"

The other cowpunchers came piling up on their horses, bring a fog-white cloud of dust that poured over Monte. And he, presently rousing with a groan, brought a cheer from them. They set him up on his feet and felt him from head to foot for broken bones. They patted his back to start him breathing.

"Put him into a saddle," said Sam Pearson. "Old Monte'll be himself when he feels the stirrups under his feet.''

So they put Monte into a saddle and steadied him there with many hands. In fact, he reached out at once with a vaguely fumbling hand for the reins and then mumbled, ''He kind of got hold of me like a wildcat, and he wouldn't loosen up.''

Here the wild voice of Louise Miller cried close by, ''Sam Pearson! You murderer, Sam, you've killed him! You've killed him!''

The foreman, still with a hand on Monte, turned and saw the girl on her knees beside the prostrate body of Mortimer. But at that moment the Easterner groaned heavily, and sat up. And Pearson took that as a signal to go.

''Let's get out of here on the jump, boys,'' he said. ''Maybe we scratched up more hell'n we reckoned on.''

He hit the saddle as he spoke, and in the center of the cavalcade struck out at a gallop for the ranch house, with the wavering figure of Monte held erect by two friendly riders. For Pearson wanted to get in his report of strange happenings to an employer who had never yet been hard on him. . . .

Mortimer, sitting up with his head bowed by shock and the nausea of deep pain, saw the world very dimly for a moment. He was aware of a warm trickle of blood that ran down the side of his face from the wound in his scalp where the braided handle of Monte's quirt had struck.

Then two soft hands took him by the cheeks and tilted back his head. "They nearly killed you!" whispered Lou Miller. "The cowards! The miserable cowards!"

He could not see her very clearly because the dazzle of the moon was above her head, and to his bleared eyes her face was a darkness of almost featureless shadow. But the moon flowed like water over one bare shoulder, where the chiffon had been torn away, during her headlong riding. These pictures he saw clearly enough, though he could not put them together and make connected sense of them.

As for what happened immediately before, he could not make head nor tail of it, and it seemed to him that he was still telling the girl that he loved her now, even now, though his brain reeled and the nausea kept his stomach working.

That was why he said, "If I were dying, I'd want to say a last thing to you, Lou. . . . I love you."

"Harry, *are* you dying? Oh, Harry,

darling?" cried the girl.

She took the weight of his head and shoulders across her lap and into her arms. There was still dust in the air, but there was a smell of sweet, soapy cleanness about her.

"I'm all right," he told her. Then the theme recurred to him, and he drove himself on to the words: "I love you. . . . D'you laugh at me when I tell you that? . . . I love you!"

"And I love you, Harry. . . . D'you hear? Can you understand?" she answered.

The words registered one by one in his mind but they had no connected meaning.

"Tell me where you're hurt," said the girl. "Tell me where the worst pain is, Harry."

He closed his eyes. He felt that he had lost in his great effort. He was not finished. He would still try to make her love him, because, beyond her, opened the gates of a new future which he could bring to the range; beyond her lay unending miles of grassland and the futures of ten thousand happy men. He felt that he was like a general who needed to carry by assault only one small redoubt and then the great fight would be won.

That assault would have to be made in the future. Now, with closed eyes, he could only mutter, "You smell like a clean wind."

She slipped from beneath his weight. He heard cloth suddenly torn into strips. Then the blood was being wiped from his face and a long bandage was wound about his head, firmly. But it gave no pain. Wherever she touched him the pain disappeared. Then she had his head and shoulders in her lap again, and one hand supported his head.

"Wherever you touch me — the pain goes," said Mortimer.

"Because I love you!" said the girl.

He regarded the words with a blank stare and found no meaning in them. "Are you laughing at me?" he said.

"I'm only loving you," said the girl. "Don't speak. Lie still. Only tell where the pain is."

"God put a gift in your hands. They take the pain away," said Mortimer. "What color are your eyes?"

"Kind of a gray, blue-green. . . . I don't know what color they are," she said. "Don't talk, Harry. Lie still."

One instant of clarity came to him. He got to his feet with a sudden, immense effort and stood swaying. "My men are back there in trouble!" he groaned. "Leave me here. Go back and stop the fight if you can."

"There'll be no more trouble. That Sam Pearson, like a coward, has made trouble enough for one night. He won't lift his hand again. But can you get into the saddle? I'll help . . . here . . . lift your foot."

He had his grip on the horn of the saddle and stood for a time with his head dropped against the sharp cantle, while the whirling, nauseating darkness spun through his brain. The orders came to him again, insistently. He raised his left foot. A hand guided it into the stirrup.

"Now one big heave, and you'll be in the saddle. Come on, up you go."

He felt an ineffectual force tugging and lifting at him; his muscles automatically responded and he found himself slumped in the saddle, his head hanging far down. There was no strength in the back of his neck. He wanted to vomit. But there was that uncompleted battle which had to be fought.

"Are you gone?" said Mortimer. "I love you!"

Then a blowing darkness overcame his brain again. He managed to keep his hands locked on the pommel; and the nausea covered his body with cold runnels of sweat. A voice entered his mind from far ahead, sometimes speaking clearly, and sometimes as dim and far as though it were blowing away on a wind. Whenever he heard it, new strength came into him, and hope with it.

It told him to endure. It said that they had reached the bridge. In fact, he heard the hoofbeats of the horse strike hollow beneath him. He saw, dimly, the silver of water under the moon. The voice said they were nearing the Hancock place, if only he could hold on a little. But he knew that he could not hold on. A sense like that of sure prophecy told him that he was about to die and that he never would reach the haven of the ranch house.

And then, suddenly, the outlines of the house were before him.

He steeled himself to endure the dismounting, to gather strength that would pull his leg over the back of the horse.

Now he was standing beside it, wavering.

He made a vast effort to steer his feet toward the faintly lighted doorway. The girl tried to support him and guide him. Then many heavy footfalls rushed out about him. The voice of Jan Erickson roared out like the furious bellowing of a bull. The enormous hands and arms of Erickson lifted him, cradled him lightly, took him through the doorway.

"Louise," he whispered. "I love you . . ."

He could make out the sound of her voice, but not the answering words. Clearer to his mind was the sense of wonderful relief in finding his men back safely, at the Hancock place. He wanted to give thanks for that. He felt stinging tears of gratitude under his eyelids and kept his eyes closed, so that the tears should not be seen.

He could hear Lefty Parkman screech out like a fighting tomcat, "Look at his face! . . . Look at his *face!* Oh, God, look what they've done to him! Look what they gone and done to the chief!"

And there was Pudge Major giving utterance in a strange, weeping whine: "They dragged him. They took and dragged him like a stinking coyote."

"Get out of my way!" shouted Jan Erickson. "I'm gunna kill some of 'em!"

The stairs creaked. They were taking him up to his room. The air was much hotter inside the house, and warmer and warmer the higher they carried him.

He began to relax toward sleep.

The girl, running up the stairs behind the men, cried out to them that she wanted to help tend him. One of the brown-faced, big-shouldered fellows turned and looked at her as no man had ever looked at her before.

"Your dirty, sneaking crowd done this to the chief!" he said. "Why don't you go back where you come from? Why don't you go and crow and laugh about it, like the others are doing? Go back and tell your pa that we're gunna have blood for this. We're gunna wring it out, like water out of the Monday wash! . . . Get out!"

Lefty Parkman left the house and sprinted away for a car to drive to Poplar Springs for a doctor; and Louise Miller went down the stairs into the hall.

The angry, muttering voices of the CCC men passed on out of her ken, and the blond giant who was carrying the weight of Mortimer so lightly. She looked helplessly into the parlor, and there saw Charles Hancock lying on his couch dressed in shorts and a jacket of thin Chinese silk, with the materials for his rum punch scattered over the table beside him. He got up when he saw her and waved his hand. He seemed made of differing component parts — prematurely old boy, and decayed scholar, and drunken satirist.

"Come in, Lou," he said. "Your boys been having a little time for themselves beating up Harry Mortimer? . . . Come in and have a drink of this punch. You look as though you need it. You look as though you'd been through quite a stampede yourself!"

She became aware for the first time of the torn chiffon and her bare shoulder. The bleared, sneering eyes of Charlie Hancock made her feel naked. But she had to have an excuse for staying in the house until she had a doctor's opinion about Mortimer's condition. The image of the dragging, tumbling body at the end of the rope kept running like a madness through her memory, and the closing eyes and the battered lips that said he loved her. For love like that, which a man commingles with his dying breath, it seemed to the girl, was a sacred thing which most people never know; and the glory of it possessed her strongly. Such a knowledge was given to her, she thought, that she had become mature. The girl of that afternoon was a child and a stranger to her in thought and in feeling.

She was so filled with unspeakable tenderness that even that rum-bloated caricature of a man, Charles Hancock, was a figure she could look upon with a gentle sympathy. For he, after all, had been living in the same house with the presence of Harry Mortimer for two long years. Viewed in that light, he became a treasure house from which, perhaps, she could draw a thousand priceless reminiscences about the man she loved. That was why she went to Hancock with a smile and shook his moist, fat hand warmly.

"I will have a drink," she said. "I need one."

"Wang!" shouted Hancock. "Hot water. . . . Take this chair, Lou. . . . And don't look at the rug and the places where the wallpaper is peeling. Our friend Mortimer says that this is a pigpen. He won't live here with me. That connoisseur of superior living prefers to spend most of his time with the gang of brutes in the big shed behind the house. Sings with 'em; sings for 'em; dances for 'em; does a silly buck and wing just to make 'em laugh; plays cards with 'em; gives up his life to 'em the way a cook serves his steak on a platter. . . . By the way, did your boys break any of the Mortimer bones?"

His eyes waited with a cruelly cold expectancy. Loathing went with a shudder through the marrow of her bones, but she kept herself smiling, wondering how Mortimer had endured two years of this. She thought of the years of her own life as a vain blowing hither and thither, but at last she had come to a stopping point. Her heart poured out of her toward the injured man who lay above them.

"I don't know how badly he's injured," she said. "I don't think any bones . . . if there isn't internal injury . . . but God wouldn't let him be seriously hurt by brutes and cowards!"

Hancock looked at her with a glimmering interest rising in his eyes. "Ah, ha!" he chuckled. "I see."

She had her drink, by that time, and she paused in the careful sipping of it. "You see what, Charlie?" she asked.

He laughed outright, this time. "I put my money against it. I wouldn't have believed it," he said.

"What wouldn't you have believed?" asked the girl.

"For my part," said Hancock, "I love living, Lou. I love to let the years go by like a stream, because . . . do you know why?"

"I don't know," she answered, watching him anxiously and wondering if he were very drunk.

He took a swallow that emptied his glass, and with automatic hands began brewing another potion. Still his shoulders shook with subdued mirth.

"I don't want to be rude, but . . ." said Hancock, and broke into a peal of new laughter.

The girl flushed. "I can't understand you at all, Charlie," she said.

"Can't understand me? Tut, tut! I'm one of the simple ones. I'm understood at a glance. I'm clear glass . . . I'm not one of the cloudy, mysterious figures like Mortimer."

"Why is he cloudy and mysterious?" she asked.

"To go in one direction for two years, and wind up on the opposite side of the horizon . . . that's a mystery, isn't it?" asked Hancock, with his bursting chuckle.

"Two years in one direction?" she repeated, guessing, and then blushing, and hating herself for the color which, she knew, was pouring up across her face.

Hancock watched her with a surgeon's eye. He shook his head as he murmured, "I wouldn't believe it. All in a tremor . . . and blushing. Mystery? Why, the man's loaded with mystery!"

"Charlie," she said, "if I know what you're talking about, I don't like it very well."

"Oh, we'll change the subject, then, of course," said Hancock. "Only thing in the world I'm trained to do is to try to please the ladies. You never guessed that, Lou, did you? I don't succeed very well, but I keep on trying."

"Trying to please us?" she asked.

"Yes, trying. But I never really succeed. Not like the men of mystery. They don't waste time on gestures. They simply step up — and they bring home the bacon!"

He laughed again, rubbing his hands.

"Are you talking about Harry Mortimer and me?" she asked, taking a deep breath as she forced herself to come to the point.

"Talking about nothing to offend you," said Hancock. "Wouldn't do it for the world. . . . Can tell you how I admire that

Mortimer. Shall I tell you why?"

She melted at once. "Yes, I want to hear it," she said.

"Ah, there you are with the shining eyes and the parted lips," said Hancock. "And that's the picture he said he would paint, too. And here it is, painted!"

The words lifted her slowly from her chair.

Hancock was laughing too heartily to be aware of her. "Mystery? He's the deepest man of mystery I've ever known in my life," he said. "There's the end of the road for him.˙ No way to get ahead. Blocked on every side in his mission of teaching us how to use the range and button the grass to the ground permanently. He's blocked; can't get past John Miller. . . . But if he can't get past Miller, at least he can get past an easier obstacle. And he does!"

He laughed again, still saying, through his laughter, "But the rich Lou Miller, the beautiful Lou Miller, the spark of fire, the whistle in the wind, the picture that shines in every man's eyes . . ." Here laughter drowned his voice.

"Sit down, Lou!" he said. "I tell you, I love an efficient man, and that's why I love this Mortimer. If he can't win the men, he'll try the women. Two years in one direction gets him nothing. So he turns around and goes in the opposite direction, and all at once he's home! Wonderful, I call it. Simply wonderful! And in a single evening! Even if he's beaten up a bit, he comes safely home and brings Beauty beside the Beast. Knew he would, too. Ready to bet on it."

"To bet on it?" asked the girl, feeling a coldness of face as though a strong wind were blowing against her.

"What did I say?" asked Hancock.

"Nothing," said the girl.

"Sit down, Lou."

"No, I have to go home. The barbecue is still running. Hundreds of people there. . . . Good-by Charlie!"

"Oh, but you can't go like this. I have a thousand things to tell you about Mortimer."

"I think I've heard enough," said the girl. "I didn't realize that he was such a man of — of mystery. But you're right, Charlie. I suppose you're right."

She felt the bitter emotion suddenly swelling and choking in her throat, for she was remembering how Mortimer, stunned and mindless after his fall, had clung still to a monotonous refrain, telling her over and over again that he loved her. She knew that he was a fighting man, and he had clung like a bulldog to his appointed task of winning her even when the brain was stunned. The clearest picture before her mind was of the two men talking in this room, with laughter shaking the paunch of Charlie Hancock as he bet with Mortimer that the tenderfoot could not go to the barbecue and put Lou Miller in his pocket. Shame struck her with the edge and coldness of steel. She turned suddenly and went out into the moonlight to where Hampton was waiting. . . .

When Mortimer wakened late that night he heard the snoring of three of the Hancock cowpunchers in an adjoining room. His brain was perfectly clear now, and only when he moved in his bed did he feel the soreness of bruised muscles.

"How you coming, Chief?" asked the voice of Jan Erickson.

He looked up into the face of the huge Swede, who was leaning from his chair, a shadow wrapped in bright moonlight.

"I'm fit and fine," said Mortimer. "Go to bed, Jan."

"I ain't sleepy," declared Jan Erickson. "Tell me who done it to you."

"A few drunken cowpunchers," said Mortimer.

"Was that big feller Wilson one of them? The feller you licked?"

"No. He wasn't one of them."

"That's good," said Erickson, "because he's taken and run away from the Chappany. He didn't like the side of the range that you showed him, and he run off to Poplar Springs on his way back home. But what was the names of the others?"

"I didn't recognize them," lied Mortimer.

"It was some of Miller's men, wasn't it?" persisted Jan.

"I don't think so," answered Mortimer. "Stop bothering me and go to bed, Jan."

"How many was there?" asked Erickson, a whine of eagerness in his voice.

"A crowd. I couldn't recognize anyone. It's all over. Forget it."

Erickson was silent for a moment, and then his whisper reached Mortimer: "God strike me if I forget it!"

A healthy man can sleep off most of his physical troubles. Mortimer was not roused in the morning when the Hancock cowpunchers clumped down the stairs with jingling spurs. He slept on till almost noon, and then wakened from a melancholy dream to find the wind whistling and moaning around the house and the temperature fallen far enough to put a shiver in his body. When he stood up there were only a few stiffnesses in his muscles. The night before, it was apparent, he simply had been punch-drunk.

A bucket of water in a galvanized iron washtub made him a bath. As he sloshed the chill water over his body his memory stepped back into the dimness of the previous evening. Most of it was a whirling murk through which he could remember the nodding head of Hampton, bearing him forward, and the perpetual disgust of nausea, and his own voice saying, "I love you!" That memory struck him into a sweat of anxious shame until the foggy veil lifted still farther. He could not remember her answer in words, but he could recall the tenderness of her voice and how her arms had held him.

Lightning jagged before Mortimer's eyes and split open his old world to the core. First a sense of guilt ran with his pulses, like the shadowy hand of the referee counting out the seconds of the knockdown. But she never would know, he told himself, if a life of devotion could keep her from the knowledge. He had gone to her ready to lie like a scoundrel, and he had come away with the thought of her filling his mind like a light. Slowly toweling his body dry, he fell into a muse, re-seeing her, body and spirit. That high-headed pride now seemed to him no more than the jaunty soul which is born of the free range. That fierce loyalty which kept her true to her father in every act and word would keep her true to a husband in the same way. She never could turn again, he told himself. And he saw his life extending like a smooth highway to the verge of the horizon. With her hand to open the door to him and give him authority, he would have the entire range, very soon, using those methods which would give the grasslands eternal life. He had been almost hating the stupid prejudices and the blindness of the ranchers; now his heart opened with understanding of them all.

He dressed with stumbling hands, and noted the purple bruised places and where the skin had rubbed away in spots, but there was nothing worth a child's notice except a dark, swollen place that half covered his right eye and extended back across the temple. He could shrug his shoulders at such injuries, if only the scalp wound were not serious. When he had shaved, he went out to the barracks shed to let Shorty examine the cut.

Shorty took off the bandage, washed the torn scalp, and wound a fresh bandage in place. "Healing up like nobody's business," he said. "Sit down and leave me throw a steak and a coupla handfuls of onions into you, and you'll be as fit as a fiddle again."

So Mortimer sat down to eat, and was at his second cup of coffee before he remembered the time of day. It was half an hour past noon and yet his CCC gang had not showed up for food.

"Shorty, where the devil are the boys?" he asked. "What's happened? You're not cooking lunch for them?"

"Well, the fact is that they sashayed off on a kind of little trip," said Shorty.

Mortimer stared at him. "They left the ranch without talking to me?" he demanded.

"They thought you'd be laid up today," said Shorty. "And so they kind of went and played hooky on you, Chief."

"Shorty, where did they go?" asked

Mortimer, remembering vividly how Jan Erickson had leaned over his bed during the night and had tried to drag from him the identity of his assailants.

"How would I know where they'd go?" asked Shorty.

Mortimer turned his back on the cook, for he knew that he would get no trustworthy information from him. He tried to think back into the mind of the gang — not into their individual brains but into the mob consciousness which every group possesses, and the first thing that loomed before him was their savage, deep, unquestioning devotion to him.

With a sick rush of apprehension, he wondered if they might have gone across the valley straight for the Miller place to exact vengeance for the fall of their chief. But Lefty Parkman and Pudge Major were far too levelheaded to permit a move as wild as that. If they wanted to make trouble for men of the Miller ranch they would go to Poplar Springs and try to find straggling groups of the cowpunchers from the big outfit.

Mortimer jumped for the corner of the room and picked up a rifle. He put it down again, straightening slowly. When it came

241

to firearms, his CCC lads were helpless, as compared with the straight-shooting men of the range. He, himself, was only a child in that comparison.

He turned and ran empty-handed into the adjoining shed. The big truck was gone, as he had expected, but the one-ton truck remained, and into the seat of this he climbed in haste.

It was fifteen miles to Poplar Springs and he did the distance in twenty minutes. As he drove he took dim note of the day. The melancholy wind which had wakened him still mourned down the valley, but its force along the ground was nothing compared to the velocity of the upper air. What seemed to be fast-traveling clouds, unraveled and spread thin, shot out of the northwest and flattened the arch of the sky, with the sun sometimes golden, sometimes dull and green, through that unusual mist. In the west the mountains had disappeared.

Three from north to south, three from east to west, the streets of Poplar Springs laid out a small checkering of precise little city blocks. Most of its life came from the "springs," whose muddy waters were said to have some sort of medicinal value. An old frame hotel spread its shambling wings around the water. A rising part of the town's business, however, came from the aviation company of Chatham, Armstrong & Worth, which had built some hangars and used the huge flat east of the place as a testing ground. Saturday nights were the bright moments for Poplar Springs, when the cowpunchers rode into town or drove rattling automobiles in from the range to patronize the saloons which occupied almost every corner.

Wherever he saw a pedestrian, Mortimer called, "Seen anything of a six-foot-four Swede with hair as pale as blow-sand?" At last he was directed to Porson's Saloon.

Porson's had been there in Poplar Springs since the earliest cattle days and still used the old swing doors with three bullet holes drilled through the slats of one panel and two through another. If Porson's had filed a notch for each of its dead men, it would have had to crowd fifty-three notches on one gun butt, people said, for bar whisky and old cattle feuds and single-action Colts had drenched its floor with blood more than once. An echo of the reputation of the place was ominous in Mortimer's mind as he pushed through the doors.

It was like stepping into a set piece on a

stage. The picture he dreaded to find was there in every detail. Jan Erickson, Pudge Major, Lefty Parkman, George Masters, and Dink Waller stood at the end of the bar nearest the door, and bunched at the farther end were eight of the Miller cowpunchers, with Sam Pearson dominating the group. The bartender was old Rip Porson himself, carrying his seventy years like a bald-headed eagle. Unperturbed by the silent thunder in the air, he calmly went about serving drinks.

Mortimer stood a moment inside the door, with his brain whirling as though he had been struck on the base of the skull. The Miller punchers looked at him with a deadly interest. Not one of his own men turned a head toward him, but Lefty Parkman said in a low voice, "The chief!"

"Thank God!" muttered Pudge Major. But Dink Waller growled. "He oughta be home! This is our job."

"It's time for a round on the house, boys," said Rip Porson. "And I wanta tell you something: The first man that goes for iron while he's drinkin' on the house, he gets a slug out of my own gun. . . . Here's to you, one and all!"

He had put out the bottles of rye and, as

the round was filled, silently, he lifted his own glass in a steady red hand.

The two factions continued to stare with fascinated attention at each other, eye holding desperately to eye as though the least shift in concentration would cause disaster. They raised their glasses as Rip Porson proposed his toast: "Here's to the fight and to them that shoot straight; and damn the man that breaks the mirror."

In continued silence the men of the Miller place and Mortimer's CCC gang drank.

Then Mortimer walked to the bar. He chose a place directly between the two hostile forces, standing exactly in the field of fire, if guns were once drawn. "I'll have a beer," he said.

Rip Porson dropped his hands on the edge of the bar and regarded Mortimer with bright, red-stained eyes. "You're the one that the trouble's all about, ain't you?" he asked. "You're Harry Mortimer, ain't you?"

"I am," said Mortimer. "And there's going to be no more trouble."

"Beer is what the man's having," said Porson, slowly filling a glass. A smile, or the ghost of a smile, glimmered in his old eyes.

"Set them up, Porson," said the low,

deep voice of Jan Erickson.

"Set 'em up over here, too," commanded Sam Pearson.

The bartender pushed the whisky bottles into place again. Every moment he was growing more cheerful.

Mortimer faced his own men. "Lefty!" he said, picking out the most dominant spirit from among them.

Lefty Parkman gave not the slightest sign that he had heard the voice which spoke to him. He had picked out a single face among the cowpunchers and was staring at his man with a concentrated hatred. Odds made no difference to Lefty, even odds of eight to six when all the eight were heeled with guns and hardly two of the CCC men could have any weapons better than fists.

"Lefty!" repeated Mortimer.

The eyes of Lefty wavered suddenly toward the chief.

"Turn around and walk out the door. We're leaving here," said Mortimer, "and you're leading the way."

The glance of Lefty slipped away from the eye of Mortimer and fixed again on its former target. For the first time an order from Mortimer went disregarded.

Among Sam Pearson's men there was a

bowlegged cowpuncher named Danny Shaw, barrel-chested, bull-browed, and as solid as the stump of a big tree. The croak of a resonant bullfrog was in the voice of Danny and it was this voice which now said, "There ain't room enough in here for 'em; we got the air kind of used up, maybe."

One of the cowpunchers laughed at this weak sally, a brief, half-hysterical outburst of mirth.

Pudge Major lurched from his place at the bar and walked straight toward the Miller men.

"Go back, Pudge!" commanded Mortimer.

Pudge strode on, unheeding. "You look like an ape when you laugh," said Pudge. "When you open your face that wide, I can see the baboon all the way down the red of your dirty throat."

Mortimer turned and saw Jed Wharton, among the cowpunchers, hit Pudge fairly on the chin with a lifting punch. Major rocked back on his heels and began an involuntary retreat. Big Jed Wharton followed with a driving blow from which Pudge Major cringed away with both hands flung up and a strange little cry of fear that made Mortimer's blood run cold. Poor

Major had gone for bigger game than his nature permitted, and the sight of the white feather among his men struck into Mortimer's brain like a hand of shadow.

He saw in the leering, triumphant faces of the cowpunchers the charge that was about to follow. The man next to Sam Pearson was already drawing his Colt. He had no chance to glance behind him at his own followers, but Mortimer could guess that they were as heartsick and daunted as he by the frightened outcry of Pudge. And he remembered the barking voice of an assistant football freshman at college: "Low, Mortimer! Tackle low!"

"Tackle low!" yelled Mortimer, and dived at Sam Pearson's knees. While he was still in the air he saw from the corner of his eye Lefty Parkman swarming in to the attack, and the blond head of gigantic Erickson. Then his shoulder banged into Pearson's knees, and the whole world seemed to fall on his back.

It was not the sort of barroom fighting that a Westerner would expect. That headlong plunge and the charge of Erickson jammed the cowpunchers against the wall. Mortimer, in the midst of the confusion, caught at stamping feet and struggling legs and pulled down all he could reach.

He put his knee on Pearson's neck and pressed on toward Danny Shay, who had been tripped and had fallen like a great frog, on hands and knees. There was hardly room for fist work. Mortimer jerked his elbow into the face of Danny and stood up in the room Shay had occupied.

Guns were sounding, by that time. As he straightened in the thundering uproar he saw a contorted face not a yard away and a Colt leveling at him over the shoulder of another man. But an arm and fist like a brass-knuckled walking beam struck from a height, and the gunman disappeared into the heap.

That was Jan Erickson's work.

Other men might dance away from Jan and cut him to gradual bits in the open, but for a close brawl he was peerless, and now his hands were filled with work as they never had been before. As Mortimer struck out, he saw on the far side of the bar old Rip Porson standing regardless of danger from chance bullets, with his eyes half closed as he shook his head in profound disgust.

Mortimer saw Pudge Major in it, also. As though the first touch of fear had turned into a madness, Pudge Major came in with an endless screech, like a fighting cat. He ran into the clubbed butt of a revolver that knocked him back against the wall. From that wall he rebounded, swinging a chair in his hands. The chair landed with a crash of splintering wood. Big Sam Pearson, who had managed to regain his feet at last, sank under the blow, and suddenly Mortimer saw that the fight was ended. Those whom Erickson had hit solidly were down, to remain down. Dink Waller patiently, uncomplainingly, was throttling his chosen victim with a full Nelson. Lefty pounded a defenseless victim against the wall. George Masters was in a drunken stagger, trying to come toward the noise of battle, but the fight was ended.

The attack had been so quick and close that most of the guns were not even drawn. Hardly half a dozen bullets had hit ceiling or floor. Not a single shot struck flesh; but the great mirror behind the bar was drilled cleanly through the center and from that hole a hundred cracks jagged outward.

"Take their guns!" shouted Mortimer. "Let them be, but take their guns! Jan, it's over!"

Some two minutes after Mortimer dived

at Pearson's knees he had eight revolvers and several large kitchen knives piled on the bar. Two or three of the beaten men were staggering to their feet. Danny Shay nursed his bleeding face in both hands. Sam Pearson sat in a corner with blood streaming down from his gashed head, which hung helplessly over one shoulder, agape with the shock, and agrin with pain.

Jan Erickson, still in a frenzy, strode back and forth, shouting, "That's what a Mortimer does. He cuts through bums like you the way a knife cuts through cheese. . . . Why don't he wring your necks? Because he's ashamed to hurt wet-nosed kids!"

"Get out of the place, Jan," commanded Mortimer, "All of you get out! There are no broken bones, and thank God for that. Get our men out, Jan!"

He turned back to the bar and said to Porson, "I'll pay half the cost of the mirror, bartender."

His voice could not penetrate the hazy trance of Rip Porson, who continued to stare into space and wag his head slowly from side to side, as he repeated, "Fourteen wearing pants and not one man among 'em . . . the world has gone to hell . . .

fourteen milk-fed baboons!"

There had to be a few rounds of drinks to celebrate the victory. There had to be some patching of cuts. So it was two hours before Mortimer rounded up his crew and had them back at the Hancock place, with the three men who had missed the fight in agonies because they had been out of it.

"Shut your faces," said Jan Erickson. "There wouldn't of *been* no fight if you'd all been there. They wouldn't of dared. . . . But the sweet spot you missed was the chief taking a dive into them like into a swimming pool; and the waves he throwed up took all the fight out of them."

Pudge Major sat with his head in his hands when they were in the barracks shed. Mortimer, on one knee beside him, patted him on the back.

"I was yella," groaned Pudge. "I was. The whole world knows that I'm yella."

"You needed a sock on the chin before you got your second wind," declared Mortimer. "And then you were the best man in the room. Ask the boys. Even Jan wouldn't take you on. Would you, Jan?"

"Him? I'd rather take on a wildcat!" said Jan.

"Jan, d'you mean that, partly?" asked Pudge.

"I mean the whole of it," said Jan Erickson. "And when it comes to working with a chair, you're away out by yourself. You're the class of the field."

Therefore Mortimer left them in this triumphant humor and drove over to the Miller place in the light truck. A Chinese servant opened the door to him but there was no need for him to enter, for John Miller at that moment came down the hall with a jangle of spurs and a quirt in his hand. His daughter was following him. And now he stood tall in the entrance, looking at Mortimer without a word.

"I dare say that you've heard about the trouble in Poplar Springs," said Mortimer. "I want to tell you that I didn't send out my men to make trouble; they went off by themselves, and I started after them to bring them back. When I found them, they'd located your people already. I tried to stop the fight, but it got under way in spite of me."

"Are you through?" asked John Miller, parting his locked jaws with difficulty.

Mortimer said slowly, "If any reprisals start, it will be from your part, not mine.

I've taken my beating and I haven't yipped. But if your fellows come on to make more trouble there'll be murder all over the range. I want to know if you think you can keep your people in hand."

"Are you finished?" asked Miller.

"I am," said Mortimer.

"Very well," said Miller, and walked straight past him.

He turned his bewildered eyes on the girl, as she seemed about to go past him behind her father. His glance stopped her. She was pale; small lines and shadows made her eyes seem older. He had stopped her with his puzzled look, but now as she stood back with a hand against the wall she was looking steadily into his face.

"I wasn't hard, was I?" she asked. "You only had to whistle and the bird flew right off the tree to your hand. Nothing could be easier than that, could it?"

"What are you saying, Lou?" he asked.

She looked down at his extended hand and then up to the pain in his face before she laughed a little. "You *are* wonderful, Harry," she said. "It's that honest, straightforward simplicity which gets you so far. And then your voice. That does a lot. And the facial expression, too. It's good enough

254

for a close-up. Ah, but Hollywood could make a star of you. . . . The way it is now, I suppose you hardly make pocket money out of the girls. Or do they run high, sometimes — the bets you place before you go out to make your play?"

"Hancock . . . there was no bet . . . Lou . . . it was only that I didn't know I'd adore you as I do," stammered Mortimer.

"You know now, though, don't you?" said the girl. "You love me all your heart can hold, Harry, don't you?"

He tried to answer her, but felt the words die on his lips.

"And d'you know, Harry," said the girl, peering at him, "that I think it was the beginning of a great love? As I went along beside you through the night, I would have given my heart. And . . . aren't you a rather rotten sort of dog, Harry?"

He saw her go by him with that quick, light, graceful step. Something made him look up as she vanished through the patio gate, and he seemed to find an answer for his question in the swift gray stream that poured across the sky endlessly, as it had been pouring ever since morning. The sun was small and green behind it.

He got back into the truck and drove

blindly toward the ranch. The subconscious mind inside him took note of the gray sweep of mist through the sky and the color of the setting sun behind it. It was not water vapor which could give that color, he knew. It was dust — dust rushing on the higher stratum of the air, headlong. Somewhere the wind had eaten through the skin of the range and was bearing uncounted tons of topsoil into nothingness.

That fact should have meant something to Mortimer, but his conscious mind refused to take heed of it, for it was standing still before the thought of Louise Miller. Then Charlie Hancock jumped into his mind and he gripped the wheel so hard that it moved under his grasp.

He brought the car to a stop at the entrance of the house. Three or four of Hancock's cowpunchers were lounging in the doorway of the ranch house. He shouldered brusquely through them, and went on into the parlor of the house, where Hancock lay on the couch, as usual, with his rum punch on the table beside him. He took off his glasses as Mortimer entered, resettled them on his nose, and then smote his paunch a resounding whack.

"Ah, Harry!" he cried. "You're the one

soul in the world that I want to see. I don't mean about battering some of the Miller boys in Poplar Springs. That'll do your reputation on the range some good, though. Tackling guns with bare hands is rather a novelty in this part of the world, of course. . . . But what's that to me? Do you know what has meaning to me?"

Mortimer picked up the rum bottle, poured a swallow into a tall glass, and tossed it off. He said quietly, "What *does* have meaning to you, Charlie?" And his eyes hunted the body of Hancock as though he were looking for a place to strike home a knife.

But Hancock was unaware of this. A wave of thought had overcome him, and memory dimmed his eyes as he said, "I'm going to tell you something, Harry. I'm going to tell you about a woman. . . . Mind you, it was years ago. . . . But when I say 'a woman,' I want you to understand '*the* woman.' Rare. Sudden. Something too beautiful to last. . . . Are you following me?"

"I follow you," Mortimer said.

The rancher had almost closed his eyes as he consulted the picture from the past.

"I saw her. I adored her. I asked her to

marry me. When she accepted me, Harry, the sound of her voice lifted me almost out of my boots. I went away planning my path through the world. And when I was about to take the prize in my hand, Harry — mark this — when I was about to take her to the church, she disappeared. Vanished absolutely. The way you say this range soil will vanish when the wind hits it just right. What took her away? A little wizened son of a French marquis with no more man in him than there is skin on the heel of my hand. She was gone. Lost to me. Love. Hope. What the hell will you have? She was all that!

"And since that day I've lain here with the rum bottle wondering how the devil I could get back at the whole female race. Can't do anything with them when you lie flat and simply think, because thought, on the whole, is beyond their ken. And therefore I had to wait until you did it for me. D'you see? You show me how women can be handled as easily as they handle men. Love her? *No!* Admire her? *No!* You simply take the woman and put her in your pocket. Who's the girl? Some cheap little chit? No, the best in the land. The proudest. The highest. The top of everything. . . .

I stood here, last night, and saw her eyes melt when your name was mentioned. I saw the whole lovesick story come swooning into her face. And as a result of what? As a result of one evening's work. Why, Harry, when I saw what you had done, I wanted to get down on my knees and beg you for lessons."

"You told her everything, didn't you?" asked Mortimer.

Hancock took off a moment for thought. The wind, at the same moment, seemed to descend and grip the ranch house with a firmer hand. The whine of the storm ascended the scale by several notes.

"Told her?" said Hancock. "I don't think that I told her anything. I couldn't say anything. I could only lie here and laugh. And admire you, Harry, and think how you'd paid off my score. And I want to tell you something, Harry. As I lay here last night I felt a deathless debt — gratitude, and all that. Wonderful feeling, Harry. The first time I've had it in my life. Absolutely extraordinary."

"I dare say," muttered Mortimer through his teeth.

"And that's why I'm glad to see you today," said Hancock. "Not because you've

259

beaten eight of Miller's best men with your hands, but because you've subdued one woman, opened her heart, put tears in her eyes, made her knees tremble, when you didn't give a hang for her from the first to the last." He broke into a peal of laughter which wound up on a gasping and sputtering.

"Close, in here," said Hancock. "Cool, but close, and that's strange, isn't it?"

Mortimer could not speak, seeing again the beauty and the pride of the girl who was lost to him.

"Chuck the door open, like a good fellow, will you?" asked Hancock. "I never had so much trouble breathing. Is the alcohol getting me at last? Well, let it get me. I'll die laughing. I've seen the proud females, the high females, the pure females paid off for me, shot for shot. And I owe that to you, old fellow."

Mortimer went to the door and threw it wide. It seemed to him that ghosts rushed up into the lamplight, into his face. Then it was as though dim horses were galloping past in endless procession, and swifter than horses ever put hoof to the ground. He squinted his eyes into the dimness knowing that the swift whirl was a dust storm rushing past him at full speed.

The range itself was melting away before his eyes.

A flying arm of dust enveloped Mortimer and set him coughing as he closed the door and turned back into the room.

Hancock was grinning cheerfully. "There she blows, Harry," he said. "There comes the dust storm you've been talking about for two years. Now you'll see if you've buttoned the topsoil down with all your plantings and plowings. Now we'll see if the range *has* been overgrazed, as you say, and what part of it is going to blow away."

The house trembled, as though nudged by an enormous shoulder, and the storm screamed an octave higher. The two men stared at each other; then Mortimer pulled out a bandanna and began to knot it around his throat.

"Get your handpicked cowpunchers on the job, Charlie," he suggested.

"It's dark, brother," said Hancock, "and the kind of lads I have don't work in the night."

"All right," said Mortimer. "The cattle I save will be my share of the stock, and the dead ones can belong to you."

He left the room, with Hancock shouting

loudly. "Wait a minute, Harry! All for one and one for all . . ."

When Mortimer stepped into the open the gale was blowing hard enough to set his eyelids trembling. It came at him like a river of darkness. He bumped the corner of the house, turning toward the barracks shed, and then the wind caught him from the side and set him staggering.

The light in the window of the shed was a dull, greenish blur. He had to fumble to find the door, and he pressed his way in, to find a jingling of pots and pans in the kitchen and the CCC men sneezing and cursing in the mist which filtered rapidly through the cracks in the walls of the shed. They stood up and looked silently toward him for an explantion.

He said, "It's a dust storm, boys. Pulled at my feet like water. . . . No man has to go out into weather like this, but if any of you volunteer to give a hand . . ."

Jan Erickson turned his head slowly to survey the group. "Leave me see the man that *won't* volunteer," he said ominously.

But not one of them hung back. They were a solid unit, and a speechless content filled Mortimer's heart, till Shorty appeared in the kitchen door, shouting, "There's gunna be plenty of grit in the flour bin and mud in the coffee, Chief!"

A louder howling of the wind seemed to answer Shorty directly and set the men laughing. They equipped themselves as Mortimer directed, with shirts buttoned close at the neck and wrist to keep out the flying sand, and with bandannas ready to pull up over mouth and nose. A big canteen to each would give enough water to wash the mouth clean for a few hours and keep the bandannas wet in case it were necessary to strain the dust out more thoroughly. Four of them would ride with Charlie Hancock's cowpunchers to help handle the cattle, which probably were drifting rapidly before the storm and lodging against the fence-lines. The thing to do was to get the weakest of the livestock into the barns and round up the mass of them in the Chappany Valley, where Mortimer's young groves of trees would give some shelter against the whip of the wind and the drifting of the soil. It was true that all this work properly belonged to Hancock's cowpunchers, but under Mortimer's control the CCC men had learned every detail of the ranch work long ago.

They worked all night.

The wind kept coming like a thousand devils out of the northwest, and into the southeast. At the farthest limit of the Hancock land, Mortimer led a group of the CCC men. They found two hundred steers drifted against a barbed wire fence, with their heads down and the drifting sand already piled knee-deep around them. There they would remain until the sand heaped over them in a great dune. It required hard work to turn the herd, shooting guns in their faces, shouting and flogging, but at last the dazed cattle began to move back toward the Chappany Valley.

Streaks and slitherings of moonlight that got through the hurly-burly showed the cattle continually drifting aslant, to turn their faces from the storm. It was like riding into a sandblast. A fine silt had forced its way under tight wristbands and down the collars of the punchers, so that a crawling discomfort possessed their bodies. Dust was thick on every tongue, and there was a horrible sense of the lungs filling, so that breathing was more labored, though less air got to the blood.

When they had jammed those steers into the Chappany, letting them drink on the way at the lowest of the two Hancock lakes, they pushed the herd into one of the groves of trees which Mortimer had planted two years before. The slant of the ground gave some protection. The spindling trees by their multitude formed a fence which seemed to whip and filter the air somewhat cleaner. Even that push against the dusty wind had been almost too much for some of the cattle. A good many of them did not mill at all, but slumped to their knees. The others, wandering, lowing, and bellowing, pooled up around the steers that went down, and presently the entire herd was holding well. But some of those that went down would be dead before morning.

It was not time to count small losses, however. It was like riding out a storm in an old, cranky ship. The cargo hardly mattered. Life was the thing to consider.

Mortimer washed out his nose and throat from his canteen and moistened the bandanna which covered the lower part of his face. He sent his contingent of riders back to find more fence-lodged cattle and aimed his own tough cow pony at a dim twinkle of lanterns high up across the valley, above the three Miller lakes. He could guess what those lights indicated, and the picture of disaster bulked suddenly in his mind greater and blacker than the storm itself.

He took the way straight up the valley, however, and rode the slope toward Miller's thousand acres of plowed ground. Heading into the wind, in this manner, it was impossible to keep his eyes open very long at a time. No matter how narrowly he squinted, the fine silt blew through the lashes and tormented the eyeballs. He had to pick direction from time to time, checking the pony's efforts to turn its head from the torment; otherwise he kept his eyes fast shut.

There were two square miles of that plowed and hay-covered cropland. He came up on the northern edge of it and found the mustang stepping on hard, smooth ground. When he used his flashlight, he saw that the border acres which edged toward the wind had blown away like a dream. The reddish hardpan, tough as burned bricks, was all that remained!

He dismounted, tried to clear his throat, and found that the choke of the dust storm had penetrated to the bottom of his lungs like thick smoke. Panic stormed up in his brain. He beat the terror down and went on about his observations. There were things to see, here, which should be reported exactly in the notebook that was his source of information.

It was a dark moment of the storm, for the wind came on with a scream and a steel-edge whistling through the hay, and the moon was shut away almost entirely. It was as though the earth had exploded and the results of the explosion were hanging motionless in the air.

He went over the bared ground to the rim of the yet standing hay. In places it was rolled back and heaped like matting; sometimes it gathered in cone-shaped masses like shocked hay; but every now and then the wind got its fingertips under the shocks and the rolls and blew them apart with a single breath. On his knees Mortimer turned the flashlight on the edge of the hayland and watched the action of the storm. At that point the life-sustaining humus was about a foot deep to the hardpan. The top portion, which had been loosened by the plow, ran down from four to six inches, and this part gave way rapidly, sifting from around the white roots of the hay until each stalk, at the end, was suddenly jerked away. In the meantime, the scouring blast worked more gradually at the lower, unplowed layer of the soil, which was compacted with the fine, hairlike roots of the range grass. Even this gave way with amazing rapidity.

The hayland was doomed. An army, working hand to hand, could not have saved it. As he mounted, the swinging ray of the electric torch showed Mortimer another horseman who sat the saddle not far away, impassive. The long-legged horse kept picking up its feet nervously and making small bucking movements of protest, but the rider held it like a pitching boat in a rough sea. Mortimer, coming nearer, saw the masked face and the sand-reddened eyes of John Miller, who was watching twelve thousand dollars worth of hay and fifty thousand irreplaceable dollars worth of topsoil blow to hell. Impassively, by the ragged glimpses of light which the moon offered, the rancher stared at the quick destruction. Mortimer rode to his side and shouted, "Sorry, Miller!"

John Miller gave him a silent glance, and then resumed his study of the growing ruin before him. Mortimer turned his mustang back into the Chappany Valley.

He passed over a long stretch of the Miller bottomland which had been plowed for onions and potatoes. The deep, black soil was withering away into pockmarks, or dissolving under the breath of the storm. Mortimer groaned as he paused to watch the steady destruction. That heavy loam had formed centuries or hundreds of centuries before among the roots of the forested uplands. Rain had washed it gradually into the rivers. The Chappany floods had spread it over the flat of the valley lands. And this rich impost which nature had spread in ten thousand careful layers was blowing headlong away, forever! It seemed to Mortimer that all America was vanishing from beneath his feet.

He hurried on down the Chappany, looking again and again, anxiously, toward the flickering line of lanterns that shone from the high ground above the Miller lakes. He had warned Miller two years ago, by word and by example, about the danger of those rolling sand dunes above the bluff. If a great wind came from this quarter, the whole mass of sand might come to life and spill over the edge of the bluff to fill the lakes beneath and sponge up the priceless water.

Out of the sweeping dimness, which sometimes blew his horse sliding, Harry Mortimer came back onto the Hancock land

and dismounted. With his flashlight he studied half a mile of terrain. On one side, some contour-plowing was commencing to blow a little, but, everywhere else he looked, his trees, his stretches of shrubbery over exposed shoulders, and the tough grasses with wide-spreading roots which he had planted were buttoning the soil to the hardpan, holding the ground like a green overcoat of varying textures.

One shouting burst of triumph filled his throat, but after that the joy slipped away from him and left his heart cold. For somehow his soul had struck roots in the whole countryside. Now hundreds of thousands of good acres all over the range were threatened, and it seemed to Mortimer that children of his body, not the mere hopes of his mind and the planned future, were imperiled.

He turned his horse up the slope, where the bluff diminished to a reasonable angle. Off to the left the headlights of an automobile came bucking through the dimness. A great truck went by him, roaring, with a load of long timbers.

Mortimer's heart sank, for he knew the meaning of that. He spurred the mustang on behind the lighted path of the truck until he reached the sand dunes immediately above the two long lakes which belonged on the Hancock land and held water for the Hancock cattle.

The sand which came on the whistling wind, up there, cut at the skin and endangered the eyes, but his flashlight showed him no portion of the Hancock dunes wearing under the storm! From the edge of the bluff and back for a hundred yards, he had planted a tough Scotch shrub which had the look of heather, though it never bloomed. For fuel it was useless. No cattle would graze on those bitter, varnished leaves. That shrubbery served no purpose in the world except to shield the ground under it. It grew not more than a foot high, but it spread in such solid masses that wind could not get at its roots.

Behind the shrubbery he had planted fifty rows of tough saplings, close as a fence. They had grown slowly, but the thickened trunks stood up now like solidly built palings against the storm. Beyond them, and stretching as far as the dunes rolled into the back country, Mortimer had covered every inch of the ground with a grass from the Russian steppes, where eight months of the year the earth is frozen, and where for four months this close-growing, stubborn grass covers the soil like a blanket of a fine weave and offers a steady pasturage for wandering herds of small cattle. For two years it had been rooting and spreading, and now it clothed the dunes behind the Hancock lakes with an impermeable vesture. The dunes themselves had been anchored, here, but the flying silt which filled the air was banking up outside the farther lines of his fence of saplings. It was conceivable that if the storm continued for days it might gradually heap the wave of sand so high that the trees would be overwhelmed; but little of the sweeping sand could ever roll over the bluff and drop into the lakes beneath.

Once more triumph ran riot through Mortimer's blood; and once more the triumph died suddenly away as he looked at the lanterns that stretched before him along the edge of the bluff.

There were far more lights than he had expected; and, now that he came closer, he found two hundred men laboring in a mist of blow-sand. Orders, yelled from time to time, sang on the wind and vanished suddenly. Here and there men were down on their knees, work forgotten as they tried to cough the dust out of their lungs.

Of course, the Miller ranch could not supply such a force of working hands as this. The men were from all the adjacent range. For the first sweep of the storm had choked a thousand pools with silt and had begun to damage the water in many a standing tank. The small ranchers in such a time of need turned naturally toward John Miller, but, when they telephoned, the ominous answer was that the dunes were crawling in slow waves toward the edge of the bluff above the lakes which served as reservoirs, during the dry season, not only for Miller's cattle but for the herds of his neighbors. That news brought men from all of the vicinity. The trucks of the Miller place carried timbers to the bluff. And the entire army was slaving to erect a fence that would halt the slow drift of the dunes. To fence off the whole length of the three lakes was impossible, so they selected the largest of the three, the one just above the Hancock property line, and here a double fence-line was being run.

John Miller himself appeared on the scene at this time and commenced to ride up and down, giving advice, snapping brief orders. He looked to Mortimer like a resolute general in the midst of a battle, but this was a losing fight.

For the whole backland, the whole retiring sweep of the dunes was rising up in a smother of blow-sand, heaping loosely spilling masses on the ridges of the dunes, so that there was a constantly forward flow of incredibly reluctant waves. And the piling weight of that sand was as heavy as water, also.

The men worked with a sullen, patient endurance, scooping out footholds for the posts, boarding them across, with interstices between the boards, and then supporting the shaky structure against the sweep of wind and the roll of sand with long, angled shorings.

One woman moved up and down the line with a bucket of water and a sponge. As she came near, the workers raised the handkerchiefs which covered nose and mouth. Some of them stood with open mouth and tongue thrust out to receive the quick swabbing with water that enabled them to breathe again. Mortimer saw that it was Louise Miller, masked herself, like a gypsy. He swung down from his horse and laid hold of the bail of the bucket.

"I'll handle this, Lou," he told her. "It's

too heavy a job for you —"

Weariness had unsteadied her, and the wind staggered her heavily against Mortimer. So, for an instant, she let her weight lean against him. Then she pulled up the bandanna that covered her face.

"It's a great day for you!" she gasped. "We laughed at you, did we? We wouldn't listen when you talked sense to us? Well, it's the turn for the dirt doctor to laugh while the whole range blows away from under our feet."

He picked up the sponge from the soupy water of the pail and swabbed the sand and black muck from her face. He steadied her with one hand against the wind while he did this.

She sneered, "We're learning our lesson, Harry. If the wind leaves us anything, we'll get down on our knees and ask you to teach us how to keep it."

He passed the sponge over her face again, slowly. "You're talking like a fool, a little, spoiled fool," he said.

She answered through her teeth: "Get off our land and stay off. We'd rather let the wind blow us all the way to hell than have you lift a hand to help us."

She caught up the pail and went on,

walking more swiftly, though the sand dripped and blew from about her feet as they lifted from the soft ground.

John Miller came up, fighting his horse into the wind, when a kneeling, coughing figure jumped up suddenly from the ground and gripped the reins of Miller's horse under the bit. With his other hand he gestured wildly toward Mortimer.

"You wouldn't listen to him!" screamed the rancher. "You laughed at him. You knew *every*thing! He was only a fool tenderfoot. God gave all the sense to the Millers! . . . But look at the Hancock place; look at the safe water; and then look at *you!* Damn you, Miller, for a fake and a fool! I hope you rot!" He dropped to the ground again, and began trying once more to cough the dust from his lungs.

John Miller drove his horse up to Mortimer. "You've got three men working with us here," he said. "Take them away. We don't need their hands. We don't need your brains. Get off the Miller land!"

Mortimer turned without a word of protest, letting his horse drift before the wind. He found Lefty Parkman and gave him the order to leave the work, together with the other two. They trooped back toward the Hancock place with their chief, and, as they went, Mortimer took grim notice of how the first sand fence was already sagging under the irresistible weight of accumulating silt. But the storm and the fate of the range had become a smaller thing to him since his last glimpse of Lou Miller. The pain of it lingered under his heart like the cold of a sword. It was not the blow-sand that kept him from drawing breath, but the fine, poisonous dust of grief.

Then the thought of Charlie Hancock and how the fat drunkard had betrayed him blinded his eyes with anger. He drove the snorting mustang ahead of his men and rushed to the ranch house. The thickest smother of the storm was coiling around him as he broke in through the doorway to the hall.

Then, as he turned toward the entrance to the parlor, he heard Hancock singing cheerfully to himself, and saw the man stretched as usual on the couch with the rum punch beside him.

"Hi, Harry!" called Charlie Hancock. "How's the little sand-blow? Been a hero again, old boy? Charmed any more girls off the tree?"

It seemed to Mortimer, as he blinked his

sore eyes, that he was looking through an infinite distance of more than space and time toward his ranching partner. The rage that had been building in him sank away to a numb disgust. Then the telephone at the end of the room began to purr.

"For you," said Hancock. "This thing has been ringing all night. The world seems to want Harry Mortimer, after ignoring him all these years."

Over the wire a strident, nasal voice said, "Mortimer? This is Luke Waterson in Patchen Valley. . . . The wind's blowing hell out of things, over here. . . . Barn's gone down, slam! Forty head inside it. Mortimer, I don't care about barns and cattle, but the ground's whipping away from under our feet. You're an expert about that. You claim you can keep the ground buttoned down tight. For God's sake tell us what to do. We'll all pitch in and wear our hands to the bone if you'll tell me how to start . . ."

Mortimer said, "Waterson, it makes my heart ache to hear you. God knows that I'd help you if I could. But the only way to anchor the topsoil is to use time as well as thought and . . ."

"You mean that you won't tell me the

answer?" shouted Waterson.

"There's no answer I can give when . . ." began Mortimer. But he heard the receiver slammed up at the other end.

As he turned away from the phone, it rang again with a long clamor.

"This is Tom Knight. Down at Poker-ville," said another voice. "Mortimer, I've always been one of the few that believed you knew your business. And now the devil is loose down here. Sand and silt in all three of our tanks. No water. But that's nothing, I've got three hundred acres in winter wheat, and, by God, it's blowing into the sky! Mortimer, what can I do to hold the soil? It's going through my fingers like water through a sieve . . ."

"I can't tell you, Tom," called Mortimer. "You need two years of careful planting, and less crowding on the cattle range . . ."

"Two years? Hell, man, I'm talking about hours, not years! In twenty-four hours there won't be enough grass on my lands to feed a frog! Can you give me the answer?"

"Not even God could help your land till the wind stops blowing."

"Damn you and your book and your theories, then!" roared Knight. And his receiver crashed on the hook.

The instrument was hardly in place when the bell rang again.

"Take it, Charlie, will you?" asked Mortimer weakly.

"I'll take it. *I'll* tell 'em," said Hancock.

He strode to the telephone and presently was shouting into the mouthpiece, ". . . and even if he were here I wouldn't let him waste time on you. For two years he's been trying to show you the way out. You knew too much to listen. Stay where you are and choke with dust, or else come up here and see how the Hancock acres are sticking fast to the hardpan!" He laughed as he hung up.

"That's the way to talk to 'em," he said. "You're in the saddle now. You've been a joke for two years. Now let 'em taste the spur. Ram it into 'em and give the rowels a twist. . . ."

Mortimer escaped from the tirade. He found himself wondering at the hollowness in his heart, and at the pain, which was like homesickness and fear of battle combined. But then he remembered the girl and the tightness of her lips as she denounced him.

He went out into the howl and darkness of the storm, and for forty-eight hours he worked without closing his eyes. Even Jan Erickson broke down before that and lay on the floor of the barracks shed on his back, a snorting sound in his throat though his eyes were wide open. A black drool ran from the corner of his mouth. Pudge Major developed a sort of asthma. His throat and his entire face swelled. He lay on his bed propped up into the only position in which he could breathe.

Mortimer gave the Chinaman twenty dollars to spend every spare moment at Pudge's bedside; his own place had to be outside, for greater events were happening every hour.

In the middle of the second day of that unrelenting wind, the last defense on top of the bluff gave way and the sand began to flood down into the third of Miller's lakes. The first two had choked up within twenty-four hours of the start of the blow. The backed-up heights of the flowing sand quickly overwhelmed the third. In the thick, horrible dusk cattle were seen, mad with thirst, thrusting their muzzles deep into the wet ooze, stifling, dying in the muck.

That was when big John Miller came up

to the Hancock house. It happened, at this moment, that Mortimer had dropped into the barracks shed to see the progress of Pudge Major and had found him slightly improved. While he was there Wang appeared, coming from the house with incredible speed.

He gave word that the great man of the range was in the ranch house, and Mortimer went instantly into the parlor of the main building. He found Charlie Hancock with his face more swollen and rum-reddened than ever, and in the same half-dressed condition, while Miller, with ten years added to his age, sat with a steaming glass of punch in his hand. He stood up when Mortimer entered.

"He wants help," said Hancock. His savage exultation at the surrender of his old enemy made him clip the words short. "I have the vote on this ranch," he added. "I have the two-thirds interest behind me, but I want your opinion, Mortimer. Shall we let the Miller cattle water in our lakes? Shall we charge 'em a dollar a head, or is it *safe* to let them use up our reserve supply at any price?"

Mortimer watched the rancher take these humiliating blows with an emotionless face.

"It is true," said Miller, "that I am on my knees. I'm begging for water, Mortimer. Shall I have it?"

"You want it for your own cattle and you want it for those of your friends?" said Mortimer.

"Too many. Can't do it," said Hancock, shaking his head.

"I would be ashamed to get water for my own cattle and not for the herds of my neighbors," said Miller. "Some of us have lived on the range like brothers for several generations."

"I'm not of that brotherhood, Miller," snapped Charlie Hancock. He added, "Can't water the cows of every man under the sky. Can't and won't. There isn't enough in my lakes."

"I put six feet on each of our dams last year," said Mortimer.

"Perhaps you did," said Hancock, "but still there's not enough to . . ."

"There's enough water here for the whole community," said Mortimer. "We've backed up three times as much . . ."

"If they get water, they'll pay for it," said Hancock. "Business, Miller. Business is the word between us. Do you remember five years ago when I wanted to run a road across that southeastern corner of your place?"

"That was my foreman's work," said Miller. "I was not on the place when he refused you."

"Why didn't you change his mind for him when you got back, then?" demanded Hancock.

"You didn't ask a second time," said the old rancher.

"Ah, you thought I'd come crawling, did you?" asked Hancock. "But I'm not that sort. It doesn't run in the Hancock blood. . . . And now I'll tell you what I'll do. I'll let your cows come to my water; but they'll pay a dollar a head for each day spent beside the lakes. Understand? A dollar a head."

Miller said nothing. His lips pinched hard together.

"This drought may last two weeks, a month," said Mortimer, "before the water holes are cleaned out and before trenches catch the seepage from the choked lakes. The people around here won't pay thirty dollars to water their cows for a month."

"They will, though," said Hancock. "They *won't* pay? By God, I want to see them get one drop of water without handing me cash for it!"

Miller took a deep breath and replaced his untasted glass on the table.

"I think you know what this means, Hancock," he said. "There are some impatient men waiting at my house, now. When I tell them what you have to say, I think they're apt to come and get the water they need, in spite of you."

"My dear Miller," said Hancock, "I occasionally have a glass, as you know, but my hand is still steady." He held out his glass of rum. The liquid stood as steady as a painted color inside it. "I've lost touch with the rest of the world, but my rifle remains my very good friend," said Hancock. "When you and your friends come over, you can have what you wish: water or blood, or both. But for the water you'll pay."

Miller looked carefully at his host for a moment. Then he turned and left the room in silence.

When he was gone, Hancock threw up a fist and shook it at the ceiling. "Did you hear me, Harry?" he demanded. "Did I tell it to him? Did I pour it down his throat? . . . Oh, God. I've waited fifteen years to show the range that I'm a man, and now they're beginning to find it out! Hell is going to pop, and at last I'll be in the middle of it. Not a rum-stew, but a man-sized hell of my own making!"

Argument would have been, of all follies, the most complete. Mortimer sat in the corner of the room with a glass of straight rum and felt it burning his throat as he watched Charlie Hancock pull on riding clothes. A heavy cartridge belt slanted around his hips, with a big automatic weighting it down on one side. He put on a sombrero and pulled a chin band down to keep it firmly in place. Then he picked up his repeating rifle, and laughed.

A siren began to sound above the house at the same time. It would bring back to the ranch house those fighting cowhands of whom Hancock was so proud and who owed their existence out of jail to his careless fondness for the bad records in their past. The sound of that siren, cutting through the whirl of the wind, would tell the true story to John Miller as he journeyed back to his ranch. And Mortimer could foretell the cleaning of guns and gathering of ammunition which would reply to it.

Hancock was saying, "Harry, in a sense it's all owing to you. I've had mental indigestion most of my life because a girl smacked me down. Except for you there'd be choked lakes for Hancock as well as for Miller. But, as it is, I have the bone that the dog will jump for, and I'm going to hold it high! Are you with me?"

"Quit it, Charlie, will you" said Mortimer. "You think you're showing yourself a man. You're not. You're acting like a spoiled baby."

"Before this baby gets through squalling," said Hancock, "a lot of big, strong men on this range are going to wish that I was never born. Before I'm through . . ."

A hand knocked; the front door pushed open, and a slight figure staggered into the hallway in a whirl of dust. It was Lou Miller. With her eyes wind-bleared and her hat dragged to the side, and weariness making her walk with a shambling step, she should have looked like nothing worth a second glance; instead, she seemed to Mortimer to be shaped and God-given specially to fill his heart. Her eyes found him and forgot him in the first instant. She said to Hancock, "My father came to talk business, I know. But he didn't get far, did he?"

"Not one step, Lou," said Hancock.

"Father came to talk business," she said. "But I've come to beg."

"You?" said Hancock. "John Miller's daughter can't beg."

"On my knees, if it will do any good," said the girl.

"Did *he* send you here?" asked Hancock, with malicious curiosity.

"He doesn't know that I'm here. But if you'll give us a chance I'll let the whole world know the kindness that's in you, Charlie," she told him.

"Ah, quit all that," said Hancock. "They've always smacked me down. If they get anything out of me now, they'll have to fight for it."

"God won't let it come to that. Not on this range," said the girl. "Let's admit that we're a rotten lot, all of us. But think of the poor beasts, Charlie! They're wedged against the fences. The sand is drifting them down. I shone a flashlight across ten thousand pairs of eyes that were dying, Charlie, are you listening to me?"

She pulled softly at his arm, but Hancock was staring up at the ceiling.

"You know something, Lou," he said. "Back there when I was alive — back there before I turned into rum-bloat and poison ivy, if you'd lifted a finger I would have given you my blood! But the way it is now, I'm finished. I'm going to get one thing out of tonight, and that's a chance to die in a scrap."

"Don't say that!" she cried out. She stood close, trying to look him in the eye and make him answer her, mind to mind. But he kept his eyes on the ceiling.

He said, "It's no good. I'm finished. But when they bury me they're going to know that I was a man. Lou, get out. I won't talk any more."

"If you go ahead," said Lou Miller, "there'll be murder in the Chappany."

"Get out," said Hancock, looking at the ceiling, "Just get the hell out."

It had been an agony to Mortimer. He took the girl by the arm and made her go into the hall with him. "You can't go home yet," he said. "You're as weak as a new calf. You can't head off into this wind."

She leaned against him for a moment, silently gathering strength, and then pushed herself away. She had not met his eyes once; she did not meet them now as she went to the outer door. Mortimer put his hand on its knob.

"Look here," he said, "I'm not as bad

as you think. You came up and let Hancock talk to you the other day. But what he told you isn't the whole truth. Will you let me speak?"

"I'll go now," she answered. "But I'll tell you one thing," she said, staring straight before her. "There wasn't any hatred in the Chappany Valley till you came. There was love!" Her voice broke. "We all loved one another. We were happy —"

He said nothing. Then she added, with a sudden savagery, "You're from the outside — Why didn't you *stay* out? Why don't you go away?"

He felt the words in his heart, where a cold pain settled. Then he pulled the door open and took her outside. Her horse had crowded against the house, head down. He helped her into the saddle and saw horse and girl reel as she swung into the wind. A moment later they were lost in darkness.

He turned and went back into the house.

"Will you listen to me?" asked Mortimer.

"I'll hear no arguments," said Hancock. "Now that I'm started I want what lies ahead."

Mortimer tightened his belt a notch. The fatigue which had been growing as a weight in his brain gradually melted away and a cold, clear river of forethought flowed through him. "Do you think your father would approve of this? Would old Jim Hancock refuse water to the cows of his neighbors?" asked Mortimer.

"Jim Hancock is an old fool," said Charlie. "And he's fifteen miles away in Poplar Springs. Who's going to get to him to ask how he votes on the business? The roads are wind-worn into badlands or else they're drifted belly-deep in silt and sand. Nobody will get to him for a fortnight. And the dance will be over before that."

"Do you know what it will mean?" asked Mortimer.

"I suppose it means *that*, to begin with," said Hancock.

He raised a finger for silence, and Mortimer heard it coming down the wind, a long-drawn-out, organlike moaning, or as though all the stops of the organ had been opened, from the shrillest treble to the deepest bass. That was the lowing of the thirst-stricken cattle which milled beyond the fences of the Hancock place, held from their search for water.

Hancock smiled as he listened. "There it is," he said. "The mob's on the stage. They're calling to Oedipus. They want the king. They're waiting for the main actor!" He laughed.

Mortimer struck him across the face with the flat of his hand. He intended it more as a gesture than a blow, but he hit with more force than he had intended, and Hancock staggered.

"Don't reach for that gun," said Mortimer.

"No," said Hancock calmly. "I know that you could break my back for me."

"I had to say something to you. Words weren't any good," remarked Mortimer.

"Ah, you think the ship is about to sink, do you?" asked Hancock, with an ugly twist of his loose mouth. "You think it's time for the rats to leave. Is that it?"

Mortimer said, "I came out here on the range to do something that the range didn't want. All I managed to accomplish was to put a prize in your hand that's worth a fight. . . . Are you hearing me, Hancock?"

"With an extreme and curious interest," said Charles Hancock.

"I'm not an expert shot," said Mortimer.

"You're very good if you take time and put your mind on it," admitted Hancock.

"Well, Charlie," said Mortimer, "if you kill a man attempting to get his cattle to your water, I'll come to you afterward. You may put bullets into me, Charlie, but I'll kill you as surely as there's wind in the sky."

Mortimer went out of the house and into the barracks shed. He said to Shorty, "You stay here with Pudge. When the rest of the boys come in, send them after me to the Miller place."

"Send them *where?*" shouted Shorty.

"To the Miller place," repeated Mortimer, and went to the barn.

Mortimer did not take a horse from the group of saddle stock. Instead, he selected a ten-year-old Missouri mule, Chico, with a potbelly that meant as much to his endurance as the fat hump means to the camel, with a lean, scrawny neck, with a head as old as Methuselah's, filled with wicked wisdom, and with four flawless legs and four hoofs of impenetrable iron.

Then Mortimer started the voyage across the Chappany Valley toward the Miller house.

The sky closed with darkness above him when he was halfway across the valley, and he had to pull his bandanna over nose and mouth, as before, to make breathing possible in that continuous smother. The wisdom of Chico, recognizing a trail, enabled the rider to keep his eyes shut most of the way. He opened them to squint, from time to time, at the drifted silt in the valley floor and the bare patches of good grass on the Hancock land, where he had planted the holding coverage to protect the soil.

Here and there, across the Hancock range, acres had given way and blown off, but the great mass of the soil had held, because for two years he had been covering the weak spots with religious zeal. Wherever he had worked, the victory went to him, but it was small consolation. There would be blood on the land before long, he was sure. And in some strange measure that was also his work. But always, as he rode, the sense of irretrievable loss accompanied him, and a hollowness grew in his heart. He had acted out with care one great lie in his life, and had found that it was not acting. But in his soul Harry Mortimer knew that the girl would never forgive him.

When he got to the Miller place he found automobiles and trucks parked everywhere, with sand drifted body-high around many of them. The patio entrance was three feet deep in drift, and when he reached the interior and tethered Chico to one of the old iron rings that surrounded the court, he stood for a moment and listened to the wind, to the mourning of the cattle down the Chappany, and to the nearer sound of angry voices inside the house. After that, he entered the place. The uproar came from the big library. He went straight to it and stood blinking the grit from his eyes and looking over the crowd.

There were fifty men in the room, and none of them were mere cowpunchers. These were the assembled heads of the ranches of the surrounding district, and they meant swift, bitter business. Hancock, if he used guns, would not live long enough for Mortimer to get at him. These armed men would attend to him quickly, and forever.

The whole noise of the argument rolled away into silence as Mortimer showed himself.

John Miller came halfway across the room toward him with quick steps. He said, "Mr. Mortimer, no man has ever been ordered to leave my house before, but in your case . . ."

Mortimer put up a weary hand. "I'm tired of your pride," he said. "I've come over here to see if I can stop murder. Will you listen to me?"

Miller said nothing. He was reaching into his mind for some adequate answer when a gray-haired man said, "Let's be open about it, Miller. He's younger than we are. He's a tenderfoot. But I've been over some of the Hancock land, and I've seen it holding like a rock. Who made it hold? This fellow did. For God's sake, let's hear what he has to say!"

"Gentlemen," began Harry Mortimer, "a dollar a head is what Hancock will ask for every steer that waters on our place. That's a good deal of money, and I don't suppose you'll stand for it. If I throw in my third of that dollar, it cuts the price down to sixty-seven cents. I wonder if that will make a sufficient difference to you. Will you do business with Hancock on that basis?"

They were silent as they listened to this proposal.

Then John Miller said, "You'd donate your third of the spoils?"

"I would," said Mortimer, squinting to clear his sight. He was very tired.

Miller said, "Suppose we call this emergency an act of God and refuse to pay a penny for the surplus which our neighbors happen to have plenty of?"

"In that case," said Mortimer wearily, "I suppose I'm with you. I've sent for my men to follow me over here. I've told Hancock that if he shoots to kill I'll go for his throat."

He got another silence for that speech. Someone said loudly, "I thought you said that you knew this fellow, Miller?"

Miller answered in a harsh, strained voice, "I seem to be a fool, Ollie. It's perfectly apparent that I don't know *any-thing*."

"If you try to rush cattle down to the lakes," said Mortimer, "you'll find Charlie Hancock and his men waiting for you, and every puncher on his place shoots straight. There are plenty of you to wipe them out, but there'll be a dozen men dead in the Valley before the business ends. Another dozen hours won't kill that many cattle out of all the herds that are waiting for water. Let me have that time to get through to Jim Hancock in Poplar Springs."

John Miller came up to him with a bewildered face, "You can't get through, Mortimer," he argued. "The trial's drifted across knee-deep with sand. No horse could live through fifteen miles of this dust storm."

"A mule could," said Mortimer.

"Suppose you managed by sheer damn luck to get to Poplar Springs," said Miller, "you couldn't get a thing from old Jim Hancock. He hates me and the rest of the ranchers. He doesn't give a hang for anything except a newspaper and a daily game of checkers. I know him like a book, and that's the truth. He'd laugh in your face. He'd rub his hands and warm them at the idea of a war in the Chappany. Mortimer, will you believe me?"

Harry Mortimer said, "Look at these men. They're a sour lot. They mean business. If you can't hold them for a few hours, they'll go down to rush Charlie Hancock's rifles. And dead men piled on one another will be all that I've gained from two years of work. . . . If I get to Jim Hancock I'll bring him back with me."

"I can't stop you," said John Miller solemnly.

A pale-faced maid ran into the library. "Mr. Miller, I've been looking everywhere for Miss Louise. She's not in the house, sir. She's not anywhere!"

"Nonsense," growled Miller. "Go up into the garret. She'll be there with some of her gadgets. That's her playground. She's still half a child."

Of this conversation, Mortimer heard only a whisper; he was intent on his own plans and problems. He went back to the patio, untied Chico, and rode out through the entrance. The dust-blast half blinded him, instantly, but he turned the mule across the sweep of the wind and headed Chico toward Poplar Springs.

Harry Mortimer got three miles of comparatively easy breathing to begin his journey. He saw the whole face of the countryside, sand-buried or sand-swept, and the trail recognizable from time to time, dots and dashes of it in the midst of obliteration.

He had passed the abandoned Carter place, with the sand heaped against the windward walls like shadows of brightness, before the storm came at him again like a herd of sky elephants, throwing up their trunks and trampling the earth to black smoke. He thought he had seen the worst of the storm before this, but that black boiling up of trouble was as thick as pitch.

He put his head down and endured,

endlessly, while Chico, through the choking smother, found the dots and dashes of the disappearing trail with faultless instinct. It seemed to Mortimer that the land was like a living body, now bleeding to death. The work of innumerable dead centuries was rushing about him like a nightmare.

Then Chico stumbled on something, and shied. Mortimer turned the shaft of his pocket torch down through the murk and saw the body of a horse on the ground. It was Hampton. He knew it by the unforgettable streak of white on the forehead.

He dismounted. Sand was heaped along the back of the dead horse, half burying the body, but the tail blew out with an imitation of life along the wind. Sand filled the dead eyes. The left foreleg was broken below the knee. There was a round bullet hole above the temple that had brought quick death to the thoroughbred. What he guessed back there at Miller's house was true. Lou had headed for town, perhaps in hope of bringing back men of the law to restore peace to the Chappany Valley. She had stripped saddle and girth from Hampton. That meant she was somewhere out here in the blowing darkness, with the storm overwhelming her. The saddle would give her a bit of shelter and a shield behind which she could breathe.

Mortimer narrowed his eyes to the thinnest slit and held up his hands to turn the immediate edge of the wind, but the rolling darkness showed him only its own face as he rode the mule in circles around the dead body of Hampton. The electric torch was like a lance-shaft, a brittle thing that elongated or broke off short according to the density of the waves of storm that swept upon him. Turning into the wind was like going up a steep hill. Turning away from it was like lurching down a slope.

After a second or third circle he gave up hope, yet he kept on looking for a sign of her. His eyes saw only splinterings and watery breakings of the torchlight, now; they were so filled with fine silt. Then a ghost stepped into the patch of the ray, and it was Lou Miller.

The wind whipped her hair forward into a ragged fluttering about her face, and she came on with one hand held out, feeling her way. She thought Mortimer was Sam Pearson and she stumbled on toward the light, crying out, "Sam! God bless you, dear old Sam! I knew you were my last chance. But I thought . . . never could find . . . beautiful Hampton . . . I had to . . ."

The wind thrust her into Mortimer's arms. She let herself go; there was no strength in her. He turned and made a windbreak for her. The storm lifted his bandanna from the back of his neck with deliberate malice, and flying sand pricked his skin with a million needle points. Now the drift came bucketing at him out of scoop shovels with a force that staggered him on his planted feet. He had to hold up the girl. She was a good weight. He thought of a loose sack with a hundred and twenty-five pounds of Kansas wheat in it. There was no poet in him. He ought to be thinking of two souls clinging to each other in this wild deluge, this ending of the world.

He knew that he should tell her at once that he was not Sam Pearson. He was a thief stealing this moment out of her life, a guilty but inexpressible happiness. The flashlight showed the dust leaping past them, giving a face to the scream of the wind.

"I *knew* you'd find me, Sam! God bless you! You're —"

"Don't say it," Mortimer cut in.

302

His voice put the strength back in her body. He turned the light so that it struck upon their faces. Her eyes held a profound wonder. The wind kept whipping her hair out like a ragged moment of light in the darkness. She still held to him.

"*You* came for me?"

He wanted to bring her closer into his arms. He wanted to tell her that he would have searched hell itself for her. But he couldn't say that. He had to be honest, like a damned fool. "I didn't come out here to find you, Lou . . . I was just lucky . . . I know . . ."

All at once she was a thousand leagues away from him, though she had taken a mere step back.

"Take Chico. He'll pull us through," said Mortimer, and helped her strongly up into the saddle.

He should have said something else. He should have made some gallant protestation, he knew. Now she was despising him more than ever. He felt that he had lost his chance and that it would never come to him again.

Chico was the captain of the voyage, for through the whirl his instinct clung to the trail; Mortimer gripped a stirrup leather and floundered on, hoping to God that his knees would not give way.

From time to time, when the sand and flying silt had choked the wise old mule, he would halt, with his head down. Then Mortimer would swab out the nostrils and wash out the mouth of Chico. Sometimes, as he worked, the light from the pocket torch showed him the wind-bleared face of the girl, like a body adrift in the sea. Yet she seemed more desirable than ever.

It was not always thick darkness. Sometimes the sky cleared a little, as long rents tore through the whirling explosions of dust, and then by daylight they saw the immensity of the clouds that rolled through the upper heavens and dragged their skirts along the ground.

They had gone on for hours when Mortimer, floundering through a darker bit of twilight, jostled heavily against Chico. The girl halted the mule and slipped to the ground, offering the reins and the saddle to Mortimer. He was staggering with weariness, but this gesture seemed to him a challenge to his manhood. For answer, he picked her up and pitched her, like a child, back into the saddle. A sweep of the flashlight revealed her angry face.

Then they went forward again. He could see now, in retrospect, that it had been merely a gallant gesture on her part, but he had been as drunk with fatigue as he was heartsick now.

An age of desperate struggle followed, with Harry Mortimer's knees turning to water under his weight; and then something cried above him in the wind. It was the girl, pointing. He was able to see, through blurred eyes, dimly, the outlines of Poplar Springs immediately before them!

A moment later they were in the town, they were approaching a light, a door was opening, they were entering a heavenly peace, with the hands and voice of the storm removed.

Mortimer lay on his back on the floor, coughing up black mud and choking on it. A young lad swabbed off his face, and said, "Your eyes are terrible. I never seen such eyes. Don't it hurt terrible even to blink? Can you see anything?"

"Get that mule into shelter and water him, will you?" said Mortimer.

"He's fixed up already," answered the lad.

Mortimer groaned and stretched out his arms crosswise. Fatigue was flowing with a shudder out of his body; the hard floor soaked it up. He closed his eyes. Afterward there were a hundred things to do. This was the rest between rounds and the hardest part of the fight was to come.

He heard a woman's voice cry out from another room, "They're from the Chappany! They've come clear down the Chappany! This is Louise Miller!"

Someone jumped across the room toward Mortimer. He opened his burning eyes and saw a man with a cropped gray head leaning over him. "Did you come down the Chappany through all that hell?"

"We did," said Mortimer.

"Bud, I'll take care of him. You run get Mr. Sloan and Pop Enderby and Jiggs Dawson and tell 'em they're going to hear what's happening in the Chappany. If it's blowin' away, Poplar Springs is gonna dry up and fade out. We don't live on nothing much else but the Chappany!"

Mr. Sloan, the banker, and Enderby, the big cattleman, and Dawson, of the General Store, were only three among thirty when Harry Mortimer sat up to face the crowd that poured into the house. They looked at big Mortimer in a painful silence, as the front door kept opening and people stamped in from the storm, then hushed their footfalls when they saw what was in progress. Now and again the voice of the storm receded and Mortimer could hear the painful, excited breathing of those people in the hall.

Nobody talked except Oliver Sloan, the banker, and he was the only one of the visitors who sat down. He was a huge, wide man with a weight of sagging flesh that seemed to be exhausting his vital forces. He asked the questions and Mortimer answered.

"How's it look in general?"

"Bad," said Mortimer.

"Hear from the Starrett place?"

"Yes. It's a sand-heap."

"Over by Benson's Ford?"

"Don't you get any telephone messages?" asked Mortimer.

"All the lines are down. Hear from over by Benson's Ford?"

"I heard yesterday. The only thing that's left over there is hardpan."

Half a dozen men drew in long breaths at that bad news. In Poplar Springs lived retired ranchers from all over the range.

"What about McIntyre's?" asked Sloan.

"The sand is fence-high," said Mortimer.

"The Hancock place . . . that's your own place, isn't it?"

"The soil is holding there. It's only going in spots."

"That's your work," nodded the banker wearily. "You said that you'd button down the topsoil; and you've done it?"

"I've done it," said Mortimer. He broke out: "I wish to God I could have helped the whole range. I wish I could have taught them. It's a poor victory to me to save my own land and see the rest go up in dust."

No one said anything until the banker spoke again. "Jenkins' place?" he asked.

"Hills sheltered that land pretty well," said Mortimer, "but the sand is spilling over the edge of the hills and gradually covering the good soil."

"Crawford's?"

"Fence-high with drift."

"The Grand ranch?" asked Sloan. He looked up with desperate eyes.

"I'm sorry," said Mortimer softly.

"It's gone, is it?" whispered the banker.

"Hardpan," said Mortimer.

Sloan pushed himself up from his chair. How many of his mortgages were on heaps of blow-sand or hardpan acres, no one could tell; but from the ruin in his face the crowd pushed back to either side and let him out into the hall.

"There's two thirds of the Chappany still holding," said Mortimer to the others. "The worst of it is that the water holes are silted up. Even Miller's lakes are gone — and Charlie Hancock won't let the cows come to his water. Cattle out there by the thousands are going to die. Is there any way of persuading Jim Hancock to give his son orders to let those cattle in to water?"

"Persuade him?" shouted Sloan from the hallway. "By God! I'll wring the orders out of his withered old neck with my own hands! We'll take the hide off his back, and see if that will persuade him!"

The whole mob poured out from the house; among the rest, Mortimer had one glimpse of the pale face of Lou Miller, and then she was lost in the crowd. They moved into the street. They flowed against the rush of the dust storm into the General Merchandise Store.

To Mortimer's watery eyes the whole store was like a scene under the sea. A score of men lounged around the stove, retaining the winter habit in the midst of the hot weather. There was constant coughing, for the fine dust which was adrift in the air constantly irritated their throats. In a corner two very old men leaned over a checker game, one with a fine flow of white hair and beard, and the other as bald and red as a turkey gobbler, with a hanging double fold of loose red skin beneath the chin. He smoked a clay pipe, polished and brown-black with interminable years of use. He was Jim Hancock. In his two years on the ranch, Mortimer had seen him only once before.

"You talk to him first," said Sloan.

Harry Mortimer walked toward the players. Someone near the stove muttered, "See the eyes of *that one?* Looks like they been sandpapered."

"What will you say to him?" whispered the girl at the side of Mortimer.

He gave no answer but, stepping to the table, said, "Sorry to interrupt you, Mr. Hancock, but . . ."

"If you're sorry for it, don't *do* it," said Jim Hancock.

Ben Chalmers, the time-tried opponent of old Hancock, lifted his eyes and his hand from the checkerboard. He stared briefly at the interloper, and dragged his hand slowly down through his beard as he returned his attention to the game.

"Do you remember me, Mr. Hancock? I'm Mortimer, from your place on the Chappany."

"Then why don't you stay there?" asked Hancock.

"Miller's lakes are choked with sand."

"I wish Miller was laying choked in one of 'em," said Hancock.

"The water holes all over our part of the range are silted up, and so are most of the tanks," said Mortimer. "There's a water famine. Cows are going to die by the thousands unless they can get water."

"Cows have died by the thousands many a time before this," replied Hancock.

"They're milling around the fence between the Miller place and your two lakes," said Mortimer.

"Let 'em mill and be damned," answered Hancock.

"More than cattle will be damned."

Hancock jerked up his head at last. "D'you see me playing a game of checkers, or don't you? Is a man gonna have a little peace in the world, or has he gotta be hounded into his grave by fools like you?"

"The men who own the cattle . . . they won't stand by and see them die of thirst. They'll cut the fence wire and let them through. It means gun fighting," said Mortimer.

"And what's that to me?" growled the old man.

"Charlie is out there with his cowpunchers and rifles to keep those cows back," the voice of Louise Miller said. "He intends to shoot."

Mortimer turned to her. She had sifted through to the front of the crowd.

"I hope he don't miss, then," said Jim Hancock. "Charlie always was a boy that wasn't worth nothing except when it comes to a shoot-up. But, when it comes to that, he's the out-fightingest son-of-a-gun I ever seen. Now shut up, Lou, and don't bother me no more."

"If the fight starts," said Harry Mortimer, "there are two hundred armed men to take care of Charlie and his boys. They'll wash over them. A dozen men may die, and your son's sure to be one of them!"

"I hope he is," answered Jim Hancock. "It'll save a lot of rum if Charlie goes now."

Sloan, the banker, stepped in. "Jim, there's been damned near enough grazing land wiped off the range to ruin Poplar Springs; and if the cattle die this town'll die with 'em. Nobody but you can give the

312

cows a second chance, without there's a war. Are you going to sit here and let everything go to hell?"

In place of an answer, old Jim Hancock reached back to his hip, produced a long-barreled, single-action Colt .45, and laid it on his lap. Then he returned to his contemplation of his next move, merely saying, "Sorry there's been all this damn' palavering, Ben."

"I don't care *what* you're sorry about," said Ben darkly. "You're spoilin' the game with all this fool talk."

A man from the crowd began to shout at old Jim Hancock with a loud voice, but Mortimer had seen enough. He felt sick and weak and utterly defeated. He jerked the door open and went across the street, leaning his body aslant into the thrust of the wind, to Porson's saloon. In the vacant lot beside it the tarpaulin housing a caterpillar tractor flapped and strained like clumsy wings in the wind.

In the saloon Mortimer found only two dusty cowpunchers who stood at one end of the bar. Old Rip Porson leaned in an attitude of profoundly gloomy thought in front of his cracked mirror. He put out the Scotch bottle and a tall glass for Mortimer.

"Ain't I seen you before?" asked Rip.

"Once or twice," said Mortimer.

"You wasn't connected with mirror-busting, a while back, was you?" asked Porson. His angry, birdlike eyes stared into Mortimer's face.

"That's him, Rip," said one of the cowpunchers. "I reckon that's Harry Mortimer, that done the kicking, and the others were them that were kicked."

"Well then, Mortimer," growled Porson. "Here's to you, and drink her down!"

He sloshed whisky into a glass and tossed it off. Instead of taking a chaser, he opened his mouth and took one long, panting breath.

Somewhere through the storm came the lowing of a cow, as though she mourned for her calf, and Mortimer's eye wandered as he thought of the milling thousands of doomed cattle up the Chappany. A bowl of fresh mint sprigs behind the bar caught his eye, with its suggestion of that green and tender spring which would not come again to a great portion of the range. He thought, also, of stubborn old Jim Hancock, all leather, without blood or heart.

"Can you mix the sort of mint julep that really talks to a man's insides?" asked Mortimer.

"Me? Can I mix a julep?" asked Rip Porson. "I don't give a damn what time of year it is, the fellow that drinks my mint julep knows it's Christmas."

"Build me a pair of them, then," said Mortimer. "Build them high and build them strong." And he laughed a little, as he spoke. A moment later he was carrying the high, frosted glasses into the General Merchandise Store. For, when he remembered how the whisky in the barroom had relaxed his own troubles, it came to him that perhaps even the iron-hard nature of Jim Hancock might be altered.

As he went in, Sloan was going out, with a gray, weary face. He looked at Mortimer with unseeing eyes and passed on; but the remainder of the crowd was packed thick around the checker game where old Hancock, with the revolver on his lap, still struggled through the silent fight against Ben Chalmers. Each had five crowned pieces. Mortimer put down the drinks at the right hand of each player and stepped back.

"It's no good," said a sour-faced man.

"You can't soften up that old codger," said another. "There ain't any kindness left in him."

The hand of Ben Chalmers left its position beneath his chin, extended, wavered for a moment in the air, seized on a piece, and moved it. Continuing in the same slow, abstracted manner, the hand touched the glass, raised it, and tipped the drink at his lips. Jim Hancock, stirred by the same hypnotic influence, lifted his glass at the same time. Hancock put down his drink with jarring haste.

"Rye!" he exclaimed, making a spitting face. "Rye!"

"I disrecollect," said Ben Chalmers slowly, "but seems like I *have* heard about folks ignorant enough to make a mint julep with Bourbon."

"Ignorant?" growled Jim Hancock.

"Ignorant," said Chalmers.

"There's only one state in the Union where a mint julep is made proper," declared Jim Hancock. "And that's Kentucky."

"The Union be hanged," said Ben Chalmers, "but the only state is Virginia."

"Kentucky," said Jim Hancock.

"Virginia," said Chalmers.

"Have I been wastin' my time all these

years with an ornery fool that don't know good whisky from bad?" demanded Hancock.

"You come from too far west to know good whisky," said Ben Chalmers. "When I think of a man of your years that ain't come to an understanding of whisky . . ."

"East of Louisville, decent whisky ain't made," said Hancock. "I'm drinkin' to Kentucky and the bluegrass, and to the devil with points east and north . . ." He took a long drink of the mint julep and made another face.

"In points east of Kentucky," said Ben Chalmers, "this here country got its start. When Washington and Jefferson was doing their stuff, Kentucky was left to the wild turkeys and the Indians."

"The breed run out in Virginia," said Jim Hancock. "They still got some pretty women, but the men went to Kentucky about a hundred years ago."

"An outrage and a damn lie!" shouted Ben Chalmers, pushing himself back with such violence that the table rocked. The kings on the checkerboard lost their crowns and shuffled out of place.

"A Virginia gentleman," said Chalmers, "wouldn't go to Kentucky except to spit!"

and he marched to the door and through it, into the twilight of the storm outside.

"That old fossil insulted the great state of Kentucky," fumed Hancock.

"It *is* a great state, Kentucky," said Mortimer. "I'll have to agree to that."

"Son," said Jim Hancock, "maybe you ain't quite the damn' fool that I been making you out. Kentucky is the only state in the country where they breed men and hosses right."

"And they breed 'em with plenty of bone and blood and nerve," declared Mortimer.

"They do," said Hancock.

"Which is why," said Mortimer, "we can't figure the reason you're afraid to go back up the Chappany and keep Charlie from killing a dozen men and winding up with a rope around his neck."

"Afraid? Who said afraid?" demanded Hancock, jumping up from the table.

"Shake hands on it, then, and we'll go together as soon as the storm gives us a chance," said Mortimer.

"Damn the storm! Why should we wait? I say we go *now!*" snapped Hancock.

Beyond the window, dimly visible through the rush and whirl of dust, Mortimer watched the tarpaulin covering the caterpillar tractor flap in the wind. Nothing on the range could move like that tractor, through all weathers, over all terrain.

"Who owns the caterpillar?" he asked, pointing.

"It's mine," said the manager of the General Store.

"Let me rent it to go up the Chappany."

"Rent it? Hell, man, I'll *give* it to you!" cried the manager. "And, by God, there's nothing else that will take you where you want to go!"

The big machine was ready, with a full tank of gas, and the engine started at a touch. Mortimer tried the controls, rear, left, and center, and the machine answered readily to the levers. Old Jim Hancock, equipped with scarf and goggles, huddled himself into as small a space as possible on the floorboards. They started forward. A great outbreak of shouting from the crowd seemed to Mortimer a farewell cheer. He waved his hand in answer and shoved the tractor against the cutting sweep of wind. He had full canteens of water and old Jim Hancock on board, and that was all he asked for, except the entire ten miles an hour that the caterpillar could make. That ten miles, adding to the cutting edge of the wind, blew the dust right through the wet bandanna that masked him, nose and mouth; it blew the fine dust down to the bottom of his lungs.

The machine hit a five-foot sand drift and went through it part climbing, part awallow, with a flag of dust blowing and snapping behind it.

They entered the wide mouth of the Chappany as the tractor put its nose into the soft of a bog, a water hole entirely clogged by drifted silt. Mortimer was backing out of this when a figure staggered up beside him, with outreaching hands.

He knew who it was. He knew instinctively, with a great stroke of his heart. He stopped the caterpillar clear of the bog, pulled Lou Miller into the machine, and put her on the floor. She must have ridden on the bucking, pitching tail of the tractor all the way from Poplar Springs, with the choking torrents of its own dust added to the blind onpouring of the storm. She was almost stifled, now, as he pulled down her bandanna and flashed his torch into a face begrimed and mud-caked to the eyes. She lay gasping as Mortimer swabbed black dust from her eyes and mouth. He put his lips to her ears shouting, "Your lungs . . . are they burning up? Can you get your breath?"

"I'm all right. Go on!" she answered.

"I'm turning back to Poplar Springs."

She caught his arm with both hands and shook it. "If you turn back, I'll throw myself out of the tractor," she cried to him desperately. "Go on! Go on! Think of what's happening on the Chappany!"

"Ay, let's go on!" yelled old Jim Hancock.

Mortimer pressed on. The wind-beaten lights of the machine showed him a ten-foot sand drift, curving at the top like a wave about to break. He put on full speed and crashed through it. Sand flowed like heavy water over the entire tractor. He was blinded utterly, but the vibration of the racing caterpillar bucketed out the cargo of sand swiftly. If the fine dust did not get to the bearings, and if the motor was not choked, they might get through.

Another sand wave heaved itself before him. He headed for it, straightening the nose of the caterpillar like the head of a spear for a target. . . .

Far up the Chappany the murk of the day's end had joined the shadow of the storm, and with the coming of the thicker darkness John Miller prepared for final action. While there was even a flicker of daylight to give the rifles of Charlie Hancock opportunity to aim he would not let his men move forward, but now the night had thickened the air of the valley to soup.

A floundering horse with a rider bent forward along its neck came by, the rider yelling, "Miller! Hi, Miller!"

"Here!" shouted Miller, and the rider turned in toward him.

He leaned out to grip the pommel of Miller's saddle, and coughed and choked for a moment, head down, before he could speak. Miller took him by the shoulders and shouted at his ear. "Shorty, was she at the Grimes place? Did you find her at Hogan's? Is there any word?"

"Gone!" gasped Shorty. "Dave Weller come and says she ain't at Parker's, neither. There ain't no word."

"The storm has her," said Miller.

He pulled up his bandanna and spat downwind. But he could breathe no better after that.

"There's twenty-one years of my life gone," said John Miller. "God be kind to her . . ." And he gave the word to attack.

The men responded eagerly, spoiling for action. They had waited long enough, they felt, and the great, mournful song of the thirsty cattle was maddening to their ears. The whole wild throng of ranchers and cowhands poured into the Chappany.

They rode with a dark determination to push Charlie Hancock and his men off the face of the earth, but when they put their eyes on the actual field of battle, some of their resolve left them. Near the edge of the Hancock lake a flat-topped mesa jumped up a hundred feet above the valley floor. To climb the boulders and flat walls of the mesa was hard work, even in full daylight without the burden of a gun; to clamber up the height through these streaks of dark and light, with a rifle to manage and good marksmen taking aim from above, looked to be very hard work, indeed. If the storm had offered complete darkness, they could have fumbled through and grappled with Hancock and his men, but as it was, in this half-light, Hancock's riflemen had an excellent chance to command the approaches to their rock.

Miller sent some of his people to climb the bluff above the lake, but when they reached the high land they were able to make out only glimpses of Hancock's men among the rocks; the distance was too great for any sort of accurate shooting. Some of the ranchers wanted to cut the fences and let the cattle go trooping down to water, but it was readily pointed out to them that Hancock would enjoy nothing more than a chance to practice marksmanship on dumb cattle before he started on human targets.

It was a clumsy impasse. The storm kept bringing them the dolorous chorus of cattle. They knew the cows were dying, going down from weakness and trampled by the milling herd. That was why John Miller's crowd wanted blood and wanted it badly, but no one volunteered to lead the rush against that impregnable rock.

There was a big rancher named Tucker Weed among Miller's following, a fellow with a voice as loud as that of a champion Missouri hog-caller. It was he who raised a shout, and drew the attention of everyone to a pair of lights that staggered up the valley in the breath of the storm.

"It ain't an automobile," yelled Tucker Weed. "No automobile could head into this storm. What is it? It ain't the old red-eyed devil himself come looking for us, is it?"

John Miller saw the lights disappear into

a sand gully, then reflect dimly on the whirl of the storm. The two lights swerved down again, pointed at the earth, and then wavered out into the level of the valley, approaching the huge, melancholy sea-sound of the bellowing cattle. The machine ran straight for only a moment, however, and then swerved to the left and headed for the rock of Charlie Hancock. . . .

The mourning chorus of the cattle behind the Miller fences had been with them for miles, but now, in a greater burst of light, as the black of the sky opened in a wide central vent, they could see the living acres that milled beyond the fences.

Old Jim Hancock stood up to see, and Mortimer steadied him by gripping his coat at the small of the back.

"Why damn my eyes!" said Jim Hancock. "Why didn't somebody tell me there was so many thirsty cows up here on the Chappany?"

They had a demonstration of another sort a moment later when half a dozen young steers, climbing over dead bodies that gave them a take-off to jump the wire, came clear of the fences and rushed at a gallop toward the water of the lake. The leader, after half a dozen strides, bucked into the air, landed on his nose, and lay still. Another and another dropped. From the top of the rock beside Hancock Lake little sparks of light showed where the rifles were playing. The half-dozen steers lay dead long before they brought their thirsty muzzles near the water.

"There he is!" shouted Jim Hancock. "There's that doggone boy of mine, up there, raising hell. Good shooting, Charlie! Good shooting, old feller! . . . But, by God, I'm gonna make you wish you'd never seen a gun!"

A sweep of horsemen poured suddenly out of the night. As Mortimer saw the masked faces and the guns, he brought the caterpillar to a halt. The cowpunchers were thick around them in an instant, and a voice was yelling, "It's the dirt doctor and old poison-face Jim Hancock himself . . . and here's Lou! She's alive!"

There was John Miller, himself, at the side of the machine; and now Lou was in his arms, while Jim Hancock shouted, "Clear away from us. Leave me get at that fool son of mine. I'm gonna teach him what comes of spoiling good beef when he ain't hungry."

Someone reached in and smote the shoulder of Harry Mortimer; someone shouted, "Great work!" And then the crowd was drawn back and Mortimer shoved the caterpillar toward the rock through a moment of darkness that swallowed the scene behind him.

The headlights sometimes showed the way a hundred feet ahead; sometimes the brillant cone choked off a stride away and they were charging blindly into the smoke and smother of the wind; then the zenith split open and light rushed back over the Chappany.

They were under the great rock, not fifty paces from the rising wall, when a whole volley of bullets struck them. Both headlights exploded into blackness. One of the metal tracks was shattered. The caterpillar began to turn clumsily.

Mortimer caught at old Hancock and dropped to the floor of the tractor as he shut off the engine. "Are you hurt, Jim?" he asked.

"Hell, no!" said Hancock. "But I guess they've shot a leg off this old tin horse of ours."

The plunging rain of bullets still rang about them until that open funnel of brillant sky above them misted over and then closed suddenly into a river of black.

"Will you go on with me, Jim?" shouted Mortimer. "Will you try to climb on with me and get to Charlie?"

"Don't be a damn' fool," said Jim Hancock. "I'll go alone. Why should you let 'em get at you with their guns?"

But Mortimer went with him. He hooked his arm around the hard, withered body of the old man and fairly dragged him through the blind current of the storm until they found the loom of rock, and then, suddenly, the wall itself. They paused there a moment, gasping, coughing as though they had just escaped from the smoke of a burning house.

Then they started up. The big boulders below gave way to the sheer wall of rock, and they had to wait for the next break in the windy darkness of the sky before they could continue, taking advantage of a fissure here and a projection there. Mortimer, keeping just below, helped the old fellow strongly up while Hancock muttered, "I'll fix him . . . beef butcher! . . . damn' fool!"

They were well up when guns crackled above them rapidly, like pitchpine burning. A bullet streaked a white scar across the rock in front of Mortimer's face; then a fist-stroke and a knife-thrust combined lanced him in the side. He had a good handhold on a projecting spur of rock, so he managed to keep his place, although that effort cost him nearly the last of his strength.

A mercy of wind closed up the gap in the sky, and in the darkness the gunfire ended.

Old Jim, agile as a dried-up tomcat, went clawing up the rock, screeching. "Charlie! Charlie! You double-jointed jackass! Put down them guns or I'll . . ."

Mortimer followed the inspired fury of the old man, but his strength was running out of him. The light came back a moment later and made him shrink as though it had been the flash of a knife. And then he saw Jim Hancock standing on the lip of rock above him, shaking one fist above his head. Men loomed beside him. The soft bulk of Charlie Hancock appeared. And Mortimer drew himself up to the flat top of the mesa. When he got there, he had to lie out flat. The pain left his side and burned only in his brain.

He could hear old Jim Hancock shouting, "Get down there! Get down there and tell 'em to open the fences up and let the cows through! Save your damned face if you can — Your ma died for you, and, damn you, you been nothing but a long, cold winter to me all your life! Get out of my sight!"

There seemed to be light still in the sky, but a darkness crawled out of Harry Mortimer's brain and covered his eyes.

After a time he saw that he was lying near a fire that burned behind a screen of boulders at the top of the mesa. A withered forearm with a bandage around it appeared in his line of sight. A hand lifted his head.

"Take a shot of this," said Jim Hancock, holding a whiskey flask at his lips.

He got down a good, long swallow of the stuff. It burned some of the torment away.

Jim Hancock said, "Son, if you die, I'm gunna have 'em hanged, every damn' one of 'em . . . and we won't wait for the law, neither."

"No," said a big voice. "We won't wait for no law!"

That was Jan Erickson. And there were others of the gang watching their chief with grimly set faces.

"Yes, sir," said Jim Hancock, "if you pass out, we're gunna string 'em up, and

I'll help pull on the ropes. So just you rest nice and easy."

It was an odd way of giving comfort. Mortimer tried to smile, but fingers of pain seemed to tear at him.

"I'm gunna lift up your head and leave you have a look at what's happening," said Hancock.

Slowly and carefully, he lifted Mortimer's head and shoulders until he could look over the sloping top of the mesa and down into the valley of the Chappany at Hancock Lake. The waters of it seemed to have living shores until his eyes cleared a little and he could see the cattle ten and twenty deep as they drank up life and new strength.

"That's good," said Mortimer. "I'm glad I saw that."

"Don't talk," said Hancock. "They've got you drilled right through the lungs, and talking is sure poison for you."

The darkness, like living shadows in the corners of a room, began to crawl out over the eyes of Harry Mortimer. If he were shot through the lungs, he had to die and he was sure that he was dying at that moment. "I've got to talk," he said.

"Shut your mouth!" commanded Hancock.

Mortimer forced out the words slowly: "Tell Lou Miller it never was a lie. Not really. I love her! Tell her, Jim . . . she's *got* to know I love her! Promise me . . ."

He seemed to be walking, then, through infinite darkness, opening doors, feeling his way down blank walls, finding more doors, opening them, and something was whistling to him far away. He opened his eyes. It was the scream of the storm that he had been hearing, but far withdrawn again into the heart of the sky.

He looked down at the big arch of his chest and the bandage which was being unwrapped by slender hands. His lips were saying, "Promise to tell Lou Miller . . ."

And a soft voice above him said, "I know — darling!"

Now, by an effort of peering into distance, he made out her face. She was so drawn and white that, to any ordinary eye, half of her beauty was surely gone; but his eye alone, which knew how to see her, found her more beautiful than ever.

"Make him stop talking, Lou," said John Miller's voice out of the darkness.

She touched the lips of Mortimer, and he kissed her hand. If there was only a few moments left, words were no good, after all. Touching her hand and looking at her was what mattered.

A crisp voice of command said, "He's lost blood. He's lost buckets, but I don't think . . . give me that probe."

A finger of consummate pain entered Mortimer's breast, his side, glided back.

"Certainly not!" said that voice of authority. "The man has ribs like the ribs of a ship. The bullet glanced around them. He'll live."

Darkness covered Harry Mortimer's eyes, but through the shadow he could hear the sudden, joyful outcry of the girl, fading rapidly from his consciousness, but lodging somewhere in his heart.

THE BELLS OF SAN CARLOS

Again, as in "Macdonald's Dream," Faust combines myth with mysticism in a striking, offbeat western drama. His protagonist, Fray Luis, is much closer to Hemingway's superstitious old fisherman, Santiago, than he is to the typical Faust knight-hero. Indeed, there is a spiritual affinity linking his story to Hemingway's classic novella, The Old Man and the Sea. *In each tale the main character seeks a special "treasure," finds it, then must struggle mightily to retain it. The old friar's sacred relic parallels Santiago's giant marlin in that each must be defended against sharks.*

The sharks of Faust's tale are gold-hungry killers, but their "teeth" — the guns and whips they use — are no less sharp and destructive. Old Fray Luis pits his spirit and his faith against these predators in his own wide sea, the deserts of the West.

"The Bells of San Carlos" affirms Faust's belief in the basic virtues of courage and en-

durance — and the drama he weaves is memorable and affecting, written with the soul of a lyric poet and the sure instincts of a master storyteller.

FRAY LUIS WAS so accustomed to his friar's robe tugging at his knees and awash about his feet that he felt naked in cotton trousers and kept looking down at them and at the thinness of his legs. As for the *huaraches* on his feet, he was used to sandals just about like them, so they made no difference, but he could not grow used to the new lightness of his step and to the absence of that windy whispering which for thirty years had been about his ankles.

He could endure perfectly well the cheap shirt with its tails worn outside his trousers, but he was ashamed to let even the buzzards see his ragged straw hat, the true peon's hat with some hand-made cigarettes tied to the brim. All through the Monotilla Mountains he had walked with his shame, and although he knew that a man about to die should fix his thoughts on higher things, still his mind dwelt more on that straw hat than on the purpose which already had taken him a thousand miles from safety. However, when he came to the sight of the valley his heart stopped, his whole world rocked and staggered before his eyes, for the tower of the convent church and the white walls around it no longer stood in the middle of the flat.

It was years since he and all the brotherhood had been driven from San Carlos de Piedras and he knew that accidental fire, six months before, had ruined the old buildings, but even if it were an empty skeleton, he had expected to see it rising high above the ground.

Instead, it was a mere stumbling heap, and it seemed to Fray Luis that all the prayers of centuries and all the sweet song of the bells from the tower were collapsed and gone from heaven as the monastery from earth. He was such a simple man that the visual loss was like a death of the spirit.

He almost doubted that this could be San Carlos, after all, but the mountains looked down on the valley with the same bald heads, the same furrowed faces.

So Fray Luis dropped on his knees, prayed for the mercy of God upon the dead and for the preservation of all the masses, all the music, all the incense smoke which had gone upward in their name, and then he rose, strengthened and comforted, and started forth across the level land.

He felt that he was walking in mortal peril. There had been a time when he knew every man, woman and child in the valley, when he could call every burro by name, and in those gentle days no eye looked upon him except with love; even the dogs which rushed out savagely at a passerby would silence their tongues when they knew it was Fray Luis.

Now the hearts of men had changed. The new regime had found new creatures to abide by the new law and there was death abroad in the land for men of the church.

His disguise had taken him safely enough through the mountains, but in San Carlos Valley every eye was apt to know him. That was why the brotherhood had wept when he departed on his mission. Now, as he walked deeper into the valley, he was trying to imagine in what form death would come to him.

It was evening. He had lingered during the last march so as to arrive at just this hour of the day, and now the night gathered over him as he came to San Carlos. The very smell of the cookery meant home to Fray Luis. For the savor of roast kid is nowhere in the world like its fragrance in San Carlos, and the pungent sweet-sour of beans never is breathed, really, except in San Carlos. The stomach of Fray Luis grew as empty as a church bell without its clapper, and he almost forgot his terrors until a clamor of dogs came rushing out from the village.

It seemed to the poor friar that they must have scented him and were dashing to put their teeth in his flesh, but then a thin ghost of a creature whipped past him through the dark of the night and he realized that it was a coyote with the town curs in pursuit. The whole clamor rushed off through the darkness and Fray Luis went straight on to the ruins.

When he reached them he had lamplight from the neighboring houses and starlight from heaven to see by, but his tears filled his eyes with darkness and he had to sit for a long time on the base of a pillar before he could look about him.

At last Fray Luis raised his head very slowly.

He could not believe that the huge old beams actually had rotted in the flame, but when he had dried his eyes, he made sure that the church and the monastery were indeed gone. It was hard to guess where one wall had stood, but as he crept about through the wreckage the plan of the old building returned to his mind and he found himself looking up to where once the flat head of the bell-tower had leaned against the stars.

The crypt entrance had lain back of that about twenty paces. He made those paces, marked the place, and then began to clear away the ruin.

It was hard, slow work. He had brought with him a short, heavy iron crowbar to help his hands, but the big flat adobe bricks are almost as tough as firebaked clay, and they stuck together in ponderous clots which he could barely lift and roll. All that night he worked. Just in the dawn, he came down to a stone pavement. Wearily he cleared a larger space, but at last he realized that he had been mistaken.

His dizzy brain had remembered steps, and now he found them, but they were steps leading up into the sacristy; not down into the crypt. No, no, for the crypt lay far off on the other side of the entire building.

By this time it was clear daylight, so that Fray Luis dared not attempt to steal off through the town. Instead, he curled himself up among the ruins and fell into a deep sleep, exhausted.

By mid-morning the intense heat had roused him. All the blood of his body was gathered in his poor old head, but in the ruins there was no shade, and he was afraid to show his face. So, through that sweltering day, he endured an agony stronger than anything he had known before. For he had drunk up all his water during the night, and this fire-hot sunshine sucked the moisture swiftly out of his body. The torment was worse even than that march of his through the mountain snows one January when he had carried medicine and good news to the little village of San José. That winter's march seemed the supreme test of his endurance, but this day was worse, burning him like coals in a brazier.

At last the day turned red, the evening rolled down like purple smoke from the Monotilla Mountains, and the stars shone once more.

Thirst was swelling the tongue of Fray Luis, but he dared not get a drink until the last noises had ended in the town. Therefore he forced his trembling hands to labor again, after he had marked, as well as he could, the probable position of the crypt entrance.

It was nearly morning before the last dogfight and serenade had ended. Then Fray Luis crawled out from the ruin to the well.

The very smell of the moisture made him impatient. He could almost have eaten the wet earth around the well where careless village girls had spilled gallons from their water-jugs.

Slowly, slowly, he turned the handle that wound up the rope and lifted the bucket. He managed so that the bucket rose with no more noise than the exquisite and tempting music of water adrip. Now it was in his grasp with the image of a star shattering and forming and wavering in the water.

Fray Luis drank with such joy that when he had to pause to take breath, his conscience smote him; never before had he taken such joy in the pleasures of the flesh. He looked up to heaven, therefore, to ask forgiveness of God, and then drank again, filled his canteen, and went back to the ruins.

In fact, the water seemed to weigh upon him more than sin. He was weak and his hands stumbled and fumbled at their work all the rest of the night and when the morning sounds told him to stop, he had still not mined down through the heaped adobe bricks to the pavement.

That second day in the open face of the furnace he endured with only the strength of patience. Forty-eight hours without food sapped the old man's strength and he looked into the northwest for that rare mercy of rain which came to San Carlos hardly more than twice a year.

Once, when he was praying for rain in the the open plaza under the eyes of the people, thunderheads actually rolled out from the northwestern mountains and within an hour, rain had fallen on the valley. It was because of that miracle that he had been chosen by the brotherhood to return to the ruins of the convent in search of the treasure.

Today he whispered his prayer and still the sky remained white-hot. Fray Luis was sure that the good saint would not favor one mortal with two signs.

He roused out of a stuporlike sleep, late in the day, with a sense in his dry throat of words just uttered and still fresh in his ear. And as he opened his eyes he saw a shadow draw back from the hollow in which he lay.

He was sure that prayer aloud, in his sleep, had brought curious eyes upon him. By degrees, his heart trembling and his breath gone, old Luis stood up half his height and peered about him, but he saw no living thing among the tumbled rubbage of bricks; so he took another sip of lukewarm water from the canteen and sat down again, giving thanks.

Thereafter, out of another drowsy trance, he aroused to find the mercy of the night already in the skies; and still there was life in him for his work. He moved with the greatest care, breaking up the adobe clut-terings and digging deeper until the crowbar fell from his hands and made a sound in its fall like the far-off ghost of a chime from the bell of San Carlos.

That disaster kept him trembling for half an hour, but still no one approached and he went on with his labor until he could have sworn he was well beneath the pavement level. Then his hand touched a stone edge as high as his knee. He was below the floor of the church.

Fray Luis had been so lucky that he had struck exactly above the crypt entrance, and now he was working on the steps. This discovery gave him fresh strength. The old man looked up at the stars and felt, suddenly, that he was not alone in his work; and now good fortune overtook him in a great sweep, for a moment later his crowbar struck through the adobe at his feet. He enlarged that hole eagerly. Some of the adobe fell inward, until the whole latter half of the steps into the crypt was clear. So, in a sort of magnificent single gesture, he arrived at the last stage of his mission. He lighted the candle which he had carried with him all that distance from the sea. It was crooked, but it lighted readily and, as he stood on the lower pavement, the vaults grew out of nothing and walked back in ordered ranges of stubby little columns.

Looking down, he found that he actually was standing on the flat gravestone of the good and great brother, Fray Tonio, and it seemed to poor Luis that the sad, patient voice of the dead man rose out of the ground, once more reproaching him for the poorness of his Latin. Fray Luis dropped to his knees and kissed the stone.

When he stood up again, he had to use both hand and candlelight to fumble his way forward into that corner where the treasure of San Carlos was hidden. Before he touched the sunken stone in the wall-corner, he looked up to pray, and knocked his head against the low curve of the vault. He pushed resolutely against the stone, and it tipped promptly, revealing a dark little niche with a bright eye gleaming out of the shadow.

Fray Luis fell on his knees again and gave thanks to God and San Carlos; then he pulled out the little silver box and opened it. The very answer to prayer was inside. He delicately lifted the edges of the holy silk which was folded inside the box and saw the yellow glint of the two finger-bones. Fray Luis leaned a moment against the wall, sick with joy. Then he closed the open niche, took the bones in their silken wrapping, and placed the parcel gently inside the leather wallet where he had carried the food for his journey.

He had risen to his feet and turned with the candle before he heard even a whisper of sound. It was the small, dry rattling made by a rolling bit of adobe on the stone steps. His candlelight shone on the faces of three savage-looking men. The shadow of unkemptness was on their chins. The hunger of years sucked in their cheeks and polished their cheekbones, and greed brightened their eyes in the candlelight.

"Ah, Domingo!" whispered Fray Luis, for he recognized one of the three; but that recognition brought him little ease for Domingo was an unholy gambler and user of the knife.

"Talk to the old wolf," said another of the men. "Talk to him, Domingo, and tell him."

The third fellow darted into the corner and ran back carrying the little silver reliquary in his hands.

"Here's a part of it!" he said, "Look, José."

"It's only the first drop from the cup," said José. "Talk to him, Domingo!"

Domingo already had Fray Luis by the shirt collar. His knuckles, edged and hard, bit into the windpipe of the friar. "Listen, Fray Luis," said Domingo, "we know that you friars lived here like fat gophers in a hole for four hundred years, and when you were kicked out you hadn't a chance to take your hoard along with you. Now they've sent you here to take a load of their treasure out to them. Instead of that, you're going to open the walls for us and show us the hidden room that's stacked with the silver bars and the vases full of gold coins and the boxes of jewels that you stole off the hands of dead women for four hundred years."

The enormity of these words left the old man calm. He said: "San Carlos be my witness, there is not a jewel; there is no gold; the only silver is this little reliquary; and the only hidden place is this turnstone in the wall."

He walked to it, pressed it, and showed them the crevice. Their hands instantly were in the hollow, finding nothing.

"And you came," said Domingo, taking a new grip on his collar, "for this little silver box only?"

"See how he keeps his face!" said José. "They learn to lie in Latin: and then its no wonder they lie in Spanish better than other men. Make him talk, Domingo."

"Fray Luis," said Domingo, "be a sensible man. If you don't show us the stuff now, you will later, and it's better to talk while your skin is still on. Though you shake your head at us and look up to heaven, there's not a saint of them all that will come down to this cellar to help you now. Will you talk?"

"I tell you in the name of heaven the sacred truth," said Fray Luis, "that there is no gold, no treasure of silver, no jewels —"

He saw Domingo take his quirt by the lash and swing up the loaded handle, and for an instant Fray Luis recoiled, but when he realized how his flesh was shrinking, he made himself sway forward to meet the blow. In his swimming vision there were pictures of saints overwhelmed with rocks, stuck full of bleeding arrows, boiled in caldrons of steaming oil, but always with upward eyes upon a glory that enabled them to forget their pain. So the old man looked up, but this blow seemed to cleave through flesh and brainpan. The breath went out of him and darkness entered.

Afterward he heard a voice saying: "You fool! If you've killed him, we'll stretch your neck for you. There never were any more wits in your hands, Domingo, than in the hoofs of a cow! He's dead! You see he hardly bleeds at all."

"Bah," said Domingo confidently. "All the blood was dried out of him years ago. You could boil down an old friar for glue. You see his eyes are opening?"

Fray Luis was rousing to a terrible pain. Still the fire ate inward through his brain and the terror ran into the pit of his belly with a dreadful nausea. He sat up. One eye was closed entirely. Something trickled down his face; the salty taste of blood entered his mouth. He remembered his Uncle Miguel taking his slender arm between finger and thumb until the bone ached: "This little one will do for the church," he had said.

And ever since, the fear of the world had lurked for Luis behind a hill. Now it rushed out upon him with the face of a dragon.

"Take him away from the town, and we'll make him talk," said Domingo, "but don't let him squeal in here; because if the people come and find him, they might be rough with us. They love this old fool because one day it happened to rain while he was praying."

So they put a dirty cloth into the mouth of Fray Luis, stuffing it in so that he could scarcely breathe, and then they lifted him by the hair of the head. He could be sure, therefore, that his prayers were silent when they carried him through the night and put him on the back of a mule, behind José.

And all the jolting way, while the pain tortured his head and the fear worked on his heart with cold fingers, he begged San

Carlos that he might be able to hold his peace about the treasure which was more valued than all the gold and jewels in the world, the blessed relics of the saint that were in his pocket. Or was it better that they should fall into the hands of thieves than to be lost with his body? No, for San Carlos when he wills can lead good men with a brighter ray than any star may cast, and at his choice he would have the holy relics again in cherishing hands.

They reached a little shanty with a shed behind it and dismounted at the open door, dragging Fray Luis forward until they stopped suddenly. The rising moon slanted into the cabin a dimness of light by which the friar partly saw and partly guessed at a dreadful figure.

There was a staggering little wooden table with a brandy bottle on it, and a big hand grasping the bottle, and an arm clad in a blue flannel shirt that was open at the breast black with hair, and then a red face loose in the jowls and hard in the nose and the brow. By the insolent glare of his eyes, the friar guessed this to be a gringo. All Americans, as Fray Luis knew, serve the devil in sundry ways, but in this terrible man he could see the complete servant of the fiend.

"What drunken gringo —" began José.

"Sew up your mouth and be still!" gasped Domingo. "Mother of heaven, it is the señor himself!"

The big man scowled up at them. "What do you mean by keeping hog-swizzle like this inside a good brandy bottle?"

"Señor," said José, "forgive the heat which corrupts good brandy as fast as flies blow a carcass."

An amazement as vague and all-pervasive as the moonshine invaded Fray Luis; for here were three armed and desperate men who shrank before that single figure by the brandy bottle.

The gringo said, in a heavy, thick voice, "What are you doing with a man so old?"

A faint thrill of hope sprang in the heart of the friar, though from this hairy monster, ugly as a tarantula inside its trap door, he expected no real mercy.

"Old, but evil," said Domingo. "With the señor's permission —"

He lighted a lantern that hung beside the door and, holding it high, showed the thin face, the blinking eyes, and the tonsured head of the man of the church.

"Ah, hell! Is that all it is?" said the gringo. "Take it away and do your dirty work out of my sight and my hearing. Vamoose!"

So they took Fray Luis into the cattle shed and tied him to the center-post. They stood near him.

"Will you talk?" asked José.

"There is no gold —" began Fray Luis.

"Try the quirt again," said José.

Domingo grinned, spat on the floor, and slashed Fray Luis across the face with the lash of the whip. The old man took breath, stunned with pain so that the scream in his throat would not come out.

"Gag him before he yells," said José. "There's no use in annoying the gringo dog. No one can tell what he will think when he's drunk, but we all have seen what he can do."

A dirty rag was pushed between the teeth of the poor friar. He began to choke, so that his eyes ached. And Domingo laid on the lash with a frenzy of pleasure. He kept stepping back and forth to give greater play to the quirt. He twisted his entire head and body with every blow, so that the friar saw only in glimpses the white shine of teeth as

Domingo grinned at his work. In his expert grasp the lash whistled in the air and struck the flesh like hand-claps.

Fray Luis tried to pray, but even in his mind there was nothing but screaming.

"He's strangling," said José, at last dusting ashes from the end of his cigarette with the little finger of the hand that held it. The little finger had a nail as long as the nail of a Chinese gentleman. "Take the gag out before he chokes."

They took out the gag. The tongue of Fray Luis ached from pressing against it. He thought in fact that he would die at once of the agony. Domingo's whip had cut him like a knife in a dozen places and still more than the pain was the horrid sense that human hands were striking him, beating down his heart, making a dog of him.

At last he could draw a clean breath and when it came from his lips again he listened, making sure that he had not screamed. At this, he knew San Carlos stood unseen beside him and at a stroke half his agony left him. He felt that if only he could see out of both eyes he would be able to look death in the face.

"Now, will you talk, old fool?" asked José.

Fray Luis said nothing. His thoughts were high above the roof of that shed. José faced Domingo. "We'll have to kill the pig, then," said José, after a moment. "Fray Luis, will you talk?"

Domingo took out a long six shooter and played with it.

"Yes, yes, I will talk!" groaned the friar.

"Out with it, then," said José.

Fray Luis held up his shaking hands. He said, in Latin: "I confess to Almighty God, to the blessed Mary ever Virgin, to blessed Michael the archangel, to blessed John the Baptist, to the holy apostles Peter and Paul, to all the saints, especially to San Carlos, and to you, brethren, that I have sinned exceedingly in thought, word, and deed."

He struck his breast three times and added: "Through my fault, through my fault, through my most grievous fault. Therefore I beseech you to pray to the Lord our God for me . . ."

A voice said: "May Almighty God have mercy upon you, forgive you for your sins, and bring you to life everlasting. Amen. But what damned bad Latin you pray in, brother!"

Fray Luis, looking toward the door of the shed, saw outlined in the early dawn

354

the hulking shoulders and the great head of the gringo. He walked into the lanternlight that filled the little place.

"Señor Charles —" said José.

"Be silent," said the renegade American. He carried the brandy bottle in his left hand, lifted it to his lips and took a swallow. Then he drew a gun. "I told you to take him out of my sight. But I could hear the whipstrokes, José, and they disturbed me. What is this fellow?"

"A sneaking rat of a friar who was prowling around the ruins," said José, "and when we make him talk, we'll all be rich. There'll be mule-loads of gold and bar silver, señor, and —"

"He won't talk, eh?" said the American.

He walked to the friar and leaned above him. With a forefinger as hard as a wooden peg he pushed back the head of Fray Luis and looked down into his face with reddened eyes.

"You came back to San Carlos like a brave old fool, did you?" asked the gringo. "And now you won't talk?"

He raised his voice to thunder. "You won't talk?" he shouted.

Fray Luis closed his eyes to shut out the frightful vision. The monster half seen in the moonlight had been dreadful enough, but standing now at his full height, his face swollen with greedy evil, his mouth slewed to the side so that the teeth looked out, he was to the friar the incarnation of the master fiend himself. Fray Luis tried to pray but the divine name which rose in his throat was altered by the movement of his lips.

"Mercy," he heard himself whispering.

In that moment he felt that he had lost his grasp on the verge of that heaven to which, through the sweet pain of martyrdom, he was about to ascend.

"Mercy be damned," said the fiend who stood above him. "Why should there be mercy for a scrawny old friar like you with callouses on your knees instead of on your hands? You were sneaking around the ruins of the church, were you? Well, then, what have you found?"

Fray Luis opened his eyes and looked up, envisioning the face of sweet San Carlos, but all he saw was the lowering gringo, more terrible than ever. Fear ran like water through the veins of Fray Luis, and tears came into his eyes. "I am unworthy, and therefore I am abandoned!" moaned the friar.

"Do you hear, you fool?" growled the

gringo. "What brought you back to the church, and what did you find there?"

He stooped down.

"Hush!" said Domingo to the other two. "What a man is this Señor Charles! He does with his voice what we could not do with a whip. The old rat is about to talk!"

It seemed to Fray Luis that he was compelled to obey the gringo. He took from its wrappings the soft little swathing about the fingerbones, the blessed relics of the saint, and held them forth. Pure as old ivory, time-polished, they lay in the palm of his hand. The blunt fingers of the gringo seized instantly upon them. Domingo and the others uttered a vague outcry that was to the friar like the laughter of devils in hell.

"This — this is the treasure, eh?" snarled the American. "Damn you, man! What *is* it?"

"Ah, señor," sobbed Fray Luis, "it is one of the keys to heaven!"

The heavy red face looked at him with a drunken leer.

"By the living saints!" said the gringo. "I think it is, for you!"

He jerked his big body about and waved a hand. "Get out, the three of you!"

"But, señor!" protested Domingo. "It is we who found —"

"Out! Out!" roared the big man.

"*Amigos* — brothers — help me!" yelled Domingo, and snatched out a heavy gun, a blue-gray flash of steel.

"Ah?" said the gringo.

He did not raise his own revolver much higher than his hip when he fired. Fray Luis heard the big half-inch slug strike like a fist. Domingo lurched back against the wall, the wind knocked out of him in a grunt. Then he slipped down. His head was between his knees. He did not move.

The gringo faced the other two as they backed toward the door. The drink kept his body wavering, and the legs sagging at the knees, but his head and his hand were steady.

"Give me a little room, José," said the gringo. "Elbow room. Room to breathe. Get over there beyond the edge of the sky. And don't come inside the horizon with me again or I'll be crowded."

He walked with his wobbling knees to the door after them; hoofbeats began; an angry voice screamed an insult out of the distance. Then the gringo came back and cut the rope that tied Luis to the pillar.

The old man tried to stand, but could not. He was much amazed when the gringo picked him up and carried him to the hut.

"When did you eat last?" asked the gringo. "There's no more belly on you than a starved sheep."

"I ate on the holy Sabbath," said Fray Luis.

"And in between?"

"I have had good water from the well of San Carlos, God and the saint be praised for it," said Fray Luis. "But now, let me die!"

"Why should you die, brother?" asked the big man, pushing the red and swollen horror of his face closer to the old man.

"Because I have given up with my own hand the salvation of thousands of tens of thousands," said Fray Luis, "and God will not have mercy on my soul!"

He began to weep. It seemed to him that the tears were the last blood in his body.

"As for the key to heaven," said the gringo, "you see that it is once more in your hand."

It was true! The miraculous relics were again in his grasp.

"The Lord giveth and the Lord taketh

away," whispered the friar. "The Lord giveth . . ."

And as he stared at the gringo, words left him.

He fell into a meditation, as wordless as the music of the wind. Food appeared. He ate and was satisfied; and he fell asleep and awakened so far cured that he could even see out of his damaged eye. The gringo loaded him onto a mule and with him rode across the flats of San Carlos Valley into the northern mountains.

"I think you can go on safely from here," said the gringo, "but if you are afraid, I'll stay with you the rest of the day."

Fray Luis smiled. "Dear son and brother," he said, "I have no longer any fear; holy San Carlos himself is my companion. But how shall I thank you for the life of my body, Señor Mister Charles?"

"Pray for me," said the gringo, "pray the devil out of the brandy bottle — and *adios!*"

He took the hand of the friar and Luis felt something very strange in that grasp, so that he looked and noticed that two fingers of Señor Charles' right hand were missing. Shot away in some battle, perhaps?

While he was reflecting on this, he discovered that the gringo had disappeared to a drumming of hoofbeats far down the valley.

Fray Luis rode softly on, still with his mind fixed far off. Soon he was into the highlands where excellent bunch grass grew and fat sheep wandered in grazing huddles behind their bell-goats.

As he rode, he touched from time to time the sacred relics in his pocket. They were safe, but only safe, he knew, because blessed San Carlos had protected them. His memory shrank from the death of Domingo — for whom he would pray — and from the face of the gringo, half bloated like the jowls of a swine and half like the beak of a vulture. He came then to think of the name of the gringo, from whose right hand two fingers were missing — and a mighty light burst upon the brain of the old friar, for the name and the missing fingers joined suddenly to make the miracle complete in his mind.

He slipped down from the mule and fell upon his knees, overweighted by the divine conclusion forced upon him. May not the most glorious deliverers take the strangest forms? And did not this miracle carry its sign and authentication upon its very forehead?

He knew only a few words of English, but now the name "Charles" rang back and forth through his brain, for surely it was the equivalent of "Carlos" in the sweet Spanish tongue.

He had been in the presence of a fleshly incarnation of the blessed saint himself! Not shining with an effulgence too bright for the human eye to endure, but darkened and dimmed by the flesh and the brandy bottle, and striking his foes down not with a silent death but through the more obvious mouth of a revolver. A single detail now remembered confirmed the miracle for Fray Luis: for he recalled that Señor Mister Charles had not sighted the gun. Blindly he had fired it, knowing that the sacred bullet would find its own way.

Tears of joy began to flow down the face of the old man, but though his eyes were blinded he had a bright inward vision of all the brotherhood, sitting enraptured as he told them his story, as he showed them the sacred finger bones and told of the living hand from which they had come.

Kneeling there, blinded by joy, he failed to see a sheep dog as it ran barking through the flock, scattering the sheep and their bell wethers here and there. When Fray Luis heard the sound of their bells, they seemed to him the chimes of San Carlos, sending the ghosts of their voices after him, music softly echoing among the hills and valleys of time, repeated with infinite, small tongues — and every separate tremor of sound that touched his ears was another blessing heaped upon him by the infinite largesse of heaven, so that he seemed to be kneeling in a shower of gold.

A note on the text
Large print edition designed by
Kipling West.
Composed in 18 pt Plantin
on a Mergenthaler Linotron 202
by Modern Graphics, Inc.